Pack

Printed in the United States of America: First Printing, 2023.
ISBN 978-1-959981-06-0 (eBook)
ISBN 978-1-959981-07-7 (paperback)

www.huckleberryrahrauthor.wordpress.com

Editor: Wes Imrisek
Editor: Elizabeth Silver
Copy Editor: Angela Grimes
Cover Art: Getcovers.com
Formatting: R. L. Davennor

CHAPTER 1

"Jade Stone, I'm going to kill you."

I stopped my run and shifted my gaze to an old man leaning against an equally old car. Back in Wisconsin, that car would have been rusted out from the yearly salt used to melt the snow and ice from the roads. This car just looked old and tired. It was light blue, so faded it appeared to be almost a pale off-white. But it didn't have rust spots. *I wonder if the man bought the car new. They look to be about the same age.*

The man, maybe in his seventies, held a gun as if he knew how to use it. He was also a werewolf with a sharp eye.

"I'm sorry, do I know you? Are you planning to just shoot and run? Or do I get a trial by my peers?" I tilted my head, knowing I should be nervous, but I figured I could outrun his aim, even with werewolf precision.

"I don't think you have any peers. My name is Matthias. I'm Quinn's grandfather. You know, the boy you were dating."

I bit back a snort. Greta's family didn't know she liked girls, but I didn't know they'd explained me away by having me be Quinn's girlfriend. I guess it made it safer for her, and Quinn always protected his twin.

Narrowing my eyes at him, I jogged in place to keep my heart rate up a bit, but his relation to my ex gave me pause. "Are you here to check in with me and my Pack?"

"I'm here to help my grandchildren move out after graduation. I'm also here to warn you that you and your...pack's...days are numbered. We've been here for generations. You're just young upstarts."

"I'll take that under advisement." I spun on my heel and headed back. I had time and distance to maintain on my watch. I could do some adjustments so that Coach didn't get suspicious, but I was cutting it close.

Matthias mumbled, "Upstart kids." Right before the gun cocked.

There was a curve in the path a quarter mile ahead. I sprinted and made the turn just as a bullet struck the tree to my right, barely missing me. I felt the heat as it passed by me, but I'd made it to the turn, and apparently, he hadn't adjusted for that. The old man may have had good aim, but I was faster.

Before heading to the car, I stopped at the dorms and made my way to Greta's room. I hadn't seen her since I'd dropped off the letter for her to deliver to her family a few weeks ago. It was early and she probably wasn't up. I knocked. After a few minutes, she opened the door.

Her eyes widened in surprise when she saw me, and she smelled of citrusy hope and vanilla interest. I tried to ignore that.

I had obviously woken her. She was wearing shorts and a button-down navy-blue pajama set. She quickly glanced at her sleeping roommate before shutting the door. "What do you want?"

Beckoning her, I made my way down the hall to the floor's common room. I didn't want to wake everyone up or take the chance of anyone overhearing us. I listened to her steps behind me as she followed.

Once in the room, I asked her, "How many of your clan are here with guns?"

Confusion poured off her, turning her previous vanilla interest to mint. A crease formed between her brows, and she rubbed her eyes. "I don't know what you're talking about."

"Your grandfather, Matthias, just took a pot-shot at me. If I hadn't sprinted, he may have hit his target. I'm just curious if you're going to support him slaughtering me and my friends."

"Jade..." She reached for me, but I backed away. Her hands dropped. "Why would I?"

"You locked me in a cage. Who knows what else you'll do?"

Several weeks earlier, she and I had gone out to the beach on a private date. It had been private right up until Boden, a crazy member of her family, had locked me in a cage while Greta and her brother did nothing to help. In the end, I learned that Greta had held the keys. She could've opened the door and set me free, but she hadn't.

"You never let me explain that. I *didn't* lock you in, Boden did that. He dropped the keys on the counter, and I pocketed them. That way he couldn't mess with you."

"But, Greta, you could've let me out at any time. You didn't. You know what? Forget it." I brushed past her and headed for the car. She didn't follow.

Once I reached Pack property, I had to go through higher security to get in. There was a gate that stretched around most of our property. It didn't go around the wooded area, but it covered the street and split our land from the public park where the hiking trails were. To get to the house, I had to drive under a huge, stylized arch large enough for construction vehicles to pass under. Made from wrought iron, like the rest of the fence, it was designed to look like trees and nature—a forest scene with birds and other wildlife. If you studied the design, you could find wolves howling at the moon in the centerpiece at the top.

The only way in was through the arch in the gate or

around it in the woods, which was a treacherous path that took miles of hiking. A car wouldn't make it. A person would have to be dedicated and careful. It was an illegal hike through land full of cliffs and hidden pits. The Pack had tried it and deemed it doable, but unlikely. Except Zee; he said it was exhilarating.

To pass through the arch, you had to get buzzed in or have a code. I had a code. Once through the gate, the driveway split. To the left was Pack House, our old, temporary dwelling that was finally abandoned a few days ago. Beyond Pack House stood the home of the previous owners of this land. They still lived on the property and, so far, were happy with the improvements we'd made. To the right was Were House, our current, permanent wolf den...our home.

I parked and slipped into the house. Before even finding food or coffee, I headed for my room, and my personal bathroom and the shower. Afterward, I changed into clean clothes, and found José and Bevin eating breakfast. They'd laid a place for me and included coffee, thank the gods. I filled them in about Matthias.

José grumbled. "That group is going to be a thorn in our side. None of the proximity sensors have gone off yet, but we'll do a visual search using the cameras after breakfast."

I shook my head. "Put Violet on it. I have classes today. Finals are next week, and I really don't want to miss this week's presentations."

Alex joined us while I spoke, and I noticed Greta and

Quinn sitting in the living room. In my haste to fill in my alphas about Matthias, I hadn't taken in my surroundings. "What are they doing here?" I snapped.

Alex blanched. "I stayed late to do some last-minute research in the library and planned on jogging home. Greta and Quinn found me before I headed out and asked if they could meet with Bevin and José. I suggested this morning because I knew that José's classes started late, and Bevin was available." They shifted in their chair and eyed the living room. "I'm sorry."

I narrowed my eyes at them, then turned my glare at the twins.

I could smell guilt coming from Alex. They stammered, "I'm sorry. Quinn *did* say you told him if he wanted answers the best way wasn't to lock people up, but to ask directly."

José's lip twitched. "So, you're to blame for the twins being here."

"No, I'm to blame," Quinn said softly. "I was hoping to talk to Bevin, José, and maybe Jade, and Alex agreed to bring us."

I flopped into a chair as Bevin placed a plate with cut-up fruit and peanut butter in front of me.

Before anyone could say anything else, Violet came up from the basement. She saw the strangers and retreated back downstairs. My phone rang and I snorted before answering it. "Yeah."

"We have a problem. There are four men at the campsite

on our property." Violet hung up. It figured; she hated dealing with people.

Then, I got a text message from her with the video feed from one of the cameras she, Zee, and Luke had set up. Pulling it up, I saw four men, none of whom were Matthias. I showed it to José and Bevin.

Suddenly, school seemed less important. "I'm going out to investigate."

José shook his head. "No, too dangerous."

Bevin placed a hand on his shoulder. "I'll go with her. We can shower first to cover our scent. We'll walk out to the back of the property and approach from the rear."

José closed his eyes, no doubt strategizing. "Do not engage with them; this is merely a fact-finding mission. Get information."

Grinning, I finished off my plate of food and grabbed an energy bar. "Of course, though they *are* here to destroy us. We know that."

At those words, Quinn perked up. "Wait, is *our* family out in your woods?"

Tilting my head, I faced him. "Is that your question?"

Greta put a hand on his arm. "Careful, Quinn. They let us in; just wait."

He nodded.

Bevin and I each showered and used soap developed by a werebear clan in Wisconsin. It covered up any scent markers on a body that gave away wereanimal indications. It had only been a week or so since I had stopped using it. We had decided that José, Bevin, and I were done hiding. We were ready to present our Pack to any wereanimal who came to our city.

There was a bit of a chill in the air, so I dressed in jeans, a t-shirt, and a zippy coat. Common hiking garb. We headed out to the public walkways. When we got to where the path neared the rear of our grounds, we slipped off the path, and back onto Pack land. We used a silent, coded door to get through the gate.

We carefully sniffed, determining if we were alone. I could find the scent trails of three of the men who had hiked in and entered our territory, but not the fourth.

Knowing we may need to shift while on patrol, we had a hidden shed built for supplies, extra clothes, and storage. We placed our clothes in the bin and found our wolves; two black shadows to search the property.

We wound our way in through the trees, and followed the trail the three werewolves left but kept searching for the path of the fourth man. The woods were oddly silent for this time of day. We were doing a stunted version of our usual sweep when something caused me to freeze.

Bevin, catching my movement—or lack thereof— paused next to me. I closed my eyes, getting a feel for the woods. I tried to figure out what was niggling at me. Finally, I opened my eyes and gazed up. There, in a tree a dozen feet ahead of us, was a man secured to the trunk. He wasn't one from the video, so there were five enemies in our midst.

He had a high-tech scope attached to his head and was quietly setting up what looked like a listening device. He was so focused on his work he hadn't noticed us.

Bevin and I backed up and he placed his paw on mine, connecting to me through my epsilon ability. *"Jade, he's alone, but we can't get up there as wolves. Can you shift and get him?"*

I closed my eyes and took stock. *Yeah, I believe so.*

"Okay, I'll stand guard."

I had trained the shift from wolf to panther a lot in high school. Since I had come to college, I had only trained once a month, maybe less. I could change form fairly quickly, but it took more of my energy than a normal shift. We had always believed the only real application was for escaping danger. *Who knew!*

I thought of Panther and let her flow over me, taking over from Wolf. The pain was much more intense than human to animal. It was like the bones truly didn't know what to do and the magic was confused. Fur retreated, only to extend again, still coarse but different. My face began to flatten, then elongate, gaining the sleek lines of my cat. Eventually, all the changes, popping, and adjusting ended, and I went from being a black wolf to a black panther.

I took a minute to stand, panting quietly. I watched the

man setting up his equipment, ready to run if I needed to, but glad to have the adjustment time.

Two silent bounds and I flew into the tree, landing on a branch just above and to the left of the man. I took his head in my mouth and jerked, hearing a snap. He fell limp before he had a chance to scream. A shiver ran down my body and I spit, hacking, before leaping back down.

Bevin put his paw back on mine. *"You okay?"*

A shiver wracked my body again before I could stop it. *Yes, I'm fine.*

"Liar."

We need to backtrack. I should cover my wolf trail with panther scent. If they find our path, they'll think you were following the panther scent, not them.

"What about recon?"

We need to get back so that José or Zee can come get that equipment. There may be something incriminating on it.

Zee—Zach—had been a lone wolf in Wisconsin. He'd gotten himself in trouble a couple of times and Bevin and I'd had to fix him up. He'd started calling us "Team Kid." When we'd started our pack in California, we ran into him here. The wolf that created him had told Zee to avoid packs at all costs. He'd decided to chance joining our pack, trusting me and Bevin.

Bevin groaned. *"When we get to the back of the property, do you have the energy to do what needs to be done?"*

Bevin meant run in the opposite direction from him. I

couldn't go back to Were House with him—not smelling of panther. Not unless we wanted this group to know our secret. I was low on reserves. I had track practice, had done two shifts, and had only eaten a bit of food.

I don't know, but I'm not risking security.

"Jade."

Bevin!

He growled low in his throat, emanating alpha power.

I whined and rubbed against him.

He closed his eyes and shook himself. Acknowledging we were in a dangerous place, his head dropped in acquiescence, and we trotted off.

Once we got back to the rear of our property, Bevin started his shift to human form. He would retrace our path. We were afraid if he went home as a wolf, the enemy would use that as an excuse to shoot a "wild animal."

Taking off in the other direction, I headed away from our property at a run before turning around and cutting back into our land by the road at the fence. I was still hidden by trees and shadow.

My lack of food and energy made me dizzy, and I wasn't sure I'd make it. I slowed my run to a walk as I passed the house of the old couple. They were sitting on their porch. She was reading a book to her husband as he sat back watching the clouds roll by. He had a glass of something cold—the condensation on the glass looked appealing—and he swayed in a rocking chair. They looked peaceful and content. Talk about relationship goals.

As the trees grew thin, I darted deeper into the property. Soon, I neared Pack House. As I slunk through the foliage, I debated stopping there. The house was empty now. I slowed behind a copse of three trees and noticed a car parked outside the house. An old car with faded blue paint.

How had they gotten the car onto the property? Pack House *wasn't* empty. I tried to contact José, but I had nothing in me. I tried again; I had to let him know. I used every drop of energy I had to connect to him.

The last thing I heard before passing out was, *"Jade?"*

CHAPTER 2

Click.

"A bullet in the brain will kill you dead, boy."

"This is our land. I ask you one last time to leave peacefully."

José's voice filled me with warmth. Wait, there was a gun pointed at his head! I had to do something, but I still couldn't do much more than twitch.

"I don't see how you have much leverage, kid."

Cracking open an eye, I saw the black of my muzzle. Panther. I breathed deeply and picked up the scents of José, Luke, and Bevin. I could also smell Matthias and his gun. It smelled like gunpowder...he'd already shot at something.

I listened hard; everything seemed quiet.

José spoke in my head. His contact almost made me jump. *"Don't move if you can stop yourself."* Our connection was still active; I must be awake.

He shifted to speaking to Matthias. "Well, sir, you are on our land, surrounded by cameras. The idea that you think I'm here alone is hilarious. If you shoot me, the footage will be given to the police, and they'll lock you up for the rest of your short life. If you walk away, you'll be fine. I warned you and your clan. You people need to learn manners."

"Cameras? Bull!" Mattias spit out. "There is no way you'd chance anything being recorded."

"Violet, love," José almost purred, "can you ask the one question we'd all love to know the answer to?"

Violet's voice came from the trees. "Hey, old man, how did you get past the security gate?"

Matthias gasped. "You put up recording devices? In a place people could see you shift?" Then I heard a thump and grappling.

Luke's voice rang out. "All clear. Keys are in his pocket."

Grunts and mumbles filled the air and a car door opened and slammed shut. I tried once more to stand, but only managed to move my head a bit.

Then José, Bevin, and Luke were there.

Luke sighed. "I always forget how beautiful she is as a cat. Can we convince her to run in panther form more often?"

José petted my head. "She can hear you. She's awake,

just *mostly* passed out. No juice left. We'll have to carry her. Bev, if you can get the haunches, I'll get her shoulders. Luke, could you get the doors and drive?"

Together they got me wrangled into the back seat of the car.

Where is Matthias?

José answered aloud, repeating my questions. "He's in the trunk."

How did you find me?

"You connected with me and then blacked out. Trippy, by the way. The connection remained and I followed it. When we got close to Pack House, we could smell the foreign wolf, so Luke and Bevin split off. Matthias came out before we could get to you."

What about the others in the woods?

"Jade, one thing at a time. Let's get you home and human first."

By then, we were at the garage, as the drive between houses was short. They decided to get me moved to the back first, and then worry about Matthias. They carried me through the house. That was the most direct route. The problem? We all forgot Greta and Quinn were in the living room. They were still there, waiting for the boys, playing cards with Alex.

José said to the house at large, "Someone make easy food."

Alex jumped up. "I can make a protein shake."

"Perfect. There are shallow bowls. Bring it out when

you have it made, then make a second."

Greta stood as if to follow Alex. "What's going on?"

José turned towards Zee. "Help Luke out at the garage." He faced the twins. "Sit. This is our business, not yours."

The command in his voice knocked them back. I was carried out to the porch and gently laid down. A bowl of cold sustenance was placed all but under my muzzle. It smelled strange and I wrinkled my nose at it. It only smelled slightly better than dead meat.

José's alpha demeanor was still prominent. "Jade, eat that now."

Slowly, my tongue extended, lapping up the chocolate and peanut butter concoction. I was sure in human form it would've tasted great, but as a panther...not so much. At least Alex had chosen a good flavor combination in theory. As I got near the bottom, the bowl was refilled. I rolled to my stomach and shook as the energy infused my body. Once the second bowl was gone, I dropped my chin to my paws, sighing in contentment. The pounding in my head I hadn't even realized was there receded.

Bevin sat next to me. "We're going to talk to Matthias. If you want to join in, you have to shift, and probably eat more. I grabbed some clothes, and José is getting a plate of food ready for you. It'll be on the dining room table when you come in." He scratched my ears and then headed inside.

Laying there, I wished they had brought a third protein shake. After another minute or so, I reached deep inside and found my humanity. The shift took a bit longer, and when I lay on the porch in my human skin, I knew I had shifted too many times without enough calories. I felt weak as I panted and trembled. My limbs felt like rubber.

I heard the screen door slide open and sniffed. Alex.

"Do you want help?"

I grunted.

They came over and grabbed my clothes. I sat up and they helped me into my shirt, undies, and jeans. I wobbled a little as I did up the zipper and clasp, but they just slipped an arm around my waist and lent me support. Alex practically carried me to the door.

"Jade, you've lost a lot of weight. You need to eat, like, more than normal, if that's possible. What happened?"

"Long story. Later."

They got me to the table, and José placed a Mexican feast in front of me. Tacos, rice, beans, and a torta on a second plate. I started to eat. Others joined me because… tacos. *José's* tacos. There really wasn't anything better. Every time I thought I had eaten my fill, there were more tacos on my plate. Finally, I glared at Bevin.

He smiled. "It isn't me." He pointed at Alex.

I whipped around to them. "What?"

They maintained an innocent face for about two seconds then busted up laughing. "It's like magic. I just slide the food on, and it disappears."

After the food, I felt mostly human and joined in the

mirth. I finally looked around and realized everyone but Luke and Zee was at the table, including Greta and Quinn.

Belly full, I leaned back and stared at the twins. I repeated my question from earlier. "Why are you two here?"

Greta tilted her head. "What was the panther?" Her voice began to shake. "Was that you? Is that why you were always so elusive about answering if you were a wolf? Is this a pack of panthers?"

Unable to stop myself, I snorted. I couldn't help it. She sounded so scared. "Panthers don't form packs. It isn't their way. Panthers are," I did air quotes, "'lone wolves' so to speak." Smiling, I huffed at my own joke. The others at the table just groaned.

Quinn narrowed his eyes. "You haven't answered her question."

"Nope. I haven't. Well, I answered part of it. We are not a pack of panthers."

Alex looked at them with a sparkle in their eyes. "I'm not a panther. Can you imagine how cool it would be, though?" They gazed up at nothing. "I'd love to be a cat. How amazing would that be?"

Chuckling, I shook my head.

José cleared his throat. "You're asking the wrong person. You should be asking me or Bevin if you want full answers." He took Bevin's hand. "We're the pack alphas. Jade is being evasive because of the pack rules. You don't give up pack secrets without express permission from the alphas."

Bevin and José shared a look and a small smile. It filled the room with love and Pack. It connected to each of us on a fundamental level. It let us know we belonged, that we were protected.

Bevin took over. "As Jade asked, why are you two here? What is your goal? It didn't escape our notice that a group from your family's clan was camping out in our forest. Your grandfather moved into our old house. And you two come in for a frontal approach. Three-pronged attack. Very organized."

Quinn blanched and Greta looked confused. Quinn said, "Our family is here? Like, on your property? Right now?"

We all could have smelled if he lied. I knew he was honestly confused.

Bevin closed his eyes, looking pained. "Why did you two come here?"

Quinn smelled scared. A sweet, candy-like odor emanated from him. "We just want answers. We've been told stories about how things work our whole lives. The way the Dynasty works. It has been run the same way for generations."

Bevin nodded. "The Dynasty. That's what your clan, your cult, calls themselves? A dynasty?"

Quinn gulped audibly. "Well, yeah. And, well, the rules are fairly straightforward. Males find a female, get married, have kids. Only the strong *then* get bitten. You only have the honor of becoming a wolf after all kids are born...for whatever reason. Girls stay at home. Boys have more freedom. It's why everyone freaked out when Greta wanted to come here for college. She came here without a chaperone. I'm not old enough to be a chaperone."

There was so much to unpack in what he said. I shifted my gaze between them, shock making me ask the obvious. "But you don't need one, Quinn?"

Quinn and Greta's scents both went minty with confusion. "Why would I? I'm a guy."

It took everything in me to keep a straight face. I probably failed.

Bevin grabbed my hand under the table. "Okay, so as a man of the…Dynasty, you can move around freely, but Greta, your twin sister, can't."

Their scents continued to be confused. The minty scent filling the room to the point I wanted to sneeze. "Well, yeah. It's the way things are with…you know…werewolves. Right?"

As I was about to answer, Bevin's hand tightened on mine. I clammed up. "What exactly are you hoping to learn? Most of the world isn't as…cut and dry as your… family." Bevin took a long, cleansing breath. I could feel him struggling to stay calm. "In our pack, men and women are accorded equal rights. That's the way in all the werewolf packs in the U.S., which I visited over the last two years."

José finally jumped in. "Men and women being treated equally is also the way of the Mexican packs." Everyone turned to him. "My family, who still live there, runs with that pack, and I ran with them once. Like the Wisconsin pack, the dominant alpha is a woman."

Thinking of my mom and dad, the alphas of the Wisconsin pack, made me smile. No one messed with my mom.

Quinn swallowed audibly and Greta sank into herself. "Okay, well, we just want to learn. I know that if I work hard, I can become a leader in my family's Dynasty. After I marry and have kids, I can earn the right to ascend to Controller, and maybe eventually to Headman."

I had a feeling he wasn't supposed to be giving away all these secrets, but none of us were going to stop him.

Bevin pinched the bridge of his nose. "The idea that you have to have kids first is just a control to ensure no females become wolves. It's sexist and ridiculous. Just something else to think about." Face hard, he stood and began clearing the dishes. Alex stood to help him.

Quinn's eyes widened and Greta's jaw dropped. Quinn whispered, "Werewolves can be born and not just created."

José put down his fork. "Who's the leader?" Obviously, he decided we were getting information not giving it.

Greta grabbed her brother's arm and shook her head, but Quinn pursed his lips, nodding. "Greta, I'm tired of all the lies. Our family isn't treating you right, and I'm starting to think they aren't treating me right, either. If they find out about Boden, he's probably dead or never allowed to have kids. I don't even know why anymore. The lore says females *can't* become werewolves, so what would it matter if a wolf had kids? None of it makes sense! I'm tired of how they treat us."

A tear ran down Greta's cheek. "Don't do this for me. I'm not worth it. I'm just a girl."

Quinn reached over to wipe the tear away. "That's why I'm doing this. You have always been worth it, G. I wish I wasn't the only one who knew it." He turned to José. "Our uncle, Jerry. He is the Grand Leader."

My face scrunched up. "Your uncle? Not your grandfather?"

Quinn faced me. "Yeah. Our uncle is the stronger of the two...the more dominant?"

Bevin returned from the kitchen. "Your...people... have invaded our land. They probably won't survive the next twenty-four hours. Are you sure you're sitting in the right house?"

Greta moaned, but Quinn's face hardened. "Yes. You warned them. I couldn't read your letter, but I heard the elders talking about it. I knew they were coming. I was going to warn you, but they arrived before I could...we could get here."

Bevin nodded. "Jade, we need to go."

Surveying the room, I realized the food was all cleared up, so I stood and followed him out to the garage. When we got to the back of the garage, we found Luke and Zee standing outside the locked door leading to our cages.

Bevin walked up in all his alpha glory, back straight, serious. "Did he put up a fight?"

Luke and Zee straightened like soldiers under inspection. Luke gave a tight nod. "A bit. He was confused that a werewolf wasn't able to escape mere humans. Once he was in the cage, he was fairly sure he could get out. When he couldn't, he was confused again. We left him there arguing about rights and lawyers."

I had never seen Bevin in full alpha-mode with the Pack. Hanging back, I basked in the wonder of it. It was both mind-blowing and spectacular to see.

Bevin's eyes narrowed. "Jade and I will go in to interview him. I want both of you in there as well. If you think of a question, connect with Jade. I want to present a two-person front, with Jade in the lead, and two for security. Having a woman ask the questions will put him off his game. His group is sexist."

We all stared at him as he laid out his plan. "I will only speak as needed. He knows I'm an alpha and Jade is…something."

Shivering, I rubbed my face. "Are you going to continue to," I waved my hand at him, "exude alpha?"

Bevin almost twitched as he took a step back, then he smiled. "Sorry about that." His power slowly trailed off.

The four of us entered the room after punching in a code to open the door. I stepped in first.

"Oh, the girl is back." His condescension oozed off him.

Bevin stopped, behind me and on my left. The other two stood just inside the door.

"Good afternoon, Matthias. I see you've come to enjoy our hospitality."

He looked around the cage and the room. "Well, nicer than what we'll put you in one day, but not the best place I've ever stayed."

I bit my cheek to stop from laughing. The gall on this guy was incredible. "I hear you enjoyed our guest cottage. What I don't get is, how did you get through our security gate?"

"You kids are so stupid." He shook his head. "You know what, I'll tell you; that's how little I care about you and your little group of idiots." He mumbled, "Kids playing at being adults. I own the security firm that did your setup. I have a back door code into every gate my company installs."

Taken aback at the audacity of him and his group, I raised an eyebrow. "All of them? And you're telling me this because…?"

"Little lady, you and these kids don't scare me. You'll be gone from here before the end of the school year. Then we can go back to doing things our way."

My second brow decided it wanted to meet up with the first. "Are the guys in the woods going to do something about us? Because if they're who you're counting on, they are as clueless as you."

"We're all wolves. You are," he sniffed, "something. I thought I smelled an animal on you before, but I'm not sure now. None of you smell like werewolves. Kids, pretending you're a pack. Calling yourselves 'alphas' and whatever word you used for yourself. You're nothing but dumb brats playing at something you know nothing about. Probably using mommy and daddy's money. A waste."

Turning to Bevin, I gave a small half-shrug. "I don't know that we'll get more out of him. Do you?"

"Sadly, no. His arrogance makes things easier."

"Ah, so here is where you let me go?"

Bevin's focus moved from me to Matthias. "No, sir." And the full weight of alpha blasted out of him as he displayed his mantle, nearly knocking me to my knees. I heard Matthias crash to the floor before I could turn and see him on his hands and knees, panting. "We warned you if you came and didn't show proper respect you wouldn't survive the encounter." His voice stayed calm and steady as he spoke. "This is when you die."

CHAPTER 3

Matthias's lip curled in a sneer. "You gonna kill me, boy? You have it in you, a willowy nothin' like you? Why, you have all that power, but I bet you'll have one of your boys do the dirty work for you."

Bevin's face stayed impassive, but I could tell he fought a sneer of his own. Implying he couldn't protect his own was fighting below the belt. Then Bevin's mouth twitched, and he smiled. "Why would I have someone less competent do it when I have Jade."

My head jerked to him. "Really?"

He gave a single nod. "We've discussed it, and now is

as good a time as any. If it fails, I can't think of a better test subject, can you?"

I rubbed my hands on my legs and debated. Ever since I'd gotten attacked in Florida my sophomore year of college, my dad had been setting up training programs. It started off as fitness, all of us young wereanimals had to be able to protect ourselves.

When I'd moved to California, most of my training had morphed into track practice. Bevin and I maintained some of our sparing practice, but not as much as Dad would've probably wanted.

Once in a while, a care package came from home with a new book of evil, a few months of training from Dad. Often he'd add something to help train my epsilon abilities. He lived to figure out how to train the weird things he didn't understand, but wanted to hone into something magnificent.

While studying for a big math exam, I'd needed a mental break. I brought up the idea to Bevin: if I can go in with Panther to heal, why not go in and harm? At first, he'd blanched, thought college had finally addled my brains, but eventually we'd fleshed out my thinking, and born was the idea of stopping a heart. The problem—this isn't something you can just go and train. This is the kind of thing that once you test it, the person you test it on isn't around to tell you, "Good job!"

With a slight tremor in my voice, I said, "Yeah, okay, I think this sounds great, Bev."

Matthias looked down at me as if I were scum. "The girl? You think she can do anything but paint my nails and curl my hair? No wait, she did a real good job of running away this morning. You've taught her well, alpha-boy. Your girl can run. Now, let me go, and stop playing a grown-up game, kids."

I balled my hands into fists and stepped forward. To work, I needed to be able to touch him. He laughed. "Look at you, girl. You're trembling like a leaf. You really should run off and let the boys handle this."

Anger swelled in my belly. I released a wave of calm, dropping everyone in the room to the floor. I heard the knees hitting the ground behind me, though I'd aimed the lion share of power ahead. Matthias had fallen and hit his head on the bars. His hand had flopped out of the cage, and he wasn't moving. It was too much to hope that that had killed him. I could see his chest still moving up and down.

Bevin's heavy breathing behind me as he gulped in fresh air told me he was fighting the effects. I darted a look, and saw he still stood, every muscle tense as he fought the effect. He nodded. "Go, do it while he's down."

I sat cross-legged on the ground and took his hand. Both Panther and Wolf rushed forward to help, black as night with glowing green eyes like mine, but I asked for only Panther. I needed Wolf to stay back and watch over me. We entered Matthias and went for his heart.

As we headed in, Panther filled me in on all his medical

issues; the man was not only old, he was a mess. His wolf tried to stop us, an old and snarly mangy gray. Panther swatted the animal to the side. It was the first time I'd entered someone and found their animal unwelcoming. It was almost as if the wolf knew why we were there.

When we got to Matthias's heart, I spoke to Panther. *Okay, my friend, I don't know how this will work, but once we stop his heart, we need to wait for a bit to make sure it stays stopped.*

Panther just nodded.

I braced myself, then stopped his heart. The action was anticlimactic from what I'd expected. I'd worked myself up to this moment, and then it just was that. I stopped it. And…nothing. His heart…stopped.

I really thought it would be a lot more than that. Maybe this is a viable way to take out our enemies. I mean, if this is it, slip in, stop the heart, and bam! Done. Why not?

Panther gazed at me, her all-knowing eyes holding a truth I felt I may be missing.

Once I felt we'd waited long enough and Matthias's heart wouldn't start up again, we began our trek out. At first, I didn't think anything of it, but then I realized it was taking too long. The ground under our feet began to slip and slide as if we were on a beach. I couldn't get any traction.

Each time I put my foot down, it sank deeper and deeper in. I wondered if I could move another step. Panther tried to help, but nothing worked. Matthias's wolf appeared again, snapping at Panther, blocking her attempts to help me. I stood in quicksand, and it was swallowing me up. I was dying with Matthias.

A low chuckle reverberated through my body as cold terror washed through me in waves. Matthias's voice echoed all around me. *You're just a girl, why do you think you can play at men's games?*

I shivered. *What happens if I can't get out?*

I started clawing and digging my way out faster. I had to get out. I sank in deeper. I scrambled, kicking and climbing. Every step forward, I slid three back.

Will I make it? Will I die in here?

No! I would make it out, I had to get out. I found purchase, I got closer, but then it became sand. Everything became sand.

CHAPTER 4

My skin was wrinkly after an hour in the tub, and I knew I had to get out. The fluffy purple towel was folded on the sink's counter, so I crawled out of the bath and wrapped myself up in its warmth. When I first toured the house, I hadn't noticed the tub had jets and a heater in it. Now that I had discovered it, I could sit in it all day and never leave. But I had to face the real world.

The thought of interacting with people made me want to crawl into a hole and pull a rock over it. I put on a pair of shorts with an elastic waist and a t-shirt with a goose on it, a pajama set my little sister had given me for Christmas.

Ever since I'd had a run-in with a gaggle of geese, and lost, my family raised geese-themed gifts to an artform. It made my little sister, Pebble, happy, and that made me happy. I really needed to be happy right then.

Climbing into bed, I curled into a ball and tried to turn my mind into a black hole of nothingness. I failed. Thinking about the last few hours felt like spikes shooting through me to my soul. The tears started up again. I tried to breathe deeply to stop them, but the wetness pooled and flowed across my nose and down to my pillow.

Just breathe.

Just breathe.

My door opened. I pretended to be asleep. I smelled José and Bevin as the door clicked shut. I smelled their concern, a soothing sandalwood, but I just couldn't right now. About halfway to the bed, one set of footsteps stopped.

The mattress dipped in front of me, and I was hauled into José's lap. "You can't hide, and you can't be alone. It won't help." He hugged me to his chest.

I tried to hide anyway, tucking my face into him so I wouldn't have to see anything.

Just breathe.

Bevin's steps approached on the other side of the bed. "Do you think she needs both of us?"

José's chin rubbed the top of my head as he nodded. He gently laid me back down on my side with my head in the crook of his arm. I curled in. Bevin spooned me from behind. Once I had them both touching me, my body finally relaxed. I felt José relax with me.

Though they were both my alphas, José was the one who was connected to my emotions. He was the one who experienced all the fun ups and downs I underwent while learning the ins and outs of being an epsilon werewolf. I'm sure he was thrilled.

At some point, they'd learned that when they both were in physical contact with me, it settled the more intense emotions and helped me control them. With them both with me, I could finally take a deep breath and think.

Bevin rubbed my arm and José said, "Can you tell me what happened?"

I groaned at the memory and all my muscles tightened. "I'm never instigating a training session again."

As he continued to give comfort, Bevin shook with silent laughter.

I leaned into him a bit, enjoying his amusement. "Can I assume you've gotten the story from Bevin?"

José shook his head. "No. I want the full story from you."

"Fine. Matthias didn't tell us much. He assumed he could violate the agreement, threaten our lives, and walk away. Bevin disabused him of his assumption." My heart started to beat faster so I paused to let myself calm down. "I told Bevin I wanted to try what we'd discussed, the reverse of healing. I need to learn if I can use it as a defense strategy, and it isn't something we can train randomly. If I can start a heart back up, I should be able to stop one, right?"

The memory made me shake and they both moved closer. Bevin's arm wrapped around my waist in a hug, and José's tightened around my back. After a few seconds my body relaxed again. I put my arm around José's waist for a bit of extra contact and he grabbed my hand.

"I used my epsilon calming to all but knock Matthias out. It was concentrated and thick. Once he was down, I grabbed his hand and entered him with Panther. We found his heart and stopped it."

José squeezed my hand. "How long does it take from the time a heart stops until death?"

My voice shook a bit. "Four to six minutes. We got his heart to stop, but waited to make sure it stayed stopped, only about two minutes. Leaving his body…it felt like we were fighting quicksand to get out. I wasn't sure we *would* get out. It took so much longer than normal. I don't know what would have happened if we hadn't made it."

Nausea rose in me again and I trembled.

Bevin's arm tightened around me. "I didn't know that. Why didn't you tell me?"

"I was scared, and we weren't alone."

"Luke and Zee wouldn't have thought less of you."

Sadness washed through me unbidden. I fought the realization that I didn't know how to explain to him what I was thinking and feeling. The tears started up again. I relived the escape, trying to get out of Matthias before he finally died. Before I could die with him.

I had to change the subject. "What happened to the other four members of the group in the woods?"

José tensed for a moment, then relaxed. "We got images from some of the cameras we have up. Greta and Quinn identified them—well, Quinn did. Luke, Zee, Violet, Bevin, and Alex went out to investigate."

Everything in me froze. "Alex?"

"They insisted."

Shaking, I closed my eyes, my nausea returning full force. "What happened?"

"Our people ended up killing three of them. One got away."

"Did any of ours get hurt?"

It was their turn to pause. "Our pack represented themselves quite well, but it was a battle, chica. Alex does need to be trained, but they've got some basic skills from the farm. I guess their dad taught them and their brother some fighting skills when they were brought up. That and they saw how animals fight. It wasn't a lot, but it helped. We'll let Owen set up a full training schedule when he arrives this summer."

Too much had happened, and I felt emptied out. I heard what he hadn't said. "Who didn't make it?"

Bevin's arm tightened around me, and I felt the sadness seeping from him. It mixed with mine.

José squeezed my hand. "Oh, chica. I'm so sorry. Zee

had never been trained for that kind of fight."

I bit back a sob. "So, they lost five of their wolves? Does the one that got away know that?"

José smiled sadly. "We'll make sure that they know."

Bevin rested his head on mine. "I don't think this new skill of yours is viable. It takes too much from you. I think it hurts your soul. I don't like seeing you like this."

José squeezed my hand. "I agree, chica. It isn't worth it. This approach is off the table. Your skills are for healing only."

Trying to melt into the bed, wishing I could forget everything from the last twenty-four hours, all I could do was agree. "Okay. Healing only. Got it."

The next day, we had a funeral service for Zee. We sat around the fire pit in the backyard. We roasted marshmallows and told stories late into the night. Bevin and I told the story of how we met him, back when he was Zach, and he was our first run as the new healing team. How he nicknamed us Team Kid.

José had a story from his sister's high school graduation. "She wanted to take a group of friends to Devil's Lake for a party. I agreed to go as a chaperone, but didn't want to go alone, and Zee happened to be in the area. I don't know why he agreed to help me out. At the time, we didn't know each other well, but Zee was an expert rock climber and could help to keep up with the gaggle of graduates." José gave a sad smile as he spoke of the trip. "He told me later it was one of the reasons he had wanted to join our Pack. He felt a connection to me and thought he could see hanging out with and…you know, being in a pack with us."

Luke told a few stories about how he and Zee would hang out together. He had one where the two of them went to the beach and Zee tried to teach Luke how to surf. Part of the beauty of the story was the water was near freezing but that didn't stop them from jumping in and trying. Once they were in the water with their boards, Luke realized Zee didn't know how to surf any better than he did. He'd just watched a bunch of videos and figured 'how hard can it be?'

The group laughed, talking about the daredevil instigating the lessons while having no idea what he was doing.

Alex had a story of Zee taking them out on a 'roughing it' weekend. Though Alex had experienced life on the farm, they'd never done much camping or living off the land. They went out into the woods for three days with only water, a sleeping bag, and a knife. Zee taught them how to create a fire, find shelter, and scavenge for safe foods.

Violet and Zee had spent a lot of time together at Pack House. Violet just said that she was going to miss him, tears wetting her face.

In the end, I handed out paper for everyone to write

words of love and hope. We threw the sentiments in the fire to send up to Zee. A family tradition. I hoped Zee was up running with the gods in heaven, enjoying the Pack runs in the clouds.

Tears streaming down my face, I wrote. *I'll miss you, Zee. Team Kid.*

CHAPTER 5

Despite Matthias's prediction, we weren't rousted out before finals. We all sat in the back of a huge auditorium and watched as José received his diploma. Bevin and I sat surrounded by the Pack, cheering him on as he walked the stage. The scent of jasmine-scent of pride filled the air at our alpha's accomplishment. After he got his diploma, we all went out for a big celebration dinner in San Francisco.

After surviving finals, Owen and Sarah drove in from Wisconsin in Bevin's car filled with a bunch of their stuff. It didn't take them long to get settled in their room.

Then Owen practically dove into the hot tub and started lamenting about the drive west.

Ignoring him, I faced Sarah. "He graduated, right?"

"Yeah, walked the stage and everything. Too bad the trip back to Wisconsin would've interrupted your finals; everyone would've loved to see you back there, and seeing him in his cap and gown was impressive."

My eyebrow rose. "Do you have any evidence? Pictures, video? I need some hard proof on this one."

Owen grabbed my foot and pulled me under the hot water.

Coming back up, I laughed, spluttering out water. He grumbled. "I got good grades, sis!"

Eyes wide, I slapped my hand over my mouth, pretending shock. "He's such a whiner. Have you decided what you'll be doing next year?"

Sarah leaned back, staring out over the pool. "Yeah, one more year at Whitewater. I'm just going to stay there. It will be lonely, but it will be easier than doing what José did. I don't have a STEM degree to transfer here."

"You'll be fine. You're so outgoing. One more year, and then you'll move here, though, right?" Owen leaned towards her as if she'd better give the correct answer.

"I think so. Do you think Bevin and José will allow a panther alpha to live in Were House?"

My face broke into the first real smile I'd had in days. "I dunno, that's a big ask. Maybe you'll have to butter them up. Offer your services as wedding coordinator."

She barked out a laugh, loud enough to attract everyone's attention. "Gods, none of you will shop, will you? It's your parents' pack all over again."

José came up to the hot tub, still in his street clothes. "What are you two discussing? I don't know if I can trust you."

Sarah swiveled. "Apparently, I need to bribe you to convince you and Bevin to accept the alpha of a different wereanimal into your humble wolf den."

Anger bubbled from him. "Wha—"

She placed her wet hand on his arm. "So, I humbly offer to help coordinate the wedding of the century *and* help with the shopping in trade for you overlooking my alpha panther status."

His eyes widened and then he started to laugh. "I've been played. The two of you together are not trustworthy."

Bevin walked up behind him, wrapping his arms around him and kissing his neck. "So, we have a wedding planner. Perfect. Now, how about we celebrate your and Owen's graduation? Let's go to an amusement park. I think we all need a day off."

Owen sat up quickly before sinking back down. "When? None of us are working yet, so Thursday?"

José nodded. "I start work at Stone Security next Monday."

I focused on José, hanging on to the side of the hot tub, and floating in the bubbles. "I think I want to look for a job this summer. Maybe at a hospital, or anything really. Just to get me doing something new."

A low growl left him. "We'll talk later. I really want you here. We will have new pack members coming this summer and I'd really like you and Bevin here as a welcoming committee."

"That's right!" Sarah said, eyes twinkling. "All the packs are sending you some of their wolves. Do you know them?"

I said, "No," as Bevin and José said, "Yes" and "Kinda."

Bevin snorted. "We met all of the North American Pack wolves over the last two years. We know them by name and face, but we don't know much about them as people. We're pretty sure who each pack is sending. We did spend some time speaking with each wolf family who decided they wanted to throw in their lot with us, but that's it."

José shrugged. "That's fair. Now, about this job. Can we talk about it later, chica? For now, let's focus on fun and relaxation. We all need a few days off."

Over the next couple of days, Sarah started mapping out what would be needed for the wedding. It being the wedding of werewolf alphas, we figured we had to invite all the other pack alphas. Most of the Wisconsin pack would probably come. Then there was José's family from down in Mexico. We hoped the new pack members from each of the other packs would join us, too. The list of invitations kept growing.

Next, there was the question of food, clothing, who would be in the wedding party, where people would stay... and then I stopped listening. Sarah jotted down ideas in a notebook with ice cream cones on its cover. The boys gave her free rein on what she thought was best, but she checked in on all the major decisions.

While Sarah set up charts, calendars, and started to make phone calls, Owen and I arranged a day at an amusement park. The grade school kids were still in school, so Thursday was the perfect day to go. We found one with rides, both dry and water, games, and lots of greasy food. Neither Luke nor Violet wanted to join us, but Alex did, making our party a group of six. We took two cars, and we were off for a day of fun and relaxation.

After getting our park wristbands, we separated into pairs, José and Bevin, Sarah and Owen, and me and Alex. We would've stayed together, but we all wanted to do different things. We agreed to meet in three hours for a snack. Alex and I went on a couple of thrill rides and one water ride. When we found the rest of the group, I was dripping wet. Alex somehow managed to go on the ride and avoid the majority of the water.

We all got in line for food and compared notes while we waited. Bevin eyed me. "Can we swap partners? I love the guy, but he won't go on Swan Dive Mountain with me."

José glared at me, as if this was my fault. "I want to survive to enjoy the degree I just earned."

Alex rotated to look at the mammoth black and red ride on the edge of the park. The screams coming as the train plummeted then twisted in a corkscrew made us all shiver. Then Alex quirked a half-smile and linked their arm through mine. "No way. Jade promised me we'd go on that after food."

Bevin sighed, resting his head on José's shoulder. "Good thing you're sexy."

José slid his arm around Bevin's waist. "And alive."

Sarah started to bounce. "Owen and I will join you two after we eat. I've been *dying*," she eyed José, "to go on that ride all day."

Owen waggled his brows. "I'm in."

We finally made it to the front of the line and ordered overpriced burgers and fries. After we ate, we agreed to meet in another couple of hours and then split up. Four of us went on the ride, while José and Bevin headed in a different direction.

After Swan Dive Mountain, an amazingly fun ride, Alex and I went in search of ice cream. We sat on a bench to enjoy the treat. The wind was blowing strong enough that I was a bit worried about the mess I was eventually going to make on my shirt.

As I finished up my ice cream, I saw a boy, maybe mid-teens, skateboarding towards me with the wind at his back. He wasn't bad, but the wind was causing him to pick up speed and wobble a bit. There was a sharp turn in the sidewalk, and I wasn't sure he was going to make it. He bent his knees and got low, leaning with the turn, but a strong gust knocked his center off balance. He wind-milled his arms, but it didn't help, and he went flying.

He landed a few feet from me, knocking his head hard. The crack reverberated through our area of the park, echoing around me. Before I could think about what I was doing, I ran over to him, and Panther rushed in to check him out. His skull was cracked and there were fragments that could pierce his brain. We quickly mended the dangerous internal bits before pulling out, leaving most of the injury intact.

When I opened my eyes, Alex gaped at me. They grabbed my arm and pulled me up, dragging me away. "What did you do?" They sounded frantic.

"Hold on." I looked around. "Help! This kid needs help."

A man ran over.

As soon as he got there, I let Alex drag me away. Once we'd moved a good ten feet away, I answered them. "I made sure the kid wouldn't die. I left most of his injuries intact." I peeked over my shoulder and saw a second man running up to the kid. "And check it out, people are helping."

Alex continued to pull me away. "Jade, we need to go."

I glanced over one more time. One of the men pulled out his phone to make a call. His eyes landed on us, but his stare wasn't focused. He seemed to be concentrating on the scene in front of him. We were walking into the wind so I couldn't hear him or what he was saying. It must be a call to 911; his motions were frantic.

As we rounded the next corner, we ran into José and Bevin.

Sniffing, José grabbed my shoulder. "What did you do?"

Lifting my hands, I saw there was blood on them. I fisted them. "There was a kid, José. I couldn't let him die."

José wrapped an arm around my waist and started dragging me from the park. "Yes, you can. He wasn't your responsibility. Bev, get a hold of the others and get home as soon as possible. I'm taking these two home before anything more exciting happens."

Bevin leaned over to get a kiss before heading off to find Sarah and Owen.

I snarled. "I didn't heal him, José, not really. He's still lying there injured. He just won't die. The kid is young. Haven't we had enough death this month?"

His eyes softened. "I know it's hard, but you have to be more careful."

CHAPTER 6

The sun shone down and there wasn't a cloud in the sky. It was a beautiful summer day, and I was sitting on a lawn chair by the pool reading a book by one of my favorite authors, Ilona Andrews. I so wanted to have a magic broom that could kick butt.

José had started work at Stone Security. He and Violet had headed into the new building this morning. Owen and Sarah were out searching for jobs for Owen and doing a driving tour of the general area. Bevin was out with Luke doing a sweep of the land.

The lemonade I drank was cool and refreshing. I

debated the pool, but the sun and the book were taking over my day.

The sliding door opened. Without looking up, I said, "Hi, Alex. Finally decided a book was the way to spend the day?"

"A book sounds lovely, but that isn't what I'm here for."

At the sound of Greta's voice, I tensed and leapt up, knocking down my drink. Closing my Kindle, I placed it on the chair and rotated to face my ex-girlfriend.

"Alex let you in?"

"Yeah. Quinn wanted to talk to them, and I tagged along. I thought I could come out here and talk with you. You're looking lovely as always in that two-piece." Her eyes tracked up and down my body.

Blushing, I realized I really needed to buy a one-piece suit. Letting Sarah dress me was easy but not always smart. I felt exposed under Greta's intense scrutiny.

Surveying the pool area, I headed towards the hot tub and away from Greta. "What do you want, Greta?"

She followed me. "You know what I want. We were good together."

"Maybe, but that doesn't change anything."

Her hand snaked out and grabbed my shoulder. She turned me to face her then pushed me against the house. Leaning into me, she kissed me deeply. For a second, I melted into the kiss with a moan, then I froze and pushed her away. "No!"

She smiled down at me with a Cheshire grin. Her hazel eyes twinkled. "You miss me, hon, admit it."

Her arms were still around me, caging me in. "I may miss the idea of you, but I can't trust you. In the end, that's what matters."

The sparkle died and she dropped her arms. "It was for your own safety...your own good. Really."

She turned away from me and I decided I was done with sitting by the pool. I grabbed my Kindle and headed inside. Greta followed.

I found Alex sitting in the living room with Quinn. Alex waved their hands as they spoke.

"The semester was great, but rough. I can't believe I survived finals."

Quinn smiled as his face softened. "Will you be getting a job this summer?"

"I think so, or maybe an internship."

I groaned as I dropped onto the couch next to them.

Alex threw an arm across my shoulders. "I know you wanted to get a job, but you have a lot to do this summer."

With another groan, I narrowed my eyes and shook my head. "Not much right now. I'm heading to the coffee shop. I'll be back later. Let anyone know if they come looking for me." I got up and headed to my room. Slipping into a pair of jeans and a shirt that said, *I'm an adult, but not like a real adult,* I headed out.

Crossing through the living room, I passed Alex and

the twins. Greta's eyes tracked my path until I reached the front door. I could feel her focus on me until the door of Were House shut. As I walked towards the gate, I pulled out my phone and sent a text to José letting him know where I was going. I figured I could walk to the café, and he could pick me up later.

The day was beautiful, and I wanted to get away. I picked up my speed and started to jog. It didn't take long to get to town.

My favorite coffee shop was close, and there wasn't a line. I headed to the counter and ordered a coffee and chocolate chip muffin from Deja, one of the baristas who'd worked there for as long as I had been a student.

"Glad to see you around this summer, Jade."

"It's the coffee and the muffins, Deja. You all seduced me into staying close by!"

She laughed. A moment later I grabbed my grub and sat down to continue my book.

Oblivious to the world around me, I felt a buzz in my pocket. I pulled out my phone and saw a message from José. He could swing by and pick me up in an hour when he was done with work. I shot off a quick agreement, got up to order an apple and get a refill of my coffee, and returned to reading.

A few bites into my apple, someone joined me at my table. I blinked and shifted my focus from my Kindle to the stranger. Sitting across from me was an older gentleman in a pale blue button-down shirt. He had dirty-blond hair and light blue eyes. His glasses were tucked into his shirt pocket, and he stared at me as if he wanted to read my mind.

With a sigh, I raised an eyebrow and said, "Sorry, not my type." And gazed back down as if I were going to go back to reading. I hoped he would get the point.

He cleared his throat. "You're so young."

He didn't get the point. "Yeah, that's only part of it, mister. You can leave now."

"I'm sorry to interrupt." He didn't sound sorry. "But were you at a park last week? An action park?"

I stopped staring at the blank screen of the Kindle and scrunched my face as I turned to him. Scratching my head I repeated, "Action park? Like a place adults go to get action? Yeah, never."

He blanched, then turned bright red. It was almost worth it for that…almost. "No! I mean like roller-coaster rides."

"Oh, amusement park." I narrowed my eyes. "Why?"

Before he answered I sent a mental knock to José.

He replied with a *"Busy, is this important?"*

Maybe. Can you listen in while working?

"Chica, first day here. Are you in danger?"

Stranger danger? Possibly. Random person has joined me and is asking questions. Should I call on Bev?

He sighed, *"No, he's running with Luke. I can get to you faster."*

The man pulled out a card and put it on the table. I didn't touch it. "My name is Doctor Ernie Everts. I work for a group of individuals who would like to meet you."

My hackles rose. "Why?"

"Well, we *think* you may have helped a child with his injuries. If we are right, we propose an exchange of information. That's it."

José's anger flowed down our connection. *"Jade! This. This is why you need to be better! Smarter. Stop trying to help people who aren't Pack."*

Listen now, yell later. And I still don't agree with you.

I sighed. "I don't know what you're talking about. I did see a kid fall, but I called for help. A man ran up to him and helped him…well, two men."

Doctor Ernie Everts looked disappointed in me. "One of those men was the kid's father. He has excellent hearing. He heard you tell your friend that all you did was ensure he wouldn't die, nothing too extreme."

Again, José's temper flowed down to me. His ire was rare, but today it was in fine form. *"What were you thinking? How could you first heal, and then talk about healing where you could be overheard?"*

Breathing slowly and working hard to maintain a poker face, I stared Doctor Ernie Everts in the eyes. "I don't know what you are talking about. The man who helped the boy, he and I were never closer than ten to fifteen feet apart. The park was noisy. I think he was just being hopeful. I may have said something about checking to make sure the kid *had* survived his injuries." I gestured to myself. "What could I have done?"

Again, the doctor gave me the look of a teacher when their star pupil gets an easy question wrong. "As I said, the father has *very* good hearing. You could almost say it's as good as an animal's. His sense of smell is good, too. You were upwind of him, and he is certain that you and he are similar in your heightened senses."

I could feel some of José's ire dissolve as his anger melted into frustration. *"Who are these people?"*

He didn't say. I looked down at his card, but it didn't have more than a name and a phone number.

"Why are you here, Doctor Ernie Everts?"

"Well, first of all, your name would be nice. Second, I would like to invite you to our compound for a visit."

José growled. *"First name only. You are not going alone."*

"I can't go today, I'm busy, waiting for a ride. I wouldn't trust going anywhere with a stranger anyway. And you can call me Jade."

"So, you won't give me your real name?"

José snorted.

"How about Friday? Give me an address, I'll drive out there with a friend."

He nodded. "Could you pack and stay for a night or two? I don't know if that would be necessary, but just in case. Our conversation may be…involved."

I could almost feel José's denial and frustration.

"I will think about it."

CHAPTER 7

Tuesday morning, I woke early, the light coming in through my window barely enough to make out the edges of my bed. As I silently left my room, I thought about my goals for the day.

Across the hall, I noticed a peg board on the wall next to Alex's door. That was new. I gazed down the hallway. There were peg boards hanging by all the doors. Whipping around, I saw a peg board up by my door with a slip of paper tacked on it.

Jade's schedule: Tuesday

I stared at the title for a full minute before I pulled

the sheet down and unfolded it. There was a full training schedule a la my dad. Aghast, I realized this must have been what Owen and Sarah had been up to yesterday. Irritated with everything, I went back into my room and changed into exercise clothes.

Once I had running shorts and a halter top on, I went into the kitchen for a water bottle, then headed over to the gym. There were new decorations there as well, including a whiteboard with our names and achievements. Apparently, Owen had been busy and had gone through our journals, because our latest numbers were filled in. I put my sheet up on the wall and warmed up.

Today's torture—er, goals—was strength training. I started with a run to warm up and then moved through the weight-training routine Owen had set up. Because I had woken up early, I had the gym to myself. This was my preferred way to do things. I didn't hate working out in a group, but when I was alone, I went into a zone and was less likely to end up on my butt.

When I finished, I headed back to the house to make coffee and grab a snack. I found Sarah in the kitchen with coffee already made. I poured a cup and joined her, drinking my liquid heaven.

"Did you exercise already?" She sounded disappointed.

"Yep! You gotta get up early."

My phone buzzed. After looking at the display, rolled my eyes and put it down. I took another sip of coffee.

Sarah watched me, then shrugged. "I half-expected you to come in and strangle your brother before you actually did anything."

"I'll admit it, I thought about it. But after Zee I know we all need to get back into a routine. I'm surprised it took him this long."

"Yeah. That really shook Owen. He won't let on to the Pack but expect him to be a wee bit worse than your dad."

Letting my head fall to my arms on the table, I groaned.

"You'll survive. He also wants to figure out all your new tricks."

"I have too many handlers, Sarah. Maybe I'll run away for a month or four. Gods!"

"Huh. I didn't think you'd ever notice."

I glared at her as I got up to grab some food. Searching the refrigerator, I found eggs, onion, peppers, and ham. I began to prepare an omelet.

Sarah came up behind me. "Do I get one?"

"Make some toast, and sure."

She pointed at my phone. "What was that?"

My eyes cut to the phone still on the far counter as I continued dicing veggies. "Greta sent me a text asking if we could talk."

"What are you going to do?"

"Probably ignore it."

Sarah's face scrunched up, then she shrugged. "Fair enough."

Ten minutes later, we were eating breakfast. She eyed me. "Do the boys know you can make this?"

"Nope! And once you've lived with José's cooking, you'll understand why I don't tell them. And honestly, this is the only thing I can manage to make well."

"That's true. Do you remember when you tried to make pancakes at my house?"

The memory flowed back, and I groaned, then laughed. "Let's not try to remember that. They were so bad. And your mom tried to eat them to make me feel better. Your dad just spit his first bite out. No amount of syrup was going to save them. So gross."

"How did you ruin such a simple recipe?"
"I have no idea. But your mom banned me from cooking at your house after that." A wide smile spread across my face at the memory.

"No, that would be my dad."

I huffed out a laugh and got up to put my plate in the kitchen. "So, what are your plans for the day?"

"After I do my torture routine? I'm going to help Owen with his resume and work on the wedding. You?"

"No idea. Shower. Figure out if José and I are really going to go to that meeting on Friday. And we've eliminated the codes from the gate, but I still feel weird about it. I don't know. I may do some research into the other contractors we used."

"Not a bad idea. Well, you stink; off with you."

She was still chuckling as I closed my door and headed to shower.

After my shower, I slipped into a clean pair of jeans and a shirt that had a hammer on it with an arrow pointing to it. It read, *This is not a drill.*

In the hallway, Bevin popped his head out of his room. I pointed to his door's new decoration. Bleary-eyed, he stared at the paper with his name on it, grumbled, grabbed it, and ducked back into his room. I snorted as I made it to the coffee pot.

José was in the kitchen preparing his lunch, wearing black slacks and a light purple button down. Looking him up and down, I let out a small whistle. "I see Sarah has been more than just my personal shopper. Looking sharp, Mr. Cortez."

A wave of pleasure rolled off him as he threw a smile over his shoulder. "Thanks, but Bevin's compliments were way better."

I rolled my eyes and took my coffee to the table. "You two are awful."

He came over and sat with coffee and a bagel. He shot a glance at the coffee table in the living room which was covered with invitations. "I know Sarah has you addressing envelopes today, but if you can find time to do any research on who Doctor Ernie Everts is, that would be great...do you think his wife calls him that?"

I snorted but wouldn't be distracted. "Wouldn't Violet

be better at that?"

"Yeah, and if you can't find anything, I'll have her do that tonight."

Luke ran into the kitchen, grabbed a travel mug, and dashed out the door with a mumbled, "Morn."

Alex came out, shoulders slouched. We watched as they made their way into the kitchen, eyes on the floor ahead of them. They selected a cup from the cabinet and filled it with orange juice, rummaged through the fruit for a banana, and then opened the fridge, and found two hard boiled eggs. Grabbing a plate, they joined us at the table, flopping into a chair next to me with a sigh.

We both just stared at them. I gently placed my hand on their shoulder. "You okay? It's awfully early for this much emotion, hon."

They started peeling their first egg, focusing on that. "I got an email from my mom. She wants me to come home for a week. It wasn't a suggestion. She said she gets that I love it here and plan to relocate, but thinks it's been too long. My family misses me. I didn't go home over winter break…or Thanksgiving break." They looked up at me, face drawn. "The thing is, I know my family doesn't care that I'm not home. It's just a weird power play."

They grabbed the salt, gave it a few shakes, and bit into the first egg.

José finished off his bagel. "Would it help if someone went with you?"

Their eyes shot up to his. "Really?"

"You're Pack. We're here for you. We will support your decision if you want to go or if you want to stay."

Violet ran in, grabbed a frozen breakfast sandwich, and threw it in the microwave. As it warmed up, she poured some coffee into a travel mug and turned to José. "Come on, work drone, we've got to go."

José's mouth twitched. "That's my cue. Got to go." He cleared his area and led Violet out the door.

Bevin trudged through to the kitchen wearing a t-shirt and shorts. He looked half asleep. He grabbed a water bottle and headed out towards the gym. Alex's eyes tracked his progress. "Why doesn't he wake up first? Eat?"

"It's our thing. Torture while still too tired to realize what's happening."

They squinted at me. "Have you already hit the gym?"

I nodded. "Torture, breakfast, shower. I'll go label envelopes while everyone else catches up to me."

"I never realized while we lived together in the dorms that your early mornings weren't hell on you. You really *are* a cat."

I gave her what I hoped was a Cheshire smile. "Think about what José said. If you need backup, one of us can go with you. Also, if you left anything back home, you could grab it and bring it here, make your room more your own."

Alex smiled softly as they looked up towards the ceiling in thought. "Yeah, maybe. You don't think with the wedding preparations it would be too much?"

I shook my head. "Some of us aren't doing as much, trust me." And with that, I moved to addressing envelopes.

Our list of names and addresses was long. As I wrote, people moved in and out of the rooms. The activity from the kitchen to the basement and the gym became a constant background of white noise. After a few hours, Sarah and Owen ended up in the basement working on Owen's resume and searching for jobs, Alex finally hit the gym for their own set of exercises, and Bevin draped himself over the couch I leaned on. After his shower, he settled on shorts and a tank top, and while I labeled envelopes, he read a book.

My phone chimed, letting me know someone was trying to get into the gate using a bad key code. We had recently changed all the passcodes, clearing them all out. The factory clearly didn't clear out the creator digits; that's how Matthias and crew got in. Violet hacked into the manufacturer's setup and did a full reprogramming of the codes, changing the base sequence allowed for the passcodes. Previously, all codes had to be a five-digit number. Now they had to be a six-digit number. She found where the creator passcode was hardcoded into the gate and cleared that out as well.

We were planning on publicly announcing all of this on the internet, better business websites, social media, and other sites, and explaining what we had found about the hardcoded creator's code. Once it was finished, we would release a freeware patch that anyone could upload, which would clear the code out. We planned on doing this from a coffee shop in the wharf in San Francisco. No reason to be easily traceable.

Grabbing my phone, I pulled up the feed from a camera near the gate and saw Quinn's car. There was an arm sticking out of the back window, tapping away at the box. I switched apps. "Can I help you?"

The arm froze and slipped back into the car.

Quinn's voice came over my phone. "Heya, Jade, it's me and Greta, we were wondering if we could come talk to you."

"And the third member of your party?"

"Just the two of us."

"Quinn, not only do I not believe you, but my app told me you tried a few codes to break in, and you're on camera. Want to try again?"

A long, deep sigh and some mumbling came over the speaker and then a shuffling sound. "We brought our dad."

Bevin sat up, checked out his outfit, and slipped off to his room.

"You brought your dad here? You think that's a smart move?"

Quinn cleared his throat. "He wants to meet you and… um, José and Bevin."

Checking out the space, I started cleaning up the invitations. There were only a few left. Ten more minutes and I could have finished them. After boxing them up, I stashed them in my room. "José is at work. If you can promise he'll behave—and trying to break in isn't behaving—I'll let the three of you in."

"Look, we're sorry about that. I'm not sure why he thought he knew the code. We'll behave. He'll behave."

"Even if he *did* know a code, that isn't a polite way to enter our territory."

A sigh. "I agree. Again, I'm sorry…we're sorry."

Though I believed *he* was sorry, I doubted anyone else in the car was.

I checked over the common area. The kitchen wasn't perfect, but it was good enough for them. The living room and dining room were picked up. Clearing the last few items of clutter, I decided it was as good as it would get.

Bevin came out of his room in black slacks and a gray short-sleeved button down. He'd assumed his mantle of power. He was magnificent. "Wow, you look spectacular. Should I let them in?"

Licking his lips, he nodded. "I'm as ready as I can get."

After releasing the gate, I turned to Bevin. "Should I change?"

His face, hard with focus on the upcoming confrontation, broke into a half-smile. "Oh, no. You're perfect exactly as you are. I'm the power, you're the show of blasé."

"That's good. I don't know if I could do what you did as fast."

"Me either." He laughed, pulling me in for a quick hug

and kiss to the top of my head.

A minute later there was a knock on the door. Bevin answered it. Quinn and Greta froze on the stoop, gazing up at Bevin in awe. I smelled the sweet scent of fear, but not from them, from the man standing behind them. He was slightly taller than the twins with the same sandy hair and hazel eyes.

After a long moment of taking their measure, Bevin stepped back to let them in. I led them to the dining room.

Bevin, José, and I had decided over spring break to stop using the werebear soap. As the twins' father walked in, he would be able to smell, as well as feel, that Bevin was a werewolf. He'd also likely smell the wolf on me. What more he could smell all depended on how well he could use his nose.

Once everyone sat down, Bevin, still oozing power, faced Quinn. "Why have you and your family come today?"

Speaking to Quinn, when we could smell that their father was a werewolf, was a show of disrespect. The power that Bevin was releasing was forcing the twins' dad to keep his eyes lowered, another show of disdain. The fact that I didn't drop my eyes showed him that I, like Bevin, was more powerful than him.

Since the twins weren't werewolves, they missed the entire powerplay happening at the table. Though, they had to notice Bevin's clothes and stiffer, more formal speech.

Quinn looked back and forth between Bevin and his

dad. His breath hitched when he realized his dad was hunched over, not answering the question. His eyes got a bit wider, then he faced Bevin. "What's happening?"

"Hopefully, you're explaining why you brought your father here. Your people came here a few weeks ago. They snuck onto our land and killed one of our pack mates. The idea of having another of your family's werewolves on my territory isn't pleasing."

Quinn's jaw dropped. "Wait, what? Who died?"

His dad spoke at the same time, his words as much a growl as actual speech. "And how many of our people died that day?"

Greta's breathing grew choppy. "What are you all talking about? Who died? What have you been hiding from us? Were you planning on sneaking onto this property to cause havoc?"

Her dad's eyes glowed as they snapped up to her face. "It's not called havoc, girl, it's called retribution. They killed your grandfather, and Jeff, and Herbert, and…"

Bevin bellowed, "Enough!" All eyes snapped to him. "We didn't just go out on a walk and decide to kill your people." He pulled out his phone and, after a few seconds, found an audio recording.

A gravelly male voice said, "Did Jason finish setting up the surveillance in the tree?"

A younger voice, maybe mid-thirties, replied. "Either way, we're going in tonight. Our intel says there are four to six wolves in there. They're all young and we should be able to take them out in their sleep."

An older voice said, "Matthias has taken up residence in the abandoned house; why can't we stay there as well? There's more than one room. Why do we have to be out here in the wilderness? I'm too old for this."

"It was *your* son who told us about this pack before we even got the letter from the supposed alpha and whatever an epsilon is. I can't believe your boy got himself bitten behind our backs, Mason. Such impudence. What are we going to do with him?"

"Leave that to me; he'll regret his decision once I'm done with him."

Gravel-voice again. "He's supposed to text when it's time to move in. I don't see why we're even waiting; we can take out these young kids. What do they have on us anyway? They're babies."

Bevin turned off the recording. "So, what you called 'killing,' I call self-defense."

The father's eyes started to move to Bevin's face but didn't quite make it. "You have the woods bugged?"

I couldn't hold back a laugh. "You think you are so superior. You have no idea what you're doing. You're a cult and we are a pack with the history that goes along with it. Our history is rich and long. You have *no idea*. What were you trying to accomplish coming here? Bargaining with us? Threatening us? Killing us? The letter we sent you was

PACK

clear. 'Come to our land, just be polite.' Was that so much to ask for?"

He turned to me and seemed surprised when he realized he could stare me in the eyes. "What right do you have to come here and claim this land?"

Bevin spoke quietly, but clearly. "We have the right set forth by the American Werewolf Packs. There were five packs in the U.S. Now there are six. They agreed to us forming this pack here. If you want to fight us, we can fight. Just realize, the one pack member you defeated was the one member who didn't have any training. I ask again: what do you want?"

The twins' father growled low in his throat. "Isn't it obvious? I want you all dead, boy. Dead and gone." His eyes widened as if he hadn't meant to say that out loud.

Quinn's face hardened. "Why did you bring us here, Dad?"

"You were a diversion, boy. Why are you so slow?" He glared at Quinn. "Get through the gate, leap from the car, in and out. These kids have nothing on seasoned wolves."

My brow lifted. "How's that working out for you?"

He snarled. Before he could say more, Greta, tears flowing down her face, asked, "How many people died?"

Bevin faced her. "Five of yours, one of ours."

She gulped. "Who?"

I could see Bevin's struggle to keep a blank face. "We lost Zee. I don't know who all you lost. If this war continues, your side will lose a lot more."

CHAPTER 8

The email came Thursday night letting me know where Doctor Ernie Everts expected me to arrive on Friday morning. The compound was in Daly City, just south of San Francisco. José didn't have to work Friday, so we both packed for three days. Our plan—our hope—was to be home for dinner Friday night.

Friday morning, I woke early enough to hit the gym. I thought I'd be alone, but José and Alex both followed shortly after me. The three of us did some cardio and then moved to sparring. We showed Alex some basics. Hand-to-hand was new to them. Then it was time for breakfast, coffee, shower, and we were off.

We decided to use the werebear soap to face this new situation. We'd discussed it, and despite our resolve, we were heading into a government agency, and this seemed like a bigger situation, especially with me having two animals.

I watched the cars blur by as we drove. "Is this as dumb of an idea as I think it is?"

José snorted. "Most ideas that start with you are."

"Hey!" I tried to be mad, but he probably could list off a dozen examples.

He chuckled. "Having you around will never be dull."

"Remember, you wanted me as part of the Pack."

"Fact. I never said I didn't. I just wouldn't mind a bit more down time. Maybe Bevin and I could take a trip together and not worry about what we'd come home to find."

"Look, buster, we've had a pack den for less than a year, and you're already worried about leaving me in charge?"

"Yes."

I flopped back, shaking my head. "You're awful, you know? I could always go back to Wisconsin…or one of the other packs. I bet they'd appreciate me."

He just continued to drive, ignoring me.

I harrumphed. "My parents left me alone; it never ended poorly."

He slid his eyes to me for a second before navigating the twists and turns to our exit. "You were younger then. Other pack members were around. You've gained skills with age, chica, become more of a firecracker. And we were always around."

Glaring at him, I decided to stop while I was behind.

We pulled into the compound. It looked like any other corporate building: muddy gray with blacked-out windows, so no one could see what was going on inside. There was fencing around the side, but I couldn't see through that either. The acronym SSLD was on the side in bold silver letters.

José found a parking spot, grabbed our duffle bags, and went to the door. It was locked. Grumbling, I took out my phone and pulled up the email, but couldn't find any more information.

José eyed the door and then swung his head to his car. "We could leave. We did our due diligence. We packed, we drove out here, and we came to the door. It's seven-thirty in the morning, earlier than I want to be conscious on a day off. We could easily go home and go back to bed."

"I don't even think I disagree with you." I picked up my bag and spun on my heel.

We were halfway to the car when the door opened, and a voice called out. "Jade?"

Slowly, I stopped, letting my head fall back. I had gotten excited about the idea of going home, sitting by the pool, and hanging out with my friends. For the first time all summer, being bored at home seemed attractive.

Swiveling around, I saw a small blonde woman standing in a brown, skirted business suit and matching brown heels.

She had on a coral silk shirt and a pearl necklace. Her hair was up in a bun, and dark glasses perched on her nose. The nutty scent of nerves wafted from her.

José grumbled, but eventually gave up and faced the compound as well.

"I'm sorry to be so informal, but I wasn't given any other name to call you. I, um, also wasn't expecting you to have a...friend...with you."

That was interesting. I'd mentioned being unwilling to come alone. Apparently, the doctor failed to mention to the people here that I would be bringing my very own plus one. I tried not to snicker at the thought of all the invitations I had filled out with their plus ones.

José slid his hand across my lower back. "Is there a problem with me being here?"

She blanched. "Oh, of course not. I'll get you on the list. We can't have you two in the same room, though. It would make the other men...uncomfortable. You understand."

José sighed dramatically. "I guess we can sleep in separate rooms for the weekend." He leaned over and kissed my temple. Then he guided me to the door. The citrus scent of amusement pouring off him made my nose tingle. I fought not to sneeze.

When we got closer to the building, I saw the woman's name tag: *Anastasia*. She led us into a small receptionist area with a desk. "Please take a seat and someone will come to show you where you need to go." She slipped behind the desk. "Can I get each of your full names?"

José grabbed my hand and gave it a squeeze. "I'm José Cortez. This is Jade Stone."

Anastasia nodded as he spoke. She wrote something down on a pad, typed on her computer, and then slipped out of the only door. A few minutes later, she came back with two official pin name tags, one that said *Cortez*, the other *Stone*.

As the minutes passed, I grew annoyed. They asked us to arrive this early, and yet they left us here to wait. I thought about getting up to storm...somewhere, when José squeezed my hand. "Chica, we have no agenda. Just relax. If they want us to sit, we'll sit."

I felt a growl low in my belly, but I leaned back and shut my eyes. José let go of my hand and started to rub my arm, using the Pack connection to calm me.

A few minutes later, I heard a man's boots clapping down the hall. I sat up before he entered the reception area. I was ready to get this day started. The man was tall, over six feet, with a short, military-type hairstyle. He wore green khaki pants and a black t-shirt. His nametag read *Vern*.

"Please follow me." He tapped his right toe behind his left heel and performed a spin.

We stood and grabbed our bags. He led us down a hall with a few offices. We turned right at a corner and I saw a door with a plate stating it was the medical suite. At the end of the hall, we turned right again. On the left, there was a wall of windows that opened into a large gym. To the right were a series of rooms. Our guide pointed to two of them. "Bathroom, bathroom, and these two will be your dorm rooms while you stay with us."

José went into the first room; I entered the second. The room was small, with a single bed and a dresser. I threw my bag on top of the dresser and headed back into the hallway.

Vern led us into the gym where there was a group of about twenty men all dressed in the same green khaki pants and black shirts. I could smell the musty scent of werewolves in the room. Not all the people, but some of them. As I searched their faces, I recognized the father of the hurt kid from the park. His eyes were fixed on me.

Chairs were set up in rows, and four in front faced the group. Vern waved us to the front of the room, while the rest of the people headed to the main block of seats. Doctor Ernie Everts was one of the people by the four spots in front.

As we walked up, I pointed out the doctor to José. I had done the research and found little; his information was on lock-down. Violet had done a deeper dive and found out that the doctor worked in the government. His file said he worked for several departments, but apparently it was out-of-date since he was part of the SSLD, whatever that was.

When we got to the head of the room, everyone suddenly moved to sit, as if that was the signal they were waiting for. José and I were waved to the front by Vern. We took two of the chairs on the edge. I took the end and José sat next to Doctor Ernie Everts.

Butterflies took up residence in my stomach as we waited in front of a crowd of strangers. I had no idea why we were there. I had expected to be shown a few rooms, maybe asked some questions. Being at the front of the class was low on my list of guesses.

José slid his hand over to mine, giving it a squeeze. He connected to me. *"Relax, chica. I don't know what this is, but breathe, and put on your game face."*

A man in nice clothes, tan pants and a black button-down, started pacing between us and the larger group. "Welcome to our center, the SSLD. I'm the director, and I hope you enjoy your introduction to our facility." Though he was talking to everyone assembled, his words were meant for me and José. "We'd like to introduce ourselves to you and hope you'll feel comfortable here with us. We're an off-book black ops branch of the Secret Service that includes beings unknown to the general population. Everyone in this room knows about werewolves, not everyone knows about what else we do. We are here to share information and hopefully receive your assistance."

He paused, his gaze raking over his men, pride filling the room. The scent of jasmine covered the other smells of the gym. This man wasn't a werewolf, but he was a leader of them. "We've invited Jade Stone to our compound because we believe she can help us with the next stage of intelligence gathering. As many of you know, we've partnered with the shifters from Australia, but so far our work has only led to failure. We believe with her help, we may find success."

José shot me a perplexed look, but I just shrugged, feeling as confused as he smelled.

A hand shot up from the group. The director pointed to the man. "Simons?"

"Director, you're talking awfully plainly in front of these norms."

Simons was a werewolf and the werebear soap was doing its job. To the group of werewolves we were sitting in front of, we smelled like regular humans, a couple of posers.

The director paused and faced us. "Is what Agent Simons says true? I thought you two were…" he waved his hands at us vaguely, "not norms."

José dropped all his guards and let his alpha mojo flow throughout the room. Nothing about him changed, except he let loose the power he usually held on a tight rein. It hit me like a hammer, but I tried to keep a poker face. Twelve people sitting in the chairs dropped to their knees, including Agent Simons. I could hear them panting. Three of the men curled into a ball and started to whimper.

I leaned over to José. "Should I have reacted, too?"

He rubbed his eyes and tucked his power away, shaking his head. He mumbled back, "You did fine, chica, just fine."

The director's brow creased as he gazed at his men. They panted on their hands and knees for a few more minutes before slowly resuming their seats. Once they were all back in their neat rows, he turned to us. "I assume you did something to prove yourselves?"

José gave a slight nod.

The director gave a curt nod back. "Good. To continue, we are attempting to develop a relationship with a shifter group in Australia."

I raised my hand.

He nodded at me.

"Is there a difference between shifters and wereanimals?"

He considered me for a few seconds before his head bobbed slowly. "In general, a were...animal is a mammal. The transformation is slow and somewhat painful to watch. Bones, skin, hair...it all rearranges. Shifters are a different animal base. In the situation we're discussing, they are swans."

My jaw dropped. "Excuse me? Swans?" The idea of a new shifter type shut down my brain. I scrambled for a question. "For what purpose?"

He chuckled. "Surveillance and secure message transfer. We could literally get eyes in the sky if we had a shifter who could fly. Shifter swans can see the stripes on a caterpillar from the clouds. The problem is, shifters are a hereditary group. From what we've learned, there aren't any that come from any outside sources, like infection or bite, like mammals do. That doesn't mean we aren't trying. For some reason, the Australians don't want to work for or with U.S. intelligence or our government."

I rubbed my temples, trying to absorb this new knowledge. I had no idea I'd actually be learning something new today.

"So, wait, why do you need me? I can't imagine what I'd bring to the table to help."

"Well, we have reverse engineered a serum that can infect a norm with this shifter swan DNA. We've come close to it working, but all of our volunteers have died. We are hoping that you can keep our next volunteer alive. It is my understanding you have the ability to heal on the spot."

My heart pounded as I gazed at José who smiled with a mixture of intrigue and frustration. He finally met my eyes and shrugged.

"Can I get more information on the shifters? Are there any books?"

José chuckled softly next to me.

"Yeah, I can show you to the library. The plan is to have the injection administered later this morning. If all goes well, you may be home by dinner." I could smell that wasn't completely true, but he was trying to put me—or more likely, the scary wolf I was sitting next to—at ease.

José started shaking his head. "No. If you want Jade to heal, she needs calories, and a lot of them. Lunch first. Don't look at her and think 'girl.' She started out-eating her sports-loving teen brother pretty quickly. If she doesn't eat, she can't heal."

The director looked at us then at the faces of his

men. "Sounds good. I'll have Vern take you to the library until lunch."

By the time lunch rolled around, I had read some about shifters and talked a lot with José about what we'd learned. There were several shifter animals around the world, most smaller flying animals, though there were some ocean-dwelling sea creatures as well. The process was more…ethereal…in how they shifted, if the book was to be believed. I wasn't sure how the people—the scientists—in the SSLD compound thought they could go from a hereditary beast to something you could inject, but it didn't surprise me that they had failed in every trial so far.

Lunch was a burger and fries with a side of salad and pudding. Both the director and Doctor Ernie Everts joined us. I finished off my tray in record time. It had been hours since breakfast and I was starving. The director seemed taken aback by how quickly I ate but, without a word, went to the kitchen and filled a second tray for me.

Once I felt somewhat satiated, I turned to the doctor. "Why have you only tried this shot on norms? Why not on one of your werewolves? They have quicker healing."

The director answered, "We only have twelve wolves in service. It's what the powers-that-be allocated to us when the department was formed. If we lose one of the wolves, we have to start over in finding a new one."

Scrunching up my face, I raised an eyebrow. "Finding? Not just creating?"

"It is part of how the charter was written. We are not allowed to propagate through biting. That way, we don't accidently create too many. The regulations are very strict. Finding werewolves is difficult, since your lot is in hiding."

José cocked his head. "Do you blame us? If werewolves came out to the general public, there would be fear, possible segregation, possible annihilation, and definitely hate crimes. There is enough of that in the world for other issues. We don't need to introduce more reasons for oppression."

The director's eyes narrowed. "Can you tell me why you two don't smell like werewolves? I mean, I can't tell the difference, but my wolves are weirded out, to use Vern's word."

José smiled. "It's a Pack secret. However, if we come back, we'll make sure to not cover up our scent. Then your wolves will have different questions to ask about poor Jade here. Or, if they really want, we can go take a shower now."

"Not necessary. If you were staying over, maybe, but as long as you two are heading home tonight, that seems a bit extreme. Can you tell me who you are? They recognized Jade's name once I said it. I guess your parents are a pretty big deal in the werewolf community. Hard not to know the name Stone. But they don't know you, José."

José shrugged. "There are enough wolves in the world, we can't all know each other. We're relatively new to the area, so that may be the reason why."

The director nodded. "So, what did you do to my wolves?"

José's mouth twitched. "I gave them my credentials. I'm

an alpha. I have a lot of power. I keep it under tight wraps most of the time. Let's just say, for a few seconds, I relaxed."

He looked at me. "Are you also an alpha? Is that why you didn't fall to the floor, too?"

I rubbed my eyes. "That is getting into a *much* longer story. Is it time to see if I can help you with your dove?"

"Swan."

"Right."

We returned our trays and headed to the medical suite. José and the director stayed in an observation room while Doctor Ernie Everts and I went into a small room with two women.

"Jade, this is Sammy, she has volunteered to get the injection. And this is Nurse Jolene."

The nurse's focus moved me. "I'm not really a nurse. I mean, I've had a bit of medical field-training. But really, I'm one of the soldiers. My real skill is that I'm not squeamish around needles. For this injection, all you have to do is poke it in the arm and *bam* you're done. My major training was sticking needles into a banana."

My brows went up and I nodded slowly. *Military excellence at work, here. Good thing most nurses go to school for years, learning so much... just so that they can poke a needle into a banana. They must have someone better than this.* I shook my head and ignored my misgivings.

Jolene grabbed the needle and filled it with the serum. She squirted a bit out to make sure there weren't any air bubbles, then she brought the needle down parallel with the floor.

Sammy started to hyperventilate. She squeaked a few times, and her wide eyes lingered on the needle.

I put up a hand to stop the process and Jolene froze. "Hold on a sec." Jolene stood like a statue, unmoving. I slipped between the two women, putting my hands on Sammy's shoulders, staring right into her eyes. "You okay?"

She nodded erratically.

"Breathe for me, okay? In for a couple of seconds, then out, slowly."

Sammy followed my directions, and her breathing started to even out.

"Look Sammy, I'll do everything I can to help this go smoothly. Okay?"

She nodded again. Obviously not a big talker. The room filled with the sickening sweetness of her panic.

"Have they explained what this is all about?"

She nodded again.

"What are you most excited about?"

She took in a shaky breath. "I want to fly, you know. They also said being a shifter may heal me." She shrugged. "I have a disease. I may not live more than a few more years. But if I do this, maybe I will."

She was starting to get distracted, but her heart rate was still high, and her breathing still ragged. Closing my eyes, I found my calm and released a small burst of it. I felt her relax.

"Better? You ready?"

She nodded again and took a long steady breath. "Thanks."
I smiled and gave her shoulders one more squeeze of
encouragement. I turned to tell Nurse Jolene she was good
to go and felt a stabbing pain in the back of my arm.
All I heard as the room began to spin was, "Oh, no!"

CHAPTER 9

José burst into the medical room as I collapsed into a chair. In the background I could hear Nurse Jolene babbling about being sorry, but I didn't care.

I leaned over, elbows on my knees, head in my hands, trying to breathe. José knelt in front of me, touching his forehead to mine. His hands rubbed my shins. "Chica, love, what am I going to do with you?"

"I don't want to die."

"Oh, chica. How do you end up in these situations?" He shifted to get his arms around me and picked me up. He growled at Nurse Jolene, "Open the door."

Doctor Ernie Everts blocked the way into the hallway. "Where do you think you're taking her?"

"Home." The snarl in his voice reverberated throughout the small room.

"No! That serum flowing through her body is our property."

"Then take it out of her." I could feel his anger and whimpered. He held me closer.

"We can't."

José's voice got very low. "Then we have a problem. Every test subject has died, and I'm not about to let her die. I need to get her home. We can help her there. She needs what we have there, and you can't provide it here."

The hallway filled with men holding large guns. My frustration started to turn into a roiling dance of dizziness and pain. "José…" I tucked my head into his shoulder.

"Mr. Cortez, you can take her to her room here or the medical suite's bed, but you will not leave the compound for thirty-six hours. That is the time it has taken each of our former test subjects to succumb to the serum's effects." My body quivered. I groaned. Pain rolled out from my gut and my vision blurred. *Thirty-six hours? So much for being home in time for dinner. Such liars!*

I felt José move, but my sense of direction grew confused as I curled tighter into his embrace.

The bed I was gently placed on was covered in shards of ice and glass. My body recoiled in pain as all the bits and pieces bit into me. My panting made it impossible to explain why I jerked.

José rubbed my forehead. "Jade, we're alone in your assigned room. I'm sorry I couldn't get you out of here. I know these beds aren't comfortable. Tell me what I can do to help. Should I call in anyone else?"

I grasped his hand as my blood turned to ice. I started to shiver. Unable to speak, I mentally connected to him.

Don't bring in anyone else. Don't mention them. This room is probably bugged.

I writhed on the bed, trying to get comfortable, freezing, panting; I just wanted to survive. My vision was gone.

The shaking continued, my body rebelling against the serum. I arched up in agony, and I groaned as the sharp edges of the bed melted into a regular cot.

"Jade, can you hear me?"

"Of course, I can hear you, why wouldn't I be able to hear you? You're right next to me."

He snorted. "Fair enough. You aren't shaking. How do you feel? Do you want some water? Food?"

I smacked my lips. "Water would be good; coffee would be better. Food…oh, yeah."

José leaned over and lifted me a little in a hug. I returned the embrace. A minute later a straw touched my lips, and I sipped some water. I heard him shuffle away and the door opened. He came back and the bed dipped. He grabbed my hand. "Jade, hon, can you try opening your eyes for me?"

It suddenly occurred to me that I had left my eyes

closed the whole time. I contemplated opening them, and I wasn't sure I wanted to. I squeezed them closed for a second then took a deep breath. Finally, I lifted my hands up to rub them, then slowly cracked them open.

I could tell the light in the room was low, but it still stung, biting into my brain. I squinted and took in a sharp breath. "I didn't lose my sight."

"Were you afraid you had?"

"I think so. I did at first, before the body shakes, and the glass shards, and the cold. Oh, gods, José. How long has it been? How much more do I have to endure?"

He pulled me into a hug, kissing the top of my head. "It's been just over thirty hours. You've been delirious for most of it, paranoid for part of it, and slept for a bit."

"Thirty hours? Is that possible? I thought you were going to say a few hours…thirty? Did you sleep at all?"

"I cuddled into you and tried to rest with you. I didn't get much sleep, but I got what I could. I was more worried about you than losing one night's sleep."

There was a knock on the door, and José got up to answer. He had a few words with the person, and then brought a tray to the bed. It was piled high with food, but not enough for two hungry werewolves.

We set to eating. The coffee wasn't half bad and the rest of it started to fill the vast hole in my gut. We'd almost cleared off the full tray when there was another knock on the door and more food was delivered.

Slowing down, I wrung my hands. "So, we can't leave for six more hours, huh?"

"That's the theory. Any idea if the serum worked?"

Frustrated with the whole situation, I shook my head.

"Why don't you grab a change of clothes and go shower? You'll feel a bit better. If it'd make you feel better, you can use the soap. I didn't yesterday so they could smell me. But you hold more secrets."

"What do you think? I'm so confused right now, I barely know which way is up."

"Well, at the park, you were identified as a wolf and 'something else.' Ben, the kid's dad, wasn't sure what you were, but he knew you were more than a wolf. He was more worried about his son than figuring out what you were. It's a miracle he picked up on your conversation at all."

I considered José's words as I grabbed my bag and headed to the showers. I decided I would keep myself a mystery. This place had done little more than frustrate me and I wasn't going to make anything easy for them. Checking my options, I found jeans and a t-shirt that read *I rule* over a ruler. It matched my mood.

My stomach growled on my way back to the room. I dropped my bag and navigated the halls to the mess, where I grabbed a tray and got my third serving of grub. José found me eating and enjoying coffee.

"You look alive and well. I wonder if we can convince our jailors to let us go."

"I can't see why not. I'm not dead yet." I tried to sound like a movie quote, but knew I failed by José's lifted brow.

"And still fully predator?"

Face flat, I gave him the look that deserved.

Doctor Ernie Everts joined us. "You look well."

I raised an eyebrow. "Apparently my wolf ate your serum for dinner."

"You really think that that's what happened?"

Grunting, I shrugged.

He coughed into his balled fist, clearing his throat. "My wolves say you still smell like a norm. Well, that isn't exactly true. They say you smell like a cool stream by a forest in the springtime. I've never heard them speak so poetically. But that isn't you smelling like a werewolf. I thought after the shower your scent would change."

"Let's just say I didn't feel like playing any of your games. I just want to go home. Since I'm obviously alive and kicking, can I go now?"

"Well, we need to know if the serum worked."

"It didn't."

"Are you sure?"

"Yes."

"How can you know?"

My head dropped down and I rubbed my forehead. "I don't know how to prove to you one way or another what I am. But I really do need to get home. If what José says is true, it's Saturday night. He needs to get home to have a day home between being here and going to work. We've given you more time than planned."

"Yes, right. Of course. But you still have our serum in you."

"No, it's dissipated. Imagine me as another dead failure, and we'll all be happier."

"Ms. Stone, would you be willing to come back and try again? It failed with you, but we still would like to try again with Sammy."

I froze, closing my eyes, and biting my bottom lip. "Let me get back to you later this week. Right now, I just need to get home and get some actual sleep."

"Fine. Fair enough. Before you leave, we will need you to sign some confidentiality paperwork, but since you're used to keeping secrets, I'm sure you're used to it. There are a few other forms, but it's all government standard."

We watched the doctor walk away. With a sigh, we finished our food, gathered our stuff, and went to see Anastasia. The paperwork took more time than I wanted to think about. Most of it was relatively straight-forward; we agreed to not talk about what we'd seen or sue them over the serum.

As quickly as we could, we made our escape to the car. The halls were oddly empty as we slipped through the building. We were lucky not to run into the director or anyone else as we escaped the SSLD compound. I felt we'd have more arguments against leaving.

Once in the car, I faced José. "Could we not share with

the others about the serum? There's enough going on with the wedding and San Mateo. Let's hold off for now, okay?"

His scent turned sour. "I don't like it, but you're the one who was attacked. I agreed to not contact Bevin while we were there, and that feels like it goes against our partnership on several levels. You can have a bit of time, but I don't promise you as much time as you may want." Once we got on our way, he did call to let Bevin know we were on our way.

As we drove home, I watched the scenery fly by—the other cars, the clouds, the trees, the birds, the flowers, the butterflies. I'd never realized before how much detail there was to see.

CHAPTER 10

When we walked into the house, the scent of warm, melty cheese hit my nose and I moaned in pleasure. I practically floated to the dining room and found a seat halfway down the table between Violet and Alex. There were a couple of homemade mac and cheese casseroles as well as other bowls and dishes, but I had eyes only for my one true love.

Chuckling, Alex passed me a tray and I scooped some of the gooey magic onto my plate. "Who knows how to make this?"

Alex returned the tray to the center of the table. "Luke."

Finally focusing on the people around the table, I found him laughing at me. "I know it's a heavy dish for this warmer weather, but it's a family recipe I thought you'd enjoy."

A growl bubbled up from my belly. "This is year-round grub. You can always make it." After stating my new Pack law, I continued to focus on eating.

Bevin asked José. "So, what happened? That was definitely longer than one day." The cinnamon scent of his frustration peppered the air.

José filled everyone in on the compound, who worked there, and what their goals were. He discussed the difference between wereanimals and shifters. As he spoke, I refilled my plate and continued to swoon over all the different cheeses hidden under the toasted breadcrumbs.

"So, do they know about other wereanimals besides werewolves?" Bevin's interest overpowered his annoyance.

José paused; I looked over to see him sipping his drink. "I don't think so. They had a lot of information about shifters, but we didn't discuss other weres."

Bevin sounded confused. "I don't understand. What happened? Did Sammy survive?"

The room got quiet. José wasn't going to lie. He'd told as much of the story as he would. I squeezed my eyes shut and put down my fork. "She had a panic attack and didn't receive the shot." My voice was low, but it carried.

The weight of Bevin's gaze sat heavy on my shoulders. I stared at my hands as I wrung my fingers. "So, what took two days?" Bevin sounded measured, as if trying to get to the bottom of things. He knew we were hiding something from him. He knew us—knew me—too well.

"They wanted us to try…again today."

It felt like a boulder was growing in my chest. All I had to do was breathe around it. I heard a chair scrape across the floor followed by footsteps. Bevin crouched by my chair, but I refused to look at him. Out of the corner of my eye, I saw when he reached out, grabbed the legs of my chair, and slowly rotated my seat until I was facing him. The chair under me complained about the awkward treatment.

My focus remained on the space between us. He reached out and took my hands. "Jade, love, why are you lying? What are you hiding?"

I was wrong; it wasn't a boulder—it was a dam. It broke, and I broke with it. I slid to the floor, kneeling in front of Bevin. I stared up into his concerned blue eyes and tears burned down my face. "I'm so tired of messing up. I just didn't want to come in here and tell everyone how I blundered again. Every time I leave the house, I come back with a tale about how I've bungled everything up again." I tried to swallow, but my mouth had gone dry. My voice came out low and rough. "I asked José to give me a few days." I dropped my chin to my chest in shame.

"How do you think you messed up?"

"On Friday, after I calmed Sammy down, I turned around to tell the nurse she was good to go, but I moved too fast…I impaled myself on the needle."

Everyone in the room froze. They must realize how badly I'd screwed up this time. I drew my knees up, dropped my head down, and hugged my legs.

I heard Bevin move. "Was Jade in danger of dying?"

A chair scraped against the floor. "Yes. But they wouldn't let us go. They had guns pointed at us when we tried. We weren't sure if they had listening devices and didn't want to give up Pack secrets. She was delusional and paranoid, but in her paranoia, she asked that I keep the Pack away. She wasn't wrong. If they knew about the Pack, they may have tried to contain everyone."

Anger boiled out of both of them. I whimpered, trying to tuck into a tighter ball.

Bevin's voice was low. "You didn't have the right to make that call on your own. What if she'd died?"

"I had to protect the Pack. If you'd come, what would have happened here? What would have happened if the San Mateo wolves invaded again?"

Both of them were leaking power, their strength slipping out, and I started to shake.

Sarah's voice cut through everything. "Boys, unless you plan on taking this outside, I suggest you stop. Now!" Her command brought them both back to the room at large.

Bevin's voice was starting to rise. "I thought you'd agree with me, Sarah."

"Oh, I do." Her face was as hard as her voice. "But I also

understand the situation. I don't understand why I didn't feel what Jade was going through, but I *do* feel what she is going through right now with you two battling it out. She felt bad before, but her guilt just may do her in, after all."

Suddenly, I was in Bevin's arms. I wasn't sure how I'd gotten there. I was still on the floor so he dropped down next to me and was trying to calm me enough to get my shaking to stop. He rested his cheek on my head but spoke to Sarah. "Can you pull her calming to help?"

"I'm worried about how much more she can take."

As the tension in the room dropped, Alex asked, "How did you know she was lying?"

Owen huffed out a laugh. "The two of them have always been like twins. They can read each other better than any two people I know. She can't hide anything from him, never could. And she wasn't really lying, just not telling the full truth. If it had been a lie, we'd all have been able to tell. But even when Jade convinces herself something ridiculous is true, Bevin can suss it out."

Hearing the lightness of the talk helped to calm me. I was with family, friends…Pack. I leaned into Bevin.

He held me, releasing a bit more of his alpha mantle, filling me with warmth. I wasn't sure what was happening, but the hollowness in me filled. He held me for another second, then I shifted to stand up. He helped me to my feet.

As he gazed deep into my eyes, I heard the unasked question. I answered with a nod—yes, I was okay. He leaned down and kissed my cheek and we both took our seats.

Shaking out my hands, I faced Owen. "He may read me well, but you can always ferret out my secrets, so don't sound so glum. You can usually get anyone to spill the beans."

He shot me a huge smile and waggled his eyebrows at me. "It's my charm. Speaking of secrets, does this mean you can now fly?"

I tried to hide the tremor in my voice as I shrugged my shoulders. "I don't think so. I don't feel different. Tomorrow I'll shower with normal soap and y'all can take a sniff and see if I smell like prey."

Owen snorted. "I hadn't thought about that. If you were infected, will your mental animals hunt the newbie?"

I shot him a dirty look and took more food. This time I grabbed some salad. It had a great-smelling vinaigrette dressing. For the rest of the meal, I listened to the others talk. I didn't have the energy to contribute but being with them helped.

After dinner, I crashed. The night before, I hadn't really slept, and my body needed down-time.

The next morning, when I woke, I debated heading to the gym. The schedule outside my door listed cardio. I decided to swim. The water was cool and refreshing. When I finally got out, a towel hit me as I climbed onto the deck. I used it to dry off and came face to face with Brooke sitting in one of the pool chairs.

Brooke narrowed her eyes, checking my body out. "You don't look broken."

"Why would I be broken?"

"For two days, your emotional state was near death. I get here and find you swimming laps."

I stopped drying my hair to gape at her.

"What? Anyway, I thought I'd get here and find you holed up in bed. So, what happened?"

She asked it so matter-of-factly, I found myself answering, giving her the full story I'd only told José.

"So, this dolt of a soldier held a needle out at you. She should have pulled it back and pointed it away from you as soon as you ducked in to help, and you now feel foolish because you assumed she was a professional? When you backed into her, not only did she stick you, she dispensed the drug. And of course, you think it's your fault."

My breathing almost stopped at the outrage in her tone. "Um, kinda."

"Grow up, Jade. She's at fault. Any ignorant clown would have known that when you asked her to pause, she should have pointed the needle in any direction but at you. That serum's probably worth thousands of dollars, if not more, and she wasted it on you. Don't feel bad; feel pissed."

I shook my head, trying to recalibrate my thinking to her take on the situation.

Before I could finish, she reached for my hand. "Show me around. I need a room—and not near your brother."

We spent the next half hour touring Were House. She ended up taking the room across the hall from mine. It looked out over the driveway but had a view of some trees as well. Once she got settled, I went to shower.

Before I made it to my door, she grabbed my arm and sniffed. "By the way, you don't smell like prey." It was nice to hear, but Brooke didn't have the most sensitive nose.

After my shower, I saw I'd missed a text from Greta. Like the last few, I deleted it, and headed for the closet. I slipped into jeans and a gray shirt displaying a black cat scowling, holding a knife, and drinking coffee. It read: *Coffee, because murder is wrong.* I made it to the living room and flopped onto a couch.

Alex came out and sat in one of the recliner chairs. "I was going to head into town for a walk. Wanna join me?"

Sliding my eyes to them, I said, "Ice cream?"

They smiled. "Sure, but I also want to see Milo at the Youth Outreach Center. They had something they wanted to talk to me about."

I perked up at the thought of seeing Milo and going to the Center. "Sure. Sounds great. I have an idea about… well, an idea. Let me get shoes on."

We walked to town discussing what Milo might want. Alex was worried. They'd been receiving counseling there and didn't want to lose that resource. I spent most of our walk trying to calm them down. It was nice having someone else to focus on.

Milo sat at the welcome desk, as usual. They were a bit taller than me, with short black hair, dyed red at the ends and spiked it. Their black eyes locked onto mine. "You brought Ms. Down Girl. Nice!"

It took me a minute to remember my first visit, and Sarah's comment to me when she saw me gaping at Milo. I hadn't realized they'd heard Sarah say, 'down girl' to me. My cheeks burned. It took everything I had not to turn tail and run.

They chuckled as they faced Alex. "Your counselor got a new job in the city proper. She won't be able to work with you anymore. I'm really sorry."

I could feel Alex panic. I moved to wrap my arms around them. I whispered, "It's okay, hon, we'll figure this out. You have...everyone."

Milo's eyes narrowed. "Are you two a couple?"

Alex tensed for a second before relaxing into my embrace. They shook their head. "No, Jade is just a really good friend. We're both single and...well...I prefer guys."

I snorted. "You don't have to apologize for your preference. I won't be offended because you don't want to date me."

Milo bit back a laugh as they nodded. "Got it." Then they looked at me. "You were with that other chick, right?"

Tensing, I let my arms drop. "Not anymore. She turned out to be...not who I thought she was."

Milo nodded in understanding.

Shortly after, we headed to the ice cream shop. There weren't many people in the establishment, which meant I could talk to one of the servers. "Hi, Milli!"

A tall, heavy-set woman with crazy red curls came up to us. Millicent was about our age—another college student staying in town for the summer. "Jade! I'm so glad to see you. What'll you have? Your usual?"

"Yes! But there's more. I wanted to see if I could commission one of your paintings."

"Really?"

"You know my friends, Bevin and José?"

"Yeah."

"Well, they're getting married on July twenty-first. I was hoping to get a piece for the living room."

Her eyes got huge. "And you want me to create it?"

Alex leaned forward. "Milli, your art is amazing. I want in on this." They shot a glance over their shoulder at me. "If that's okay with you."

My face broke out in a huge smile. "Sounds good to me. We can get an even bigger piece that way."

Milli stopped breathing and stared at us with wide eyes, and then she squealed. I grinned, happy to make someone's day better.

CHAPTER 11

Monday morning, I sat at the dining room table eating a bagel and drinking my coffee when Bevin joined me. He and José had been tense most of the day Sunday until they'd gone out running together as wolves. They'd come back scraped and looking sore and went directly into their room. No one had seen them for the rest of the evening.

"Sorry for causing the tension between you and José." I gazed down into my mug. "I wasn't thinking." My hands were wrapped around my coffee for warmth.

He finished adding jelly to his cream cheese and bagel,

and took a bite, chewing slowly as he considered me. After taking a drink of his coffee, he replied, "You weren't thinking, and you were also scared. You feel better now. I'm not sure what happened, but I'm pleased about that."

I opened my mouth to answer, but he raised his hand and continued, "I'm not happy with the situation. If you ever pull a stunt like that again...I don't know. Just don't. You're that sick, you call me. I don't care about anything else; you call me." I nodded. "Okay. I made that clear to José, as well."

"Was that what the fight in the woods was about?"

"That was me needing to blow off steam and him agreeing to it. Then we came back and—"

"Stop. I don't think I need to hear any more."

His face blossomed into a mischievous grin. "Fair enough. But there *are* good parts."

"Bevin! Gah! It's like hearing about Owen. Just no."

He leaned forward and continued to eat, then leaned back. "Give me your arm, oh, newly winged one."

I rolled my eyes, but did as he asked. "I know Brooke already cleared you, but sometimes her nose can be as shallow as her personality." He sniffed. "Yeah, nothing. Just wolf and panther."

Sarah and Owen came in and joined us, along with Alex and Brooke. As we finished, Sarah pulled out her huge book of wedding madness. Eyes dancing and wearing a wicked grin, she rested her gaze on me. "Okay, Jade, we need to find dresses."

I swallowed the last of my food. "We do?"

"Yes, we're in the wedding party. Haven't you been paying attention to anything?"

"Well, kind of."

She glared at me. "The boys decided on two groomsladies and two groomsmen. It was that or, like, ten of each."

My brow wrinkled. "Who gets the groomsladies and who gets the groomsmen?"

Bevin threw his arm around me. "I decided to get the ladies since we're going with you and Sarah. I've spent most of my life hanging out with you two. The men are Owen and Luke. If we opened it up to more ladies, the list would never end, what with our sisters, the rest of the Pack, and so on…this is easier."

"But a dress? I could wear a tux. I could be a groomsman."

Bevin's eyes narrowed. "Nope. You clean up well."

"But I'll be next to *Sarah*, in a matching dress. No one cleans up *that* well. What have I ever done to you?"

"Do you want the list chronologically, or in alphabetical order?"

Brooke gave me her back, facing Sarah. "Can I join in the shopping?"

Sarah brightened. "Sounds great!"

I gaped at them in horror.

We perused three stores, and none had dresses that matched the wedding color scheme: purple and gray. From what I could tell, the dresses in this store wouldn't work, either. Ready to leave, I moved towards the exit.

Brooke reached out and grabbed my arm. "Gods, you *are* horrible to shop with. Here, hold this." She handed me a knee-length bodycon dress in the exact right shade of purple. Ruching went from the right shoulder, down across the body and around the back where it fanned out down the center of the skirt in pleats, each pleat sporting a row of small beads. Clear jewels adorned the top of the ruching in the front.

Frozen like a statue, I stared at the dress, taking it all in. Finally, Brooke pushed me, grumbling, "You're impossible. Go to the middle changing room; there are a few dresses already there. Try them on."

I stumbled a few steps before catching my balance and making my way to one of the three dressing rooms. One door was shut. I assumed it was taken by Sarah. In the changing room, I quickly stripped, and pulled on each of the dresses.

After I struggled into each contraption, I stepped out to compare with Sarah. There was one that actually looked better on me than Sarah, which shocked us all, but overall, I was getting discouraged at the findings.

Brooke smirked. "Try on that last one. The one I handed you."

I grumbled but did as I was told and went to try it

on. I was tired of trying on dresses and ready to go home. I slipped into the dress and found that there was a side zipper, so I could actually manage to get the thing on myself. I had gone out half-naked in a few of the selections, scandalizing some patrons of the store. Checking myself out in the mirror I looked…well, like me, but in a purple dress. I was not good at this.

I wiggled to get everything in place. I left the room with a dubious look on my face. Sarah looked great, but she was supermodel-gorgeous so that was a given. Brooke placed us next to each other and had us pose in a few positions. Then she got some accessories, and more accessories, then switched them out. Necklaces, purses, tiaras, bracelets, earrings—it wouldn't end. I was pretty sure they were testing how much I would put up with.

It was too much. I broke. "Gods above. Sonnara save me! For the love of all that is sacred, are we done yet?"

Brooke smirked. "I win."

My jaw dropped as I glared. "Are you kidding me?"

Sarah smiled. "I figured you wouldn't let us do more than two accessories. Brooke figured you'd let it go for at least fifteen minutes. Go change, we'll figure out the rest." She leaned over and kissed my forehead. "You look amazing."

I rolled my eyes and went to change.

At home, Bevin was in the living room with Alex. "Can I see what you found?"

Sarah pushed the dress bags to Brooke who slipped off to her room. "No." She said it with some finality. "No seeing the dresses until the day of the wedding."

Bevin sat up, putting his book down. "Why not?"

"Bad luck?"

"That doesn't make any sense at all. You aren't the bride."

"There isn't a bride. I figured you and José are wearing matching tuxes, so this is the only outfit surprise you get."

He shook his head and the scent of cinnamon wafted from him; he was annoyed. "Whatever." He looked at me. "How was dress shopping?" As his gaze shifted, so did his scent—to citrusy joy.

I harrumphed, then fell into one of the couches with a sigh. "They messed with me."

My phone buzzed and I pulled it from my pocket. I let my hand with the phone flop back down on the couch.

Bevin's laughter faded. "What?"

"They want me to return on Friday to help with Sammy." I rolled my eyes. "I told them I would get back to them sometime this week. It's just a reminder text so that I don't forget. They need to get things set up."

"You aren't planning on going, are you?"

"Why not? What could happen? It isn't like I'll get injected again. They'll inject the norm no matter what. If my intervention is the difference between life and death, don't I *have* to go?"

"No, Jade, you don't. It isn't your responsibility to keep every norm alive. You have to learn this. You went there, you almost died. The way I see it, they have two options. They find other medical help, or they figure out making shifters out of norms isn't possible. Obviously, this didn't work with you, so maybe this really is just a hereditary thing."

"Life and death, Bevin. I could be saving that girl's life."

He moved over to my couch and squatted down next to me. "Please think about this, Jade. Last time you entered that compound, you almost died. I...I can't lose you. José is my life, my soul, but you're in there, too. You always have been."

Closing my eyes, I draped my arm across my face. I knew I had to go despite his touching words. I was pretty sure Bevin knew as well.

On Friday morning, I drove Bevin's car to the compound. José had to work, so Bevin insisted on joining me. We both showered with the soap to cover our scents. I did it because I was still annoyed with them. Bevin, because he didn't trust them.

Anastasia met us at the door and only paused a beat when she saw Bevin. She took his name and within seconds had a name tag for him. We thought about having him wear José's, but then decided we didn't want them asking too many questions about our pack.

The director came to collect us this time. I had eaten a large breakfast, so we went straight to the medical suite.

"Who's this fine gentleman you brought this week? Where is José?"

I peered at Bevin over my shoulder before looking up. "This is Bevin. He and I grew up together and have studied medicine together."

"Can he do what you can do?"

Bevin huffed. "No one can do what Jade does."

"He can take care of me. I trust him."

"You don't trust José?"

Shaking my head at the ridiculousness of the statement, I chuckled. "With my life, obviously. But he's at work today."

"Is Bevin a…"

"So many questions! Can we just do what we came here to do?" I let the frustration fill my voice. "Maybe we could let Bevin do the injection, then I won't have to worry about the serum ending up in the wrong person again."

A wave of shock emanated from Bevin, but the sound of his footsteps didn't falter.

"Sorry, ma'am; we can't have any unknowns in the room with Sammy."

"I'm an unknown."

"Fair. Okay, any *more* unknowns."

We arrived at the medical suite. I went to the room with Sammy and Nurse Jolene. Bevin followed the director into the observation room. I heard Bevin's mental knock.

Yeah?

"Can we stay connected? I'd feel better."

Sure.

Sammy seemed calmer this time. She met my eyes. "You survived. You're the first to get the injection and survive."

"Yep. Now let's make you the second."

Her face broke out into a grin. "I'm so excited. You're totally going to make this work. I, like, totally can't wait to fly!"

"Right. Okay, Jolene?" I sat down and let Nurse Jolene do her thing.

The administration of the serum went without a hitch, and we moved Sammy to a bed. She started to freak out when her vision dimmed, but I told her that had happened to me, too. A few minutes later, she felt cold and began to toss and turn as if her bed were uncomfortable. She shifted to her side and swiped the bed. "Is there…did someone break glass on this bed? Or are there ice shards? I still can't see."

Reaching over, I grabbed her hand. I sat on a chair next to her bed and let Panther flow into her. I released a bit of calm and slowed down her heart, which was beating too fast. Her blood pressure skyrocketed. We went about putting out fires as quickly as they popped up.

I felt Bevin more than I heard his voice in my head. *Jade, you need to let go. It's been twelve hours and you need food.*

I pulled out. The room spun around me like a carousel. I would have collapsed, but Bevin caught me. Sammy lay, fitful, but asleep on the bed. She mumbled about being attacked and exams. *Is this the paranoia stage?*

While I'd worked on her, someone had gotten monitors

attached to Sammy. Her vitals all looked good. After getting a read on her wellbeing, I tucked against Bevin's chest. "I can walk."

"I don't think you could stand on your own. They showed me where your room is. You're going there. I've sent for food. You're eating and resting."

"But…"

"No!" he growled and released a bit of alpha essence. It flowed over me, silencing me. My whole body quaked.

I tried to stand on my own and, as predicted, I couldn't hold myself up. Bevin went to lift me. I gave him a pitiful look.

He growled. "Take a bit of my energy so that you can walk, but not too much. I don't want to be at a disadvantage."

I did. He staggered and then caught himself. After that, I managed to get my feet under me with Bevin's arm around me in support.

When we got to my room, several trays laden with food awaited us on a small table and the dresser. Bevin helped me to sit on the bed and we both dug in. Once the trays were empty, he stacked them on the table and sat next to me. "You need to sleep. If you don't take care of yourself, you can't take care of anyone else."

"Have you slept?"

"No. I was watching over you for most of the time, though the director did give me a tour of the facility and I met some of the people. It's an impressive place."

"Did they give you a room?"

"Yep, but we're going to share this bed, like when we were six. I think we both need Pack right now. We'll sleep better."

Something deep inside me relaxed. The bed wasn't big, but we puppy piled as best we could. I was up against the wall, back to Bevin. He finally gave up trying to get comfortable and wrapped an arm around me. "That way, if I fall off the bed, I'm taking you with me."

A moment later, he woke me up. I protested, but he was insistent. "It's been almost eight hours. It's time to get back to Sammy. They say she's doing good, better than any other norm, but the next ten to twelve hours are critical."

Stretching, I sat up. "Sammy, right. Food first. Let's head to the mess hall. Do we have time to shower and change our clothes first?"

"Yep. And make sure to use this." He handed me the werebear bath products. "They don't know what to make of us. It's probably my favorite part about being here." Bevin was obviously as paranoid as I was about the room being bugged.

We made ourselves presentable and went to find breakfast.

The director joined us. "I see Sammy is still with us. This is the best case we've had, besides you. The others who made it this far weren't as stable as she is now."

I nodded as I stuffed more bacon into my mouth. If nothing else, the pancakes they made were better than anything I could make...though, that wasn't saying much.

He cocked his head at me. "I just don't understand you. You eat more than any of my men. Your werewolf ate the serum like it was candy. You sat stock-still for twelve hours, yet you look like a twig I could break over my knee."

Under his breath, Bevin mumbled, "Doubt it."

"What's that, son?"

Bevin shook his head. "Sorry, just thinking. She's scrappier than she looks. People always underestimate her, but she's been training her whole life. I wouldn't bet against her too quickly."

"That so?"

"That's definitely so."

I was getting a bit annoyed with them, so I stood to clear my tray. From there, I headed back to the medical ward. In the hall, Bevin caught up with me. "Hey, sorry. Didn't mean to frustrate you. Just pisses me off when people underestimate you because you're a girl."

"Sometimes that's half my opening strategy."

He laughed. "Fair enough."

In the examination room, I resumed my post next to Sammy. She slept soundly, and her vitals were right on target with where they should be. Just before I placed my hand on her, a man burst into the room carrying another man. Vern. His shin bone was sticking out of his leg, and he was passed out from the pain.

"Where's the doctor?" the supporting agent demanded.

"I don't know. What happened?" I quickly assessed the situation.

"We were sparring. He did this move, and we heard

a crunch. I can't explain it." He got Vern on the table, then backed up to the wall. His face was white, drained of all color.

I turned to Bevin, a question in my eyes. He searched my face, then gazed at Vern's leg. After two beats, he gave a sharp nod.

After a calming breath, I went into business mode. "I may need you to do some bone alignment. It will help speed things up. I'll also need more energy. Monitoring Sammy is one thing; this is major work." "On it," Bevin agreed, and I got to work.

Bracing myself, I placed my hands on Vern's arm and Panther slipped in. As I closed my eyes, we moved to the leg. First thing was to stop the bleeding. Then we moved to the soft tissue and muscles. I heard Bevin speaking with someone and then a hand on my shoulder. Wolf drank in as much energy as she could as Panther and I continued to repair skin and muscle. The work was slow.

We moved to the bone before the soft tissue healing progressed too far. Bevin had aligned it at first, but the placement was a pinch off. We adjusted it and began knitting it together. I started to feel lightheaded when another hand reached out to touch me. Once again, Wolf drank deeply. The surge of power almost made me lightheaded in a different way. Whoever they were, that wolf was strong.

Once the bone healed to my and Panther's satisfaction, we moved back to the soft tissue. The tear was a mess. I reached for Bevin. *Can you align the torn skin edges?*

A third shot of energy filled me before I felt the repair was done and Panther and I could slide out. My heart beat faster and I panted as if I'd just run a marathon. I sat hard on the first chair I could find.

Bevin knelt in front of me. "You okay?"

I nodded.

"That was freaky cool. Usually, we can't see what you're doing in such detail."

Smiling, I said the first thing that popped into my head. "Drink, food, then Sammy."

"Are you up to it?"

"Yeah. It's what I'm here for. I'm not letting her slip away because I got distracted. I just need calories. I *so* want one of Tanner's chocolate shakes. I can practically see it dancing in front of me."

He rubbed my knees, chuckling as he stood. Before he could turn and ask, the director, along with a table with two trays of food, a chocolate shake, and coffee appeared in front of me.

"Ma'am, that was magic. When we were told you could heal, we all were skeptical. What you just did for Agent Vern...he would have been out of commission for months, but his leg looks good as new."

The chocolate shake was good—not Tanner-good, but it hit the spot. As for the rest of the food, the next time I looked down, it was gone. Story of my life.

"I'm glad I was here. It's my special skill. I think I'll get back to Sammy."

The director's eyes bulged as he gaped at the empty trays. Bevin, standing behind him, bit his lips to stop himself from laughing.

I moved back to the chair by Sammy's bed and took her hand. Closing my eyes, Panther and I triaged her situation. Though the digital displays gave her good readings, she had some internal trauma. Nothing major, but enough small pieces that, if put together, could snowball later on. We slowly made our way through, patching and repairing what we could find. An aneurysm was developing in her brain. A weak spot had formed in her aorta. Her appendix, which had been fine when we'd left last night, was about to rupture as well. We fixed them, item by item.

Still connected to Bevin, I gave him a running catalog of my repairs. He grumbled as the list continued.

I pulled out when Sammy was finally stable. The room was dark. My body had stiffened to the point where I wasn't sure I could move. Groaning, I tried to stand and fell back down on my butt. Suddenly, Bevin was there, taking my hands. He pulled me to my feet.

"What time is it? How long has it been?" Feeling weak, I leaned on my alpha.

"You were in there for almost another fourteen hours."

"I'm so tired, and I hurt. Can we go home?"

The director, who stood at the doorway, said, "Of course

you can. You aren't a prisoner. I think at this point you've done what you can do. More than any of us expected. Is there any chance you could come back on Monday? We'd love a report of what you found and what you did. Also, I don't know...*we* don't know what will happen next. We hope this worked. We hope she'll shift. But we'd like you to be part of it."

"Let me get back to you tomorrow."

Bevin, arm around me, held me up. "Let *us* get back to you later."

The director narrowed his eyes. "So, you *are* the other alpha. We've been taking bets as to whether you and Cortez were both alphas, or just Cortez. I've said from the start you hold yourself too much like a leader to not be an alpha. Good for you, boy. Good for you."

CHAPTER 12

On Sunday, José, Bevin, and I discussed the pros and cons of helping out. We decided getting more information about shifters would be good since they'd developed the serum in our backyard. Sammy's training would likewise occur nearby and any information we could glean would be in our favor. We also figured, if she could fly, they could potentially spy on us. It wouldn't be hard to find out where we lived. Preparing for that would be in our best interest.

Then there was my love of facts, and any information we could add to our library was a benefit. The alphas decided that Bevin and I would spend a few hours each morning at the compound, and then return. I wouldn't be doing any more healing. My only medical job would be to monitor Sammy's progress.

"José, you didn't see that man's leg. The bone was sticking out. What do I do, just turn away?"

His face hardened. "Chica, they aren't Pack. You are there as a silent observer, not a participant. They have a doctor. Where was he anyway? You didn't mention him in any of your reports of your second trip."

I shrugged and we both faced Bevin. "I never saw him during this latest trip. He wasn't there, from what I could tell."

"Well, that should be your first question tomorrow when you get there. When Agent Vern showed up with his broken bone, why wasn't Doctor Ernie Everts there to fix him up? Was that all a setup for you? Pretty daring, if it was."

Bile rose in my throat, and I felt the blood draining from my face at the prospect. They knew I was keeping Sammy alive, but how could they have guaranteed I could—or would—have helped Agent Vern? If it had been nothing more than an evaluation of my skills, they had risked potentially crippling a perfectly healthy and skilled soldier for the sake of an experiment.

José wrapped an arm around me. "You are sometimes too naive, chica." He kissed my cheek. "This is why you follow our lead, got it?"

A shiver made its way down my spine. I nodded. "But at

this point, they know I can heal. I don't see why I shouldn't heal someone who needs it. I'm training to be a medical doctor and vet, for Sonnara's sake! It's good practice."

He growled low. "You are there only to learn and observe, or you don't go. Do you understand? Can you handle that?"

I rested my head on his arm, biting back another snarl. "Yes."

The next morning, after hitting the gym, eating breakfast, and getting ready, Bevin and I headed out. Bevin checked out my shirt. *I am only responsible for what I say, not for what you understand.* He scratched his chin. "In a mood already?"

"I don't like being tested."

At the compound, Sammy was sitting up and all smiles. As we entered the medical suite, she leapt down from her bed and flew at me, engulfing me in a huge hug. That contact was enough for me to identify her as *other*. The serum had worked. Happy to see her alive and well, I squeezed her back.

"Thank you, thank you, thank you, thank you! I survived. I'm the first. Now we wait to see if it worked."

"It did." The words were out of my mouth before I thought.

Everyone in the room froze and Bevin groaned.

Sammy's eyes got huge. "What?"

Dread flowed through me like waves of ice water. I shook my head. "Sorry, I still need coffee. I meant, I'm *sure* it did." I laughed nervously. "Look at you. You got the shot, you're bouncing and hyper. I'm sure it worked. Now you just need to wait for whatever triggers the next bit. Do you know what that would be?"

She visibly relaxed with my words. "No. I should probably go find one of those books to read, but I'm just too excited...and hungry. Are you hungry? Maybe we could go find food."

Bevin snorted at the question, but I just nodded. The three of us headed to the mess hall. Once we were seated, the director found us and joined our party. "It's amazing. You did a wonderous thing. Sammy's up and active. She passed all the medical tests. She's the picture of health and vitality."

Finishing my coffee, I smiled at the compliment. "I was wondering if I could sneak off to the library again. I'd like to read up on shifters some more, see if I can figure out what to expect."

"Great idea! Maybe all three of you can go. While you're there, can you write up a report on what you did with Sammy? I'd like to know what happened with her medically."

I'd almost forgotten I'd promised to do that. "Of course. Do you want it digitally or on paper?"

"For now, on paper. We can discuss digital access at a later date."

I could almost imagine. Two nobodies off the street with

access to their network and databases? Never. Shooting a side glance to Bevin, I could almost see him having the same thoughts.

"Maybe Sammy could help with the reports, I bet she'd be interested in what happened during the time she was in your care."

"Actually, Sammy may be better off in the gym. If the serum worked, she should begin to learn the limits on her new abilities. She's probably faster and stronger. A new training program should be set up, and the sooner she starts, the better for all involved."

The director's eyes narrowed. "The daughter of pack alphas. Friend of alphas. You really know what you're doing, don't you?"

My head dropped to my left hand, and I massaged my forehead. "Some days more than others."

"Ms. Stone, what would you say if I were to offer you a job?"

I froze mid-rub. After a minute, I slowly turned to look at Bevin. His face was stony as he stared into space. Shaking off my paralysis, I finally took in air and answered, forming my words slowly. "Thank you for the offer, but I would need more information and time to consider."

He slapped my back heartily. "Of course, you will. Go to the library. Read. You can take a few books home if you'd like. There's a logbook by the door; we just ask that you return whatever you borrow. I'll have Anastasia write up what I'm thinking for a job offer so that you can take it home and have whomever you want check it over. No rush on an answer. I can understand how working for the government may not be your first choice for a job."

I narrowed my eyes at him. "One more thing. Where's the doctor?"

"Doctor E? He isn't technically part of our department. He's part of a sister department and we only borrow him a week each month. It's hard to find doctors we can hire full-time to work at our level of clearance. The vetting process is tricky."

With that he left, accompanying Sammy to the gym. Bevin and I said our goodbyes as we headed to the library.

There were a few promising books. I grabbed three and Bevin pulled down two. After skimming the ones I chose, I put one back. An hour later, Anastasia came in with a packet and left it on the table, then silently left. I eyed the packet like a feral animal sat next to me and decided I would wait until I got home to open it up. After another hour, Bevin and I wrote the titles of the books we had in the log and went to the gym windows to watch Sammy train.

The books suggested that Sammy would probably shift in another week. Like us, a shifter's first shift was linked to the full moon, which was the following week on Thursday. I was somewhat convinced that Bevin could call her out if he used his power, but I wasn't sure if he wanted to. As we watched her, I linked up with him.

Hey.

"*Hi.*" His answer came slow, like he knew I was up to no good.

Did you find out anything in what you read?

"*A bit, but I'd like to read more and discuss it with you in more detail.*"

I think it's linked to the full moon. At least for the first shift. That's next week. But I read that an alpha's push can force a shift. My guess is, you could flood the room with your power and force her to shift.

"*Why? Why help them more? I thought we just wanted to observe and learn.*"

We could see the shift. We could see what happens next. We could decide if we want to stop coming here.

He sighed loudly. "*It can't be in front of everyone. The director—who has guessed I'm alpha— Sammy, you, me... that's it. I don't want to put on a show.*"

I don't disagree.

We dropped the connection and watched Sammy run an obstacle course. It was simple; nothing like what Dad or Owen would put together. When she finished, we entered the gym and found the director. Pulling him aside, I said, "We have an idea, but we need a smaller room and just the four of us."

His eyes narrowed. "Why?"

Bevin's voice dropped low. "Let's start with privacy, and then we'll explain. If you don't like the idea, then we'll drop it."

The four of us moved to one of the smaller workout rooms. There were no windows, and with the cinderblock walls, I couldn't imagine a camera. I quickly filled the director and Sammy in on what I'd read.

Sammy's brow bunched and she pouted. "But there are no alpha swans here. How does that help?"

The director only nodded. "Sammy, stay in the middle of the room." He grabbed my and Bevin's arms and pulled us to a wall. Then he bobbed his head.

"Wait," I called out. "Her clothing will get in the way. Sammy, I know this sounds odd, but face away from us and take off your clothes. Maybe get down in a crouched position."

The small room filled with the cinnamon and minty scent of her annoyance and confusion. "I have to be naked? In front of all of you?"

"It's one of the things we get used to—*you'll* get used to."

"But I'm not used to it. Can I...would it be possible if...maybe...can it just be me and—wait. Who's the alpha? I...I just don't want to strip in front of so many people."

I sighed, but realized she had a point. The director and I left the room, leaving Bevin and Sammy alone.

About ten minutes later, Bevin opened the door, and the director and I returned. A black swan padded around in the middle of the room. She was almost pure black, except for her beak, which was a bright orange, and some white feathers tucked beneath her wings. When she spread her wings, there was a white stripe down the edge of each.

She suddenly let out a loud musical sound, almost like a pleasant version of a squeaky toy, if that were possible.

"Ms. Stone, please seriously consider my job offer. We need someone who has the ability to be medical staff, consultant, and trainer. You are a wonder, and I barely even know you." The director's voice held a level of awe I wasn't prepared to hear. The sincerity in his voice rang true.

Bevin and I just stared at him as he gaped at the swan padding around the room.

Facing Bevin, I considered the situation. "She'll need to learn how to fly. Did you read anything about that?"

"I saw a chapter header in one of the books. I'll check it out tonight, but we need to get going."

"I agree." I looked at Sammy. "Sammy, you should be able to control the shifting now. You just need to focus hard on the form you want. If nothing else, think about one body part, like your hand, and focus on getting that body part shifted to the form you want it to be."

Before I'd finished talking, a mist formed around her, dark gray. A couple of seconds later, a naked Sammy sat on the floor, vibrating. She quickly slipped on her clothes. "Oh, my God, that was the coolest thing ever! Thank you, Jade and Bevin. Will you two come back tomorrow?"

Bevin nodded. "Yeah, that's our plan. Make sure you eat enough calories to cover shifting. You'd be surprised how much it takes out of you."

"Is that why I'm so hungry?" She gazed back and forth

between us as she asked.

We both said, "Yes," at the same time.

While we'd said our goodbyes, the director had been on his phone. He apologized for not walking us out, saying he wanted to stick with Sammy to make sure she didn't pass out and that she got enough food. After watching me eat a few meals, he had an idea of what was needed. We agreed with his plan and told him we knew how to find our own way out.

Before we left, Anastasia stopped us and said she had an employment package for Bevin as well. While his brow knit in confusion, I just laughed. "Apparently we don't hide our teamwork very well."

We got home in time to eat lunch with Alex and Brooke. Owen and Sarah were out surveilling the property and everyone else was at work. The intercom buzzed, and Alex checked their phone, freezing when they saw who it was. Then their heart rate increased.

Pulling out my own, I saw it was Greta and Quinn.

Alex put down their phone. "We don't have to invite them in."

"Do you know why they're here?"

"I think Quinn wanted to talk to me, and Greta usually comes to get away from their family."

I could understand that. "It's fine. What does Quinn want?"

Alex blushed and Brooke smirked.

I waved my hand. "Never mind. I'm going to finish eating and go read in my room."

Brooke's disappointed voice dripped all over me. "Hiding from the ex? How typical."

My face dropped. "I want to read about the shifters. It'll be distracting out here."

"You're avoiding the girl I warned you about."

"Are you really going to say, 'I told you so'?"

"If the shoe fits."

I grabbed my plates and brought them into the kitchen, but before I even got to the sink, there was a knock on the door.

Brooke said sweetly, "I'll get it."

Placing my dishes in the sink, I leaned on the counter, dropping my head and breathing deeply. Bevin came up next to me. "It'll be fine. Let's go to my and José's room and look over the job offers."

I nodded but didn't move. I didn't want to be here... didn't want *them* to be here...didn't want *her* to be in my territory. The day had already been too long.

"Hello, you two. Greta, long time no see. And this must be your brother, Quinn? I'm Brooke."

The door shut and I heard people move into the living room. I could go out the back and enter the hall from the other way. It would be cowardly, but...no, the books and contract were still on the dining room table.

Pulling up my big girl panties, I gave into the inevitable.

I grabbed the books and envelope and tried to ignore the living room.

Quinn's voice rang out. "Jade, Bevin! Heya, how're you two doing?"

I paused, and slowly spun on my heel to face the living room. "Good. What brings you back to our neck of the woods?"

"You know, escaping the insanity of our family."

"Do tell." *Gods, Jade, why are you asking?*

"Well, after the last…well, after they came here, the story being told was they came here on a peaceful mission, and you went rabid. I had Violet send me the audio and played it for Jerry, the leader, and, well…now things are ugly. He realized that it wasn't you going teenage rebellion, and now he's embarrassed. That's probably worse."

This wasn't going to be a short conversation. I relented and sat down on one of the couches. Bevin ran to the kitchen, grabbed some sodas, then joined me. "Thanks," I whispered.

"After our grandfather arranged the attack, and subsequent slaughter, there are only four wolves left, if you count Boden, which I guess Jerry is doing. Boden would have been punished severely, but now he's needed as a soldier in this 'war,' as Jerry calls it. The thing is, Boden isn't sure he wants to be part of it."

"Where do you stand?" I couldn't help asking.

The searing gaze he shot Alex was answer enough, but

he still answered. "I don't like what the Dynasty is doing. They could've pulled back and remained peaceful. That's what you did. None of you have traveled to San Mateo. But no, they had to come here and try to take all of you out. Like, kill you. It's wrong. I can't support that."

Greta, who had been focused on her hands, finally looked up. "We want to join you guys."

Brooke's eyes narrowed. "You know that you won't get Jade back even if you jump ship and join our Pack, right?"

Greta glared. "Oh, you think she'd rather be with you?"

I was about to speak, when Bevin laid a hand on my knee and shook his head.

Brooke scoffed. "Girly, you are so playing the wrong card. Jade doesn't want you, she doesn't want me—praise be to Mondara—I don't know that there is *anyone* she wants right now. Too much drama. But what she really wants is people around her she can trust. At the end of the day, she *knows* she can trust me."

Deciding that was my cue, I grabbed my books and envelope. "I also would like to be able to speak for myself. Quinn, thank you for the information. Anything else you can tell Alex, Brooke, or Bevin would be great. I have some research to do." With that, I slipped away.

Before I got far down the hall, Bevin grabbed my arm and dragged me into his room. There was a small round table and four chairs in the corner. We sat and opened our employment envelopes. We had similar offers. They wanted us to work as many hours as needed to get the job done as medical and training consultants. They knew we were still in school and would work around our schedules.

There was nothing in the contract that stated we would have to give up secrets about the packs, how they worked, or pack membership. There was nothing in there about giving up personal information. They knew we were something— well, they knew Bevin was a werewolf—but didn't care to know specifics.

The final line indicated the rate of pay. I read it and put the paperwork down. Bevin and I just stared at each other for a minute, mutely.

It was enough.

CHAPTER 13

That night, José, Bevin, and I sat down and discussed the job. The way it had been written allowed for a lot of freedom. During the summer, we could just work during the mornings. We might work some afternoons, but mostly we'd be expected to be on call as needed.

The biggest thing we'd worried about was Pack security, and the contracts spelled out that this job wouldn't infringe on that. It was like the director knew about packs and their secrets and having us work for him was more important than learning about us.

To be certain, we sent a copy of the contract to my parents

to have their lawyers look it over. They said they'd get back to us. Getting a job with the government was a big decision.

The next day we returned, as part of our original agreement to help Sammy. We wanted to try to teach Sammy how to fly. According to our research, training a swan shifter to fly was inversely related to the age of the new shifter. The young took to the skies like it was the freedom they'd always dreamt of. The older the new shifter, the more likely they'd developed the frontal lobe of their brain and understood the risks involved in heights...and falling...and eventually death. Their transition from land-traveler to sky-glider was, un-shockingly, more difficult.

Sammy figured out how to shift back into a swan. She padded about in her black swan form, flapping her wings, and honking out her melodious song. All around smiled at her joy. Before her shift, she was gleeful about flying. However, when we reached the top of the building, she froze, refusing to leap.

Reevaluating our approach, we went to a calisthenics obstacle course built on the opposite side of the building from the parking lot. She started on a platform ten feet high. She waddled to the edge, extended her wings, and glided down. We all yelled for her to flap, but she was frozen until her feet hit the ground. On landing, she stayed in her open-winged position for a couple beats before collapsing to the ground.

She began to talk in the squawking of the black swan.

None of us understood her. She approached Bevin and gazed up with her small, beady eyes.

"Do you want me to help you up?"

She bobbed her head. He lifted her up to the platform, and we repeated the exercise. Over and over and over. By trial number…a lot, she finally flapped her wings…once. Her landing was a few feet further down the training field. When Bevin lifted her, he placed her on a platform higher up. When Sammy took off, she flapped her wings a few times and coasted further down the obstacle course before landing with tucked wings. We called it a day.

Sammy shifted and dressed. The director invited us for lunch, but we needed to head home. We hugged Sammy and congratulated her on a successful first day in the air.

"I don't feel very successful. I froze like an idiot."

Bevin wrapped her up in a hug. I knew how wonderful those hugs could feel. "It was your first day. You'll learn. Don't worry. You stepped off a perch and eventually flapped your wings and tucked them in on landing. In my books, that's three skills. It was wonderful. Don't be too hard on yourself, my friend. No one thought you'd do it in a day."

"Will you be back tomorrow?" She gazed up at him with large eyes.

I shook my head. "I don't know. We have a contract we need to sign or not sign. Once we've come to a decision, we'll come back. Either to return the books, or as employees."

Her face turned serious as she seemed to consider my

words. "I hope this isn't goodbye." She gave us each one more hug, then ran off.

On the way to the car, my phone buzzed. I checked the display and rolled my eyes, then pocketed the phone.

Bevin's eyes narrowed. "What was that?"

"Nothing."

"Jade."

"Bevin." I mimicked.

He rolled his eyes.

"Fine. It's just Greta texting to ask if we can get coffee or ice cream."

"How many texts has she sent you?"

"I don't know. A few. I just ignore them."

He shook his head as we got to the car. We drove home and shifted our conversation back to the ins and outs of bird flight, or rather, controlled falling. Hours and hours of falling. When we got home, we joined the others for pizza. I wasn't sure who had decided to order pizza, but I was pretty excited to see it.

We were about to clean up and head out back to the firepit when my phone buzzed. I checked the display, then simultaneously clicked the gate open and ran for the door. I was halfway out when the others followed, asking me who I'd seen and what was going on.

I didn't answer, I just ran.

A car pulled up and Fred, Bevin's dad, and his two sisters emerged. I leapt into his arms for a huge hug. I didn't care that

Bevin deserved the first hug; I took it. Fred laughed as Bevin hugged his sisters and performed introductions to Alex.

Fred set me down and gave Bevin a hug.

Bevin and I helped empty the trunk and then led everyone inside.

Feeling like my face was going to break from smiling, I asked, "What are you doing here? Did anyone know you were coming?"

"Nope. We just decided you may want more help before the wedding of the century. New pack, first gay alphas, wedding by the ocean, a war is a brewing. Am I missing anything?"

"Shifter swans?"

He tapped my nose. "Cute."

I laughed. My happiness at seeing this rock of normalcy was overwhelming. "I think we should put them in Owen's wing, no?"

Bevin nodded. "Absolutely."

We led them down the hall and gave them three separate rooms. We had the space and saw no need for doubling up the girls.

"Can we swim?"

Bevin nodded. "Mi casa es su casa, mis hermanas. Now, enjoy."

They disappeared into their room. Fred dropped off his bags and came out.

We made our way to the dining room. Fred and I took seats, while Bevin went to the kitchen to grab drinks and more food. "Where's Janet?" I asked, surprised Bevin's dad had come without his wife.

Fred kept his eyes on his son while he spoke. "She stayed back for a week or two. She couldn't get as much time off work, and figured she'd get here around the fourteenth. She'll still have a week to help with final preparations."

Bevin placed a load of sodas and a board with crackers, meats, and cheeses on the table before collapsing onto a chair. "Dad, can you look over a contract for us? We've sent it to Hazel and River to have their lawyers look it over, but since you're here, you're better."

Fred smiled. "Sure, why didn't you send it to me in the first place?"

"Honestly? I know how busy you usually are at work. River often knows when you are available, and if you had time, he'd send it your way. And we only sent Jade's contract, not mine."

"You both have one? What's this about? Can you start at the beginning?"

We did. I took lead, but Bevin interjected bits and pieces, fleshing out the story.

"Wait." Fred shook his head in disbelief. "Shifter swans are a real thing?"

Laughing, I got up and went to grab the contracts. They were still in the boys' room on the table. When I returned, I handed the contracts over.

Fred did a cursory skimming of the papers and his

brows popped up. "Wow, this looks…wow. They really want the two of you working for them. The Secret Service—LD? What does the LD stand for?"

"We never asked. It's a secret division that has werewolves."

Fred snorted. "Lupine division."

I groaned and dropped my head to the table. "That is horrible. They'll have to rename it."

"Probably not. I bet no one knows that's what the LD stands for. It's antiquated. It will remain a mystery as they bring in their new mythical beasts." He tapped the papers down. "I do want to give these a more thorough reading, but I should have them read quickly enough. I can text River that I'm here and checking them over. No reason to pay another lawyer."

"Thanks, Dad."

"Now, how is alphahood treating you?"

Bevin made a face. Fred turned to me.

"He's doing a mediocre job." I shrugged with a smirk. "I guess. I mean, if I'm forced into doing a job evaluation."

Fred smiled. "Excellent. And school?"

We both made unhappy sounds, and Fred beamed.

"Now, I brought some gifts from Wisconsin." He handed a package to each of us.

Not trusting anyone from my old Pack, I slowly opened the gift as Bev opened his. Bevin laughed, showing me a block of Wisconsin cheese in the shape of a wolf. I sighed figuring what I'd find. Sure enough, inside my wrapper was another block of Wisconsin's finest, this time in the shape of a goose.

We spent some time discussing the San Mateo clan and what we had done and were doing about them. It was good that they were down to the three experienced werewolves and one less experienced one. But we all worried they would rush out to make more.

"Have they left any more surprises for you since school ended?"

Bevin's face hardened. "Violet checks the cameras often and we do our sweeps. We haven't found anything. We figure they're regrouping after the twins' grandfather messed up. His attack wasn't sanctioned. If it had worked, he'd have been a superstar, but he failed and they are weaker for it."

"Are you going to let the twins join you? That Greta and Quinn duo?"

Bevin shrugged. "It's a hard decision. We don't want to do more to incite them. Then there's the fact that the twins aren't werewolves and won't be unless we change them. I don't know if we're ready to start creating more wolves. But do we want to send Greta back into that world? Do we want Quinn to be pulled in and probably turned by them? It isn't a quick and easy answer."

Fred took his son's hand. "It sounds like you and José are doing a great job. You aren't jumping into decisions.

You're thinking, talking, and trying to foresee future consequences."

"That's how you raised me."

Squeals of delight came from the back as Bevin's sisters splashed in the pool.

Releasing Bevin's hands, Fred reached for mine. "So, how are you after you got injected?"

I slumped. "Why doesn't anyone believe me? I'm fine. Everything worked out in the end, didn't it?"

Fred gave me a piercing look. It felt like he could read my soul. Squeezing my hand, he faced Bevin. "You're taking good care of her?"

I growled. They both ignored me.

The side of Bevin's mouth twitched before he could get it under control. "Mostly. She's more of a handful than we'd figured, but we don't want to have to face the Wisconsin Pack, so yeah, we're taking care of her."

Fred gave the work contracts his seal of approval, so Thursday morning, Bevin and I drove in with the contracts signed. We stayed until lunch to help with flight school. By the end of the morning, Sammy was jumping off the highest platform.

I told the director I was heading out of town Friday, but Bevin would be around the following week. We knew the full moon would happen during my trip with Alex, but the timing was the best with everything that was happening with work and the wedding. Alex and I figured we could slip away for a few hours and take a run in a nearby woods.

For now, Bevin and I were both still using the soap to cover our scents. We weren't sure if it was needed for Bevin, but my weird mixture was something we didn't want to explain.

CHAPTER 14

The following weekend, Alex and I headed to Iowa to visit their family.

The plane ride was nicely uneventful, and Alex's dad, Marty, was waiting for us outside the airport.

"Hey, squirt. Get in the back."

"Hi, Dad. This is my friend, Jade."

"Yep. In the back." He didn't even look at us as he slid into the driver's seat of the truck.

There were seats inside the truck. It was a double row four-door truck with seat belts and air conditioning. But what he meant by 'the back' was the bed of the pickup truck.

Alex and I climbed into the bed with our bags and held on. Most of the ride was fun, except for the part where he drove eighty or more miles an hour down the interstate for twenty minutes.

It was eighty-five degrees and humid with the sun beating down. When the truck slowed, I half wished for the air conditioning.

Alex knocked on my mental door, something I wasn't sure they'd ever done before.

Yes?

"Sorry about this. I should've warned you."

No worries. We'll survive, even at this speed.

I saw them snort, even if I couldn't hear it. The ride became more enjoyable when we finally got to country roads and slower speeds. When we reached their family farm, it was huge and beautiful. Pink and red flowering trees lined the driveway circling the main house. I could smell lilac and honeysuckle bushes. The scents brought me back home to Wisconsin, and a part of me wished my old family home lay around the corner. Despite missing my friends and family that I wouldn't see. I sank down into the aroma for the ride up the driveway.

Further back from the house were a few pole barns and fields—lots and lots of fields. Being mid-June, they were merely sprouting; nothing was high enough to identify, at least for me. I could smell the cows in the air, and see a fenced area where goats were running amuck. This farm did so much. Evergreens grew along the property's edge, and their smell, too, reminded me of home.

When the truck came to a halt, we hopped down, carrying our bags with us.

"Alexandra, everyone is out working; you know where to go. Jade will stay with you in your room."

"Okay, Dad. Anything you need us to do?"

"Not right now, but maybe later." And with that, their dad disappeared into the middle barn and Alex led me into their large white house.

We entered through a mudroom. Alex kept on their shoes as we walked into the kitchen. "We only take off our shoes if we came from the barn and have house shoes available."

"Got it."

The kitchen was huge. There was a wall of top and bottom cabinets in a warm cherry wood with a double sink under a window that looked out over the fields. They had the largest refrigerator I'd seen outside of Were House in a lovely avocado color. It matched the stove, microwave, and sink. In the center of the kitchen stood a large oak table which could easily seat fifteen people. An orange-and-rust-colored runner lay in its center. It smelled like there was a roast cooking and my stomach grumbled. Alex giggled.

"Don't worry, dinner is at three and supper is at eight. We'll be eating soon."

Checking my watch, I saw it was one-thirty.

Around the corner, there was a large living room and

hallway. Alex pointed. "There's a bathroom, a laundry room, and my parents' bedroom down this way. You can also get outside through a back door. The rest of the bedrooms as well as another two bathrooms are upstairs."

I followed them upstairs, and they showed me the two bathrooms as well as the room we'd be sharing. It was large, with a queen-sized bed. The walls were a light pink, and the bedding yellow with small white flowers. Against one wall stood a white desk with shelves over it containing a few books and some dolls. The desk matched the bed and dresser, painted with small flowers and hearts in red and purple paint. It was all so…juvenile.

Back home, Alex had decorated their room in dark woods and blues—nothing like this room. Their bedding at Were House was blue and gray, and we'd gone downtown to find posters with images of artistic renditions of outdoor scenery.

I rotated, taking it all in. "This was the room you grew up in?"

"Yep."

"Why didn't you ever…I dunno, paint it? Update it? It looks like the room of a middle school girl. It isn't at all you…or am I missing something?"

They flopped down on their bed, landing on their back, arms out. "Nothing in this town or house felt comfortable. It never seemed to matter. I never knew I *could* feel comfortable."

Sitting on the corner of the bed, I tried to imagine

them in the room as a teen, smiling and peppy, hiding their feelings of prickly discomfort. "How bad will this be? Can we explain to them who you are now?"

"It won't matter. None of them will listen."

"Will my using 'they/them' make it harder for you?"

"It doesn't matter. They won't hear it. This was probably a bad idea coming here, bringing you, all of it." Their voice came out a low monotone and they emitted an earthy scent of defeat. Beaten down before we'd even begun our stay.

"Well, we're here for a week, and there's a full moon before we go home, so the best we can do is try to have some fun." I tried to make my voice light but wasn't sure I could cheer them up.

They sat up and gave me the most dubious look I'd ever seen. Bevin would have been proud.

Their door slammed open, and a young girl, maybe about nine or ten, ran in and tackled Alex. The girl looked like a miniature version of them. "You're home! You're finally here. I'm so happy you came home. This place sucks when you're away. Will you stay?"

"What's up, Sher? What's so bad?"

She sighed and flopped back in the exact position Alex had just left. "I don't know. Mom and Dad suck, Tisha is all about the boys. Tyson started off freshman year great, but his grades slipped. And without you here, I have to watch Skip."

Alex smiled down at their small doppelganger. "That's it, then? You just don't want to watch the Tasmanian devil!"

They leaned over and tickled their sister.

"Hi, Sher, I'm Jade." I held out my hand.

The girl sat up and gave me the stink eye. "My name is Sherry. Only Alexandra can call me Sher." She crossed her arms over her chest and tilted her head away from me.

Okay, then. Dropping my hand, I had to bite my cheeks to stop myself from laughing.

"Sherry Elizabeth, that is no way to talk to my guest!" Alex gazed down at their sister, their face hard.

The girl dropped her arms and looked like she was about to cry. "But Alex, she called me *your* nickname."

"It was the only one she had. It's what I called you. What else was she going to say?"

Sherry slumped, then straightened and gazed straight into my eyes. "I'm sorry, Jade, friend of my sister Alexandra." She stood and gave me a slight bow. Then she spun on her heel and flounced out of the room.

My mouth dropped open and I didn't know what to say.

Alex rubbed my arm, drawing me back to the here and now. "Don't worry about her, she's a bit melodramatic."

My butt hit the floor as I slipped off the bed, laughing. "You think?"

Alex joined in my mirth.

Shortly thereafter, we were called for dinner, and I met the rest of Alex's siblings.

Dinner was a roast with carrots, onions, and potatoes. Checking out the table, I saw sides of rice, salad, and peas. At the far end, still steaming, sat two loaves of homemade bread, and it looked like there was a dessert waiting for curtain-call.

Everyone wanted to hear about college, so we spent the meal filling them in on dorm life and classes. Though they knew we'd been assigned the same room, but they didn't know I was a junior with a similar major.

Alex's mother gave me a soft look. "You were in the same classes and could study together?"

"Yes, ma'am. Two each semester."

Alex put down her fork. We'd convinced them to eat more, but they still weren't eating enough. Now that they were home, they were already back down to almost nothing. "She's studying vet sciences, but it's only one of her majors. She's double majoring in pre-med as well."

They all turned to face me. Their dad spoke to his plate. "Another smart one, huh." He didn't sound pleased.

Alex faced their sister, Tisha. Tisha had the look of their mom: tall, lean, with dark hair. "What are your plans now that you've graduated?"

"Like you care."

"What does that mean? Of course, I care."

"I don't remember seeing you at graduation. My phone is free of any texts from you, sister mine."

"Phones work both ways. I texted you at the start of the year, but after you didn't respond, I stopped trying. Now that I'm here, I'm hoping to get a response."

"Whatever."

"So, college?"

"Not everyone is going to waste Dad's money like you, *Alexandra*. I'm more considerate." Even though Tisha sounded annoyed, her scent gave her away. Citrusy amusement. Was she happy to be embarrassing Alex in front of her family?

Alex slipped their hands under the table and fisted them. "Right, okay. So, no college. Are you getting a job or helping out around here?"

"How about you stick around and find out?" And with that, she pulled out her phone and ignored the rest of the group.

I investigated the faces of the people around me. Alex's mom and dad didn't seem to care, Sherry was busy managing the youngest kid, Skip, and Tyson was gazing up at me.

Alex took a few more bites, shifted their attention to their parents, who were ignoring the kids, then to Tyson. "How about you Ty, how was your first year of high school?"

"Great! I made a ton of new friends. I don't know what your deal was when you went, but it's great. You just needed to get your nose outta the books. Once I did that, things turned around."

After massaging their temples, Alex gave up and focused on eating.

Dessert was apple pie with vanilla ice cream. I offered

to help clean up. Pearl, Alex's mom, looked scandalized. Instead, Alex and I went out to take a walk.

There was a path that led around the farm. "Why did your mom insist you return? What was the purpose? No one is spending time with you."

"Control. I didn't come home for Thanksgiving or winter break. I hadn't returned yet for the summer, and that was just too much freedom for them."

"Is this what life was always like?"

They shrugged. "Some nights. Tisha's gotten bolder, Tyson used to be more studious. I've always been meek. I just never saw a point in fighting them."

"I don't want you to be meek back home. That isn't your role. We all like when you see things and challenge us. it's important for the Pack."

"I know. But I can be myself back home with the Pack, can't I?" They looked around, waving their arms, encompassing the farm. "Here, with these people who raised me, it's different. I feel like I'm a stranger. You've let me out and I don't think I can be put back in that box, even if I wanted to…and I don't think I want to. You and Bevin…" They seemed at a loss for words.

I wrapped an arm around their waist. "Good. I really like the real you."

CHAPTER 15

The next few days were a weird combination of fun and stress. Time with Alex's family was stressful. When they were off working the farm, Alex and I toured the nearby town. We took Sherry to a water park. We visited a haunted cave and then went to a strawberry farm to pick fresh strawberries.

The full moon was on a Thursday, and we were flying out Friday. Thursday morning, we decided to go to a woodsy area Alex had liked hiking in when they were younger and run during the day. A two-to-three-hour run should get the itch out of our system.

After breakfast, Tisha came up to Alex and sneered. "Yeah, run away again today with your friend. You're such a disappointment to the family, Alexandra. All the money you've wasted from Mom and Dad. What are you even going to do with that degree of yours? Will you come back and support the family? No. You're going to stay in California like a selfish brat." She pushed Alex in the chest. "No respect for anyone. No love for anyone but yourself."

She flipped her hair over her shoulder and stalked out of the kitchen.

The sharp gingery scent of shock washed over Alex, quickly replaced by an earthy scent of sad acceptance. I wrapped my arm around them. "None of that was true. She's jealous that you've gotten away from this small town and lashed out, that's all. Come on, let's go run."

They nodded, but I didn't think they really heard me.

The drive to the wooded area took long enough for Alex to work through the confrontation with Tisha. Once there, we let our wolves out. Her wolf was as white as mine was black. We looked like negatives of each other, and if anyone saw us, we'd make quite a sight. I let Alex guide us. They knew this land and taking the lead would boost their confidence.

The smells were different, reminiscent of my old pack's stomping grounds. Alex had only been wolfy in California, so they had a whole new world to explore. We started off with about an hour of running and stretching our muscles. After jumping some fallen trees, we found a stream, and when Alex paused, I plowed into them so that we both flew into the water. The splash was huge and after their initial yelp, we splashed and played. Eventually, we crawled out and flopped down on the grass.

We found a rabbit trail and replenished our energy, then returned to the water to clean off. The time flew as we ran and played. As the sun arched through the sky toward the horizon, I signaled Alex, and we turned back towards the road. We found the car and our clothes and let our humanity back out, hiding the wildness of the black and white wolves before they were seen. Dressing quickly, we grabbed the bag lunch from the car and sat on the grass to eat.

Alex glowed with excitement. "That was fun. I had no idea how different it would be here. I mean, I knew our senses were better, but everything was *so* different. The scents, even what I saw."

"Oh, yeah. Our first run when Bevin and I got to college was a trip. I mean, I'd been in other places, but we were in a new state, just me and Bev, everything was different… just so weird."

They gazed at the woods. "I know, it smells like home here. I mean, I know California is now our home, but not my original home. Does that make sense?"

"Yeah, I know what you mean. It feels a lot like my

home back in Wisconsin, too."

Alex leaned in and sniffed me. "The forest smells like you." They blushed. "That's why it makes me think of home and safety."

I leaned in and put my head on their shoulder. I didn't know if I'd ever gotten a nicer compliment.

We cleaned up and headed back to the farm. We'd missed dinner, but that was fine with both of us. Good food wasn't worth the stress of spending more time with Alex's family. Every meal was a new battle to be maneuvered and missing one was a relief.

We went up to their room and packed our bags. Despite how homey the run in the woods felt, we were both excited to return to California.

At seven, we were called down to the kitchen for supper. It seemed early, but what did I know about farm living?

The meal was a feast of fried chicken, potatoes au gratin, green beans, mac and cheese, salad, corn on the cob, and brownies cooling on the stove. It all looked and smelled amazing, though the mac and cheese wasn't Luke's mac and cheese. The visit may have been socially awkward, but I had no complaints about the cooking.

"I know you two missed dinner, so I wanted to make sure your last meal was filling. I know you girls are leaving early enough that you called in a cab, so let's enjoy this last bit of time together."

The irony of enjoying time when the family had ignored

us for the last week was, I hoped, not lost on anyone. But it probably was.

We ate. I got through my first plate and started fantasizing about the second. I reached for the chicken and my stomach cramped. My hand fisted and I pulled it back.

Alex's family was talking and focused on their own plates, so only Alex saw my aborted reach for food. "You okay?"

Everything in my body felt wrong. I shook my head. "My stomach just cramped...and the room is spinning. Could your mom be trying to poison me?" I was only half joking.

"I don't think so. What should we do?"

"Could we head out behind a barn? If things get bad, I may want to pull out a friend."

"Yeah, smart." They surveyed the table before pulling me up.

Their mom's brows dropped. "What's wrong, hon?"

"Um, I think we left something out in the car. We'll be back."

"Oh! Okay." The first benefit of everyone ignoring us this trip—we could slip away, and no one cared.

Doubtless we disappeared from everyone's notice as quickly as we walked from the room.

We got outside and Alex had to practically carry me out to the barn. I could feel my phone buzz but couldn't deal with it right now. I was trying to focus on radiating peace. With Alex's family, Alex, and three alphas, at least one obviously trying to contact me, I had too many things to worry about. Talk about too many cooks in the kitchen.

When we got tucked away behind the third pole barn, which also had a shed creating a double block, I stripped off my clothes. I got to my hands and knees, but before I could do anything, my stomach cramped again. I rolled to my side, panting.

Curling into a ball, I tried to control…anything. I felt like I had nothing in my power I *could* control.

Somewhere off in the distance, I heard Alex's voice. "I don't know what's wrong with her. She's writhing on the ground, clutching her middle, panting."

Pulling in my knees, I groaned, trying to make myself as small as possible.

"I don't think it's the moon; we ran for a few hours this afternoon. Yeah, I don't know, it's weird. Yep. Right. She started on her hands and knees, she couldn't do it, just fell over."

It felt like my insides were melting. I closed my eyes. I pushed myself up to my butt and hugged my legs. Tucking my head between my knees, I tried to breathe.

Alex's play-by-play continued. I felt like I was the main attraction to some weird event. "She's up on her butt now, but her breathing is still rough. She looks like she's in a lot of pain."

My arms felt like they were made of lead. I let them drop to the ground. My mind began to float, followed by my body. I felt hollow.

"Her arms dropped, and now there's a weird cloud

around her. A mist? Yeah, maybe. Yeah, grayish or black. Yeah, it *is* getting darker. Wait, how did you know what's happening to her? What? Are you sure? What do I do? Okay. See you tomorrow. Bye."

Crap! I knew what this was, now.

In a panic, I reached out to José. I was disassociating in a mist of confusion, but I didn't care, I called out to him.

José!

"*Chica, what are you doing? You need to stay focused on what is happening to you.*"

I don't want this. Make it stop.

"*Oh, honey, I can't.*"

There was no longer any pain. It was done. I was a swan. It was such a different shift than my mammals. I was going to have to do a lot more research.

José was still in my head. "*You still with me, chica?*"

Yes.

"*So much pout in a single word.*" I could hear his amusement through our connection.

The world looked so weird. I started to pad around and let out a melodious honk. Frustration and wonder at being in a new form. I really didn't think I'd had a black swan and now here I was—wings, feathers, and a beak.

Alex's eyes were practically hearts, they were so enamored. "You're gorgeous. I love swans. This is amazing. And you're still black."

I extended my wings.

"Oh! Your wings are white. That's so cool. Can you fly?"

I tried to glare at them but failed. I could barely move in this new body. I knew what we'd gone through for days with Sammy. I tucked in my wings and padded around for a few more minutes.

José's voice came to me again. *"Will you be okay?"*

I sighed internally. *I'm going to need therapy. I'm so happy you, Bevin, and Fred are there. I think I'll need all of you.*

He chuckled. *"You'll be fine, chica. Have you tried finding your humanity?"*

I'm about to.

Finding a dark spot, I closed my eyes and focused on my fingers. A weightless feeling took over again, and Alex gasped. I hoped that meant the mist was back. Then it felt like a boulder was placed on and in me, as all the weight returned. "Whoa, that sucks."

Hearing my voice, I slapped my hands over my mouth—yep, those were lips—feeling my face, my body, and then I found my clothes. I put them on.

I stayed put in the grass, panting for a few minutes. Alex sat down next to me. "You okay?"

I grunted.

"That really isn't an answer."

Rolling to my side, I struggled up to a sitting position. "I just…I had hoped that the serum hadn't worked. I didn't feel different. I didn't smell different. And now I have another item to add to my list of oddities."

Alex grabbed my hand. "I think it's wonderful. I know you're reeling but think about the advantages." They leaned down and sniffed. "You know, I still don't smell it on you."

At the moment, I couldn't see any advantage, but I was willing to allow their enthusiasm to burn away some of my ire. The fact they couldn't smell the bird on me would be interesting later.

We finally returned to the house in time for the brownies to be cut and passed out. I was starving, but we'd raid the kitchen later. For now, brownies would do.

I wasn't about to tell Tanner, but Pearl's brownies were almost as good as his shakes.

CHAPTER 16

We landed in the San Francisco airport. Upon exiting the plane—besides being overwhelmed by the sheer number of people embarking and disembarking the planes, muscling for position in food lines, scrambling to find entertainment or gate information—I smelled werewolf, and it wasn't us. Alex had never stopped using the bear soap, and while we traveled, I had used it, too. Why bring other soap on our trip?

We headed toward the exit, and I found the source: a man, a woman, and a teenage girl. I grasped Alex's arm and dragged them until we were directly behind them, and I could overhear their conversation.

It sounded like they were in the middle of a disagreement. The man was shaking his head. "I don't want to call back home for the number and searching our bag will take too long. Let's rent a car, take a few days to explore, and then we'll check in."

The girl's voice was uncertain. "Is that safe?"

The older woman took her hand. "I'm sure it's safe. Look, we'll sight-see from the redwoods down to Santa Cruz. After that…"

It was enough. "There's no 'after that.' It isn't safe."

They stopped in their tracks and spun to face me, their expressions and scents hostile. I could sense more than see them sniff.

Though they'd been speaking softly, softer than even Alex could probably hear, I was pretty certain this family were some of the new members of our Pack, and I had to warn them of the dangers in the area.

The man's eyes narrowed as he looked me up and down, irritated. The woman looked back and forth between me and her phone while the girl slipped behind the couple. Smart girl.

Top lip lifting in a partial snarl, the man's chin rose, and he glared down his nose at me. His hands fisted as he sneered. "It isn't polite to listen in on other people's conversations, girl."

"Fair. I have a ride. The drivers are José and Bevin, maybe

they could provide my credentials since right now mine are…" I raised my arm to my nose to sniff it, "…hidden."

The man looked unconvinced, but the woman held out the phone to him as she faced me. "Are you Jade Stone? Daughter of Hazel and River Stone?"

Alex's jaw dropped. "Jade, how do these people know you? How do *you* know them?"

With one hand on their shoulder, I held my other out. "Can we head out to the car? This can all be explained, I promise. You can still take your few days, a week even, to tour, but let's do it safely, please. I'd hate for your first experience in our fair territory to be dangerous."

The girl finally poked her head out from behind her mom's back. "But how did you know we were coming today?"

Throwing my hands up and out in a rainbow pattern, I wiggled my fingers. "Magic!"

Alex's face dropped as they deadpanned, "We just flew in from my family's place in Iowa…pure chance."

The girl's parents laughed.

"So, I'm Jade, this is Alex." I held out my hand to be shaken this time. They obviously weren't going to just follow me blindly.

The woman took my hand. "I'm Holly, this is my husband Nick, and our…daughter, Madeline."

The girl huffed. "You can call me Maddy." Her voice was unusual and at one point it dropped in pitch, and she cringed as if in pain.

We shook with each of the introductions and then we headed out to the front of the airport to find the boys. The family was finally willing to trust me.

When we found them, José and Bevin leapt out with matching expressions of shock and pleasure. I performed quick introductions. We all looked back and forth between the number of people in our party and the car the boys had brought. The car was a small sedan.

José made an executive decision. "I'll take you to Were House, someone else will come to get this lot. I can give you a quick tour of the area or take you directly home, up to you."

"Do we have to stay at…Were House? Or can we find our own home?"

"You can live wherever you want, but the housing market is horrible. We have a huge den. We have single rooms, but we also have some two-and three-bedroom suites with living spaces, including a small kitchenette. If you want to have a more luxurious meal, you would need to join us in the main kitchen, but you could have a private family meal most nights."

The gingery scent of shock wafted from them. Nick leaned in, head tilted. "Is this for real? Our own space within the den? Separate, but together?"

José wrapped an arm around his shoulders. "Why don't I take you home and give you a tour? You need to relax and unwind. No decisions should be made at an airport."

Once all the bags were packed into the trunk and the

family was packed into the car, José whisked them away.

I faced Bevin to ask about our ride, but before I could, he wrapped me in a huge bear hug. I wanted to ask but gave in to the need for the connection. Over my head, he asked Alex, "How has she been?"

"Good. Once she shifted back, I think she tried to ignore what happened."

"That tracks."

Oh, that. I snuggled closer to my alpha, letting him absorb some of my grief.

"How did you know she was hurting? She seemed so happy to me. Even smelled happy, especially when we got off the plane and out of the airport." Alex sounded perplexed.

Bevin's chest vibrated with amusement. "I don't know. She and I just always know. Even when we don't know ourselves, we know each other. Did you know she called out to José when it was happening?"

"What?"

"Yep."

"Not you?"

"Well, if she depended on only one of us for all her needs, then we'd be a hollowed-out shell in under a week."

I pushed away and punched him in the chest. "Jerk."

He leaned down and kissed my forehead. "Better?"

"No. How are we getting home?"

A horn honked and Owen pulled up in Luke's car. We

tossed our bags in the back and climbed in. We let Alex take the front. I still needed physical contact with Bevin.

Before taking off, Bevin asked, "Can I see her? The swan?"

I thought for a second, then nodded. "It would be easy enough to bring you into my mental landscape. Shifting into a swan in the car seems...ill advised, especially the getting naked first part."

Owen growled from the driver's seat, "So, I'm the chauffeur for two dead people in the back seat?"

Bevin raised an eyebrow. "More like asleep, and you and Alex can discuss Iowa or what they'll find back home. So many stories to tell."

Bracing myself, I tuned out the rest of the banter and took Bevin's hand. I had been avoiding my mental landscape for a while. Shortly after realizing I had two animals, I created a mental world for them. A cabin, a campfire, and a small lake in the background. It was a place for me to go when I needed to communicate with my wolf and panther. I could bring other people in, as well as their animals.

When my ex-girlfriend became a wolf and a part of her got stuck in my mind, I created a sort of prison, so her emotions didn't overwhelm me. Beyond the frustration of having anyone's emotions take over, no one needed to know the emotional state of their ex-girlfriend. The area she took up always made me a bit sad.

As soon as I was comfortable, Wolf went to invite Bevin and his wolf. We had a real collection of black beasts in my space. He gazed at our two wolves, my panther, and the locked-down mound under the cone of silence.

Bevin cocked his head. He sniffed. "It seems different."

Giving in to the inevitable, I opened myself up to the prison, and realized he was right; it wasn't fighting me in the same way. "When we're home, maybe I'll have Sarah and José help me unwind the protection and we can try to figure out what's changed."

The ghost-Piper, the image of my ex-girlfriend connecting me to her, felt different. If I focused on it... her, I could feel her, hear her, know what she was doing, but something about the prison Sarah and José had set up was off. If the ghost-Piper got out, I wasn't sure if I could control her on my own. A shiver ran down my spine at the memory of the last time she'd almost taken over my senses.

"Good. Now, I see our three beasts. Where's the new one?"

I relaxed and twined my fingers with his and rested my head on his arm. I rolled my head up to stare into his shining sapphire eyes. The concern and love I saw there grounded me. I straightened my spine and got us turned around. We strolled until we came upon a lake with some logs along the bank. We sat on one and watched my black swan paddling happily. The three beasts had followed us, but they stayed respectfully back.

"Jade, she's lovely."

"I know. She looks like Sammy's. I'm just... overwhelmed, I guess."

"You'll be able to fly one day."

That thought sent a small thrill surging through my body. "And you'll get to train me."

He groaned.

"Why didn't you offer to drive the new family? Their daughter is trans, isn't she?"

"She is. It's why they wanted to come here and join our Pack. Their Pack tried but didn't know how to help. She didn't transition as young as I did, only a few years ago. It's been harder for her. She was accepted into college at San Francisco State University. I guess other places, too, but she figured she'd have the best hope of figuring things out here."

"But why didn't you drive them?"

"Because, Jade, you needed me."

I slowly brought us out of my mindscape. Bevin squeezed my hand once we returned to awareness of the real world. My stomach growled, letting me know I hadn't eaten enough for my mental acrobatics. A glance out the window informed me that we were close to home.

Whispering, I asked Bevin, "How many know?"

Owen, never one to mince words, answered for him. "What, that you're a bird-brain?" My head fell back, and he chuckled. "Well, your alphas know. Sarah told me because we don't keep secrets. I don't know about Violet or Luke, but you should tell them. Since it just happened last night, they might not know yet."

Bevin squeezed my hand tight. "You certainly keep things interesting."

CHAPTER 17

With the car parked, Owen turned to face me. "One last thing. While you were playing around in Iowa, two of the Packs, Massachusetts and Colorado, sent their wolves. I think you'll like the guy from Colorado, he's a trip."

"Alex, is that why you're so nervous?" Since Bevin and I had exited my mental landscape, their scent had taken on a nutty carnival smell.

They bobbed their head but didn't look at me. "So many new people, it's a bit overwhelming. I psyched myself up for over a month to prepare to move into the dorms."

"Okay, how about this: we'll walk in together, just the

two of us, arm in arm. A new duo from Arcoíris. None of the new folk know us, we'll be our own new wolves."

They finally moved, facing me. "You are such a dork... would that be okay?"

"Of course."

Owen opened his door and popped the trunk. "I've got the bags. I'll drop them in the hall by your doors."

Bevin gave my knee a squeeze. "If you don't mind, I'm going to slip off to find Mr. and Mrs. Ocean. I'd like to talk to Maddy and her parents. I didn't even ask if she's gone wolfy yet."

I scrunched my nose. "She hasn't and she won't...no seed of a wolf. I'm sorry, I didn't even think about that. But you can add that to your discussion with them."

Bevin's head dropped. "Okay, thanks. Sometimes I wish I didn't know as much, but maybe it's better that I do. I'll add that to what I tell them."

We all piled out and the boys went in first. I threw my arm over Alex's shoulders, and they slipped their arm around my waist. Holding on tight to hide their fear, we entered the house.

I was surprised to see Quinn sitting in the living room with Fred, Luke, and two other wolves I didn't recognize. We could do introductions later. As we sauntered through and to our hallway, I smelled jealousy, and assumed it was Quinn's. When we'd made it to our doorways, I leaned down and kissed Alex on their cheek and whispered, "Way to go."

We each took our bags into our rooms. I spent a few minutes relaxing. I splashed water on my face, and then decided to face the gauntlet.

My first stop was the kitchen. An unknown man had taken up residence—a tall and dark werewolf with black curly hair. Without turning around, he asked, "What'll it be?"

Ingredients were strewn everywhere. Lost in the myriad of options, I stood dumbstruck. Arms wrapped around me from behind and the voice of my savior said, "Make her a chocolate shake."

I collapsed back into Sarah's arms, practically swooning at the thought of a chocolate shake.

She laughed and dropped me into a kitchen stool. "It's right up there with Tanner's."

My eyes narrowed at the person who'd taken over the kitchen. "Who are you and how do you know Tanner's recipe?"

He turned and grinned. "I'm Oscar, and we went to the same culinary school."

"Wait, Tanner went to culinary school? Why didn't I know this?" I thought for a few minutes. My eyes narrowed as he placed his concoction in front of me. I took a tentative sip and groaned in pleasure. I thought I'd pass out right there. "Marry me!"

Oscar asked Sarah, "Is she talking to me or the shake?"

Sarah shrugged. "I'm not really sure. She likes girls, but for a good chocolate shake she may switch teams."

I tuned them out to enjoy my moment with the shake.

Once the shake was halfway gone, I focused on Oscar. "When you say culinary school, do you mean parents? Are you Tanner's brother?"

His face broke out in the most mischievous smile. "Damn, girl, he was right."

Sarah gaped at us.

Dropping my hands to the counter I bit my cheeks to stop myself from laughing. "Okay, who won the pool and who knows?"

"Tanner won, he said you'd figure it out quickly, and only you two know."

"No one else figured it out? How many of these chocolate shakes have you made?"

"Plenty."

"Well, then, let's see how long it takes the others. I mean, Fred has to know; he must be loving this."

Oscar's eyes twinkled. "I see why my brother loves you. You're fun."

I nearly choked on the shake. "So, what do you do? And why decide to move from the east coast here?"

"How did you know I was from the Massachusetts Pack?"

"I'm clever; now stop changing the subject."

"I'm a stay-at-home dad. I cook and clean."

I nearly slid from my stool into a pile of goo. "You cook? Are you planning on cooking for all of us? Like this? Are you better than Tanner?"

"You'll have to let me know." His warm voice blanketed

me along with his amusement. He handed me a second shake before I could ask. "As for why…"

As the seconds passed, I sighed. "Tanner asked you to come watch over us, didn't he? He's worried about us."

"Well, he asked about you specifically. I'm sure he's worried about all of you, but his specific request was for you, child."

Sarah rubbed my back as my head fell to my folded arms. "I can take care of myself."

Sarah's rub turned into a pat. "You keep telling yourself that, champ. Maybe one day it'll be true."

Two mini versions of Oscar ran in, followed more slowly by a beautiful woman. She sat down on a stool next to me. She looked as fit and athletic as Sarah, if a bit older. The kids ran to Oscar, demanding attention and food. "Hi, I'm Sierra, Oscar's wife. These crazy bundles are Ginger and Seth."

The sound of young children filled my heart with joy. We were beginning to feel like a real pack, with families and kids. "Have they been to the pool?"

"Oh, yes. They're thrilled to live in a house with a pool and so many people around. We love the den you've designed with single rooms and family units. It really is something spectacular."

"Thanks."

Oscar leaned over to give his wife a kiss. "She figured it out in under five minutes. Tanner knows his girl."

"But of course."

Alex wasn't wrong. It was going to take some time to get used to a Pack Den with so many people.

Sarah and I took our shakes out to the pool so I could tell her about my adventures in Iowa.

Eventually, I became aware of Quinn and Greta. I wasn't sure why they were there. Maybe Quinn wanted to see Alex, but I didn't want to see Greta. I felt her eyes on me as soon as I sat for lunch. Alex and the twins ate in the living room, there weren't enough seats around the dining room, but my skin itched under the other woman's intense gaze.

After lunch, and once Quinn and Greta left, we headed out to the gym.

When Owen had designed the gym of his dreams, it included both inside and outside torture areas. Our outside exercise equipment wasn't as elaborate as the SSLD, but he had come up with some leaping challenges for the panthers, so our structure did have height.

As we headed out, I slid my arm into José's. "I can't believe everyone is following us out. I know I said I had a presentation for anyone interested, but...I mean, why is *everyone* interested?"

"Chica, they're all new and curious, what did you expect?"

Though my heart beat faster, they were my new Pack, and they'd all learn eventually. The more they knew now, the more they could aid me in the future.

Most of the people who followed us out didn't know what was about to happen; only those of the original Pack did. José agreed to give background while Bevin stayed with me.

I moved to the tree line, and, turning my back to the group, I stripped and let my swan out. It took a few minutes for me to wrap my mind around calling a new animal in a new way. I sat on my butt, holding my legs, and imagined my arms becoming wings. *I needed to begin learning how to fly.* If Sammy was any indication, the process was going to be long, and the sooner I started, the better off I'd be. I'd done some exercises in my mindscape on the plane, but I wasn't sure if that'd help.

After my shift, I stood stock-still while the shock washed over me. It was a lot, and with three animals, my sensitivity had grown again. The smell and sound of the full crowd came crashing down on me as I stood there, frozen. I spent a moment filtering out everyone's chit-chat. My head still swirled and the struggle threatened to take me under.

Sarah came up next to me and placed a hand gently on my back; Bevin did the same. The strength of two alphas gave me the power I needed to put my blocks up. Even with them, I took a few minutes to decompress before fully embracing my feathers.

The structure's ramp led to a landing roughly ten feet high. It didn't seem so bad, but as a panther, I was good with heights. I continued up another ramp to the fifteen-foot-high platform. I shook out my wings to a chorus of ooh's and ah's. That felt good. I flapped my wings and the action seemed awkward, yet natural at the same time. I visualized flying. I'd watched several videos and tried to see myself as a swan, soaring through the air.

After sensing the air currents, I leapt and flapped my wings. I actually lifted off! I flapped again and glided on a current. Elation flooded out of me as I realized I was doing it. I was flying. The clouds floated by on a breeze, it was amazing. Suddenly, I realized I didn't know how to control altitude, direction, or speed. I panicked.

How do I get off this ride? I can't turn! How do I stop?

My cruising ended when I hit a tree and crumpled to the ground.

CHAPTER 18

"Honk!" I let out a mellifluous protest to my ungainly landing. I shook my head and swore I saw stars.

"Jade!" Bevin slid on his knees at my side. "Are you okay?"

I closed my eyes and focused on my humanity.

He squeaked and jumped back a bit. "Someone bring her clothes."

A boulder settled on me with the shift. I shuddered as my body adjusted to the weight change. A minute later, I sat on the ground, naked, hugging my knees.

The new Pack members surrounded me as Sarah ran up with my clothes. My head hurt and my body ached, but

175

I managed to slip on my shirt. I got my jeans pulled on, then Bevin helped me to my feet.

Bevin bent in close. "You okay?"

"Yeah. I have to learn how to fly." I leaned in and placed my head on his shoulder. "We need to hold a Pack meeting. I can't believe I'm saying this, but we need to fill everyone in."

Chuckling came from a few feet away as José's voice rang out. "I would like to have everyone meet in the Pack meeting room in one hour."

I watched as everyone filed towards the house. Most came over to smile at me or give me a kind word. Though there were a lot of new faces, it was nice to see Oscar and his kids, and Maddy and her parents. I was already starting to connect with some of the new Pack members.

Oscar grabbed my hand. "My word, finally a story to share. I'll have a plate ready for you when you make it into the dining room." Then he kissed my cheek. Grabbing his kids' hands, he headed for the house.

When the only people left with me were José, Bevin, Owen, and Sarah, I slumped.

Sarah's arms wrapped around me from behind. "You're a sexy bird, but you need to learn to avoid the trees. I know as a panther they help, but that's not how it works when you have feathers."

"Wow! You really have spent too much time with Owen. You're starting to sound like him."

Owen cheered, "That's my alpha!"

We all just stared at him. His smile didn't falter.

Chuckling, she squeezed me. "I can feel that you're mentally okay. Physically?"

I nodded. "Yeah. Just embarrassed. It was fun for a couple of minutes, but *ouch*. There are mechanics to flying: up, down, left, right, oh, and stop…you know, without a tree."

Owen's eyes lit up. "I am so on this one, sis."

I groaned. "I know what I said sounded like a cheat code for a video game, but it isn't. This is me, as a bird, flying."

Owen winked, spun on his heel, and sauntered away.

José grabbed my hands. "I've been debating an official Pack meeting anyway. What's on your agenda, chica?"

I huffed. "Well, me. They need to know the basics about epsilon wolves."

He nodded. "Okay, then we have a plan. Let's get food."

We made our way to the house and, true to his word, there was a bowl of gumbo waiting. It smelled divine, almost as good as the New Orleans Café in town. The others had to raid the kitchen for their own grub.

After fortifying myself with two quick bowls, we made our way to the Pack meeting room. This one was a bit different than my parents'. There were three doors, one in the back that led to Were House and two on the sides. The two side doors faced each other halfway down opposing walls and led outside. One led to the front driveway and the other headed to the woods. The doors to the outside were mainly for safety.

When you entered from the back, the floor sloped down towards the raised stage at the front. This made it easier for everyone to see whoever was talking. Like the Wisconsin Pack's meeting room, there were loveseats, couches, bean bags, and side tables scattered around the room. There were a few round high-top tables with stools if people would rather sit that way. We'd wanted to allow for everyone's seating preference.

The room was painted a sky blue with dark blue accents. Several high windows allowed in natural light. We were debating artwork for the walls or a rotation of kids' drawings. We had time to decide.

Entering the room, I made my way to the stage with José while the others found couches. Slowly, the rest of the Pack joined us.

Sarah had agreed to watch the kiddos during the meeting since she wasn't a werewolf and already knew all of the information. We had one demonstration we wanted her for, but she didn't have to be in the room for the rest. There was a kids' playroom with games, a huge TV, and electronics in the basement.

As José and I sat on the edge of the stage, the room filled. Everyone was curious about our first Pack meeting.

Before José began, his face broke out in a smile. I could feel the joy emanating from him seeing his Pack before him; it filled the room, and everyone's faces glowed with his happiness.

"I want to welcome you all to California, the dangerous Wild West, and to our Pack. I know joining us was a gamble. We're young, we're new, but I believe this Pack will be great. A family. I know the wolves from Florida aren't here yet, but I think it's important that with so many new faces, we begin to form Pack bonds. Once all the new wolves are here, we'll have a bonfire out back and perform an official Pack welcome. You're all part of the Pack, joined with me, but we'll do a ceremony to the gods and have them welcome you as well. As for today, I want to quickly tell everyone what I know of each of you and let each of you introduce yourselves. Then I want to give a few warnings about moving to the Wild West."

José spent a few minutes giving a brief warning about the Dynasty wolves, facts about each of the wolves who had been living in California for the last year, and then a quick introduction of the new faces. He then asked anyone who wanted to provide a longer introduction to please do so.

Oscar stood up first and introduced himself and his family. Everyone seemed relaxed, and a wolf I didn't know turned to him and asked, "Why did you choose to move from Massachusetts to California, my man?"

Oscar's smile slowly grew, spreading to encompass his full face. "My brother suggested it to me."

I snorted and José gave me a confused, questioning look.

Oscar winked at me before sitting down.

Holly stood next and introduced herself and her family.

"Before I'm asked, my daughter is transgender. She asked that I tell you all because you'll smell it on her, and she wants you all to use 'she/her' pronouns. This is important to her and to us. We moved here because she's going to college here and we hope that it will be easier for this Pack to adjust. Our old Pack was making an effort, they were doing their best, but we needed more. Better."

She sat before anyone could ask her anything.

The wolf I didn't know stood. He was tall, well over six feet, almost as tall as Bevin. He had sandy blond curls, and dark eyes. His lazy grace made me think of the surfers I had seen at the beaches. "I'm Phoenix, Phoenix Storm. I came here from Colorado, where I was an adventure guide. I'm hoping to start up a new branch of the company here. We're, like, expanding. I'm here for new adventures, mis amigos."

I bit my cheek. I couldn't laugh at his over-the-top outrageousness, but I knew Bevin and Owen could read me like a book. Bevin's eyes sparkled as he watched me.

Before anyone could react, Alex stood. "I know I'm not new to those from here, but I was recently bitten and changed to a wolf within my first few months in California. I'm not one of the alphas, and being part of a Pack is pretty strange to me, so I thought I could introduce myself as well. My name is Alex. I met Jade in college and, like I said, I was attacked. José and Bevin let me join the Pack and, along with Jade, they've been helping me learn what it means to be a werewolf, to be Pack." They turned to Holly and her husband Nick. "Like your daughter, I smell one way and prefer something else. I go by 'they/them' pronouns. Anyway, hi everyone." She quickly sat and turned the color of a ripe tomato.

Bevin, who had been sitting next to them, wrapped them in a hug and whispered softly in their ear.

Brooke stood next. "I'm Brooke. You'll get to know me one-on-one. I'm original Pack, but like Owen, I've been off at college. This is fun. Can we learn about Jade now and get back to the pool?" She rolled her eyes. "Really, Jade? A bird?"

I couldn't stop my laughter this time. "Okay, yeah. I know that's what brought all of you so quickly to this room, but that isn't where I want to start."

I spent a few minutes explaining to the group what it meant to be an epsilon wolf, some of my abilities, and my role in the Pack. I was about to demonstrate my powers with a blast mental "hello" when Owen jumped up.

"Are you kidding me? Haven't I seen you pass out enough? Did you even think about bringing food with you to this little show?" He turned to Bevin and shook his head. "Will she ever learn? I mean, really. She needs a keeper!"

My head fell back, and I growled at the ceiling. "I had a big lunch."

"Yeah, after two shifts."

My head snapped down and I glared at him. "It isn't like I've never done this."

Oscar got up. "How about I go whip up a shake?

Would that work?"

I stopped protesting. "On the other hand, I *could* use some extra fortifications."

Everyone in the room, who had started to tense up at the sibling bickering, laughed and relaxed, except José. He spoke to Oscar. "You need to see this, too."

Oscar gave a small smirk. "I have a good idea of what our young Jade can do, and if I need it, she'll give me a private lesson."

José's eyes narrowed. "Your brother sent you, you say?" Then his eyes widened, and he grabbed my arm in a vice grip. Slowly, he turned to me. "You're obsessed with his chocolate shakes. His brother? Like…you *know* his brother? *We* know his brother?"

I laughed and a chuckle came from Fred's direction. "Why, yes, my fearless leader, we *do* know his brother." The door clicked closed as Oscar left the room. "Why do you ask?"

José let out a long laugh and released my arm. "Okay, time to give yourself a headache."

That sobered me up a bit, but not enough to lose my smile. Facing our Pack, I explained, "Please don't all freak out. This will be weird, but it's our best secret, and our best tool." With that, I closed my eyes and found the connections.

If you think about me, create a door—if I understand the process—and knock gently, you can initiate a mental communication. I can also let you see our connection so that we can find each other.

I dropped the connection and opened my eyes. The room had gone very still. The scent of snickerdoodles and sweet candy filled the room, wonder and fear. Slowly, the snickerdoodle scent won out as the Pack's fear dropped away.

Eventually, knocks came as one by one they figured it out.

I did get dizzy, but Oscar's chocolate shake came to the rescue, fortifying my reserves.

"When we're in communication, you start to smell like me, so this isn't completely stealthy, just so you know."

Once everyone had a chance to connect with me, I explained the healing and calm. Owen ran down to the kids so Sarah could join the meeting. We figured two shows with one example. We showed the Panther Soul Share by having Sarah demonstrate the calming in the room.

José had to catch me before I fell over and handed me the remainder of his shake. *How could he have shake left over?*

Phoenix's eyes roved from me to Sarah. "Whoa, babes, you two are trippy!"

Sierra smiled up at me. "Are you available for putting our kids down for nap time?"

Nick snorted. "Or insomnia?"

Violet, who had been quiet up until then, raised her hand. José nodded at her. "Can we now discuss why our panther-wolf just crashed into a tree?"

CHAPTER 19

Monday morning, Bevin and I drove into work together. Sammy had been studying flying and was improving.

I found her eating breakfast and decided to join her. I felt like I was turning into a hobbit, having a second breakfast whenever I could sneak it in. "Morning, Sammy. Can we talk before you find your feathers?"

"Sure. What do you want to discuss? I think I'm getting better at flying. I jumped off the highest platform in the training center yesterday. I'm thinking about going for the roof today, but I'm not sure. I mean, it sounds exciting, but..."

I laced my hand on her arm. "Sammy, maybe less caffeine?"

She laughed. "Yeah, maybe."

"I thought we could start writing down impressions of your first flight to create a training manual. If everything goes as planned, the director will want to create another swan, and I think documenting your experience would be good. What do you think?"

"Do I, um, have to do the writing?"

I gave her an encouraging smile and Bevin covered up a snort. "No, I'll write. Or Bevin will. We just need to ask a bunch of questions to make sure it's all correct. You may need to read it over, though."

"Oh! I can do that."

"Maybe we can spend an hour or so each day after breakfast before flight school. Then Bevin and I will do the actual writing at home so that we don't *miss* flight school."

"Oh!" She let out a squeal. "That sounds amazing! You'll use what I'm doing and learning to create a flight manual."

My poor sensitive ears. I flinched. "That's right."

We used the phone's voice recorder to help track Sammy's quick speech and topic jumps. Sammy did *not* jump from the roof. Her fear of heights was still too strong. Her take on flying, however, was interesting. She talked about her fear and how she learned to feel the air currents.

We grilled her on her first few days, her feelings during controlled falls and figuring out how to turn. What muscles she used, and what it felt like to use her muscles, wings, and feathers to circle the compound.

In her excitement, she told us a few stories about her first few landings—both the worst failures and best successes. I told Bevin if anyone heard my snorts on the recording, then he wouldn't live it down.

On the way out, we told the director about the training manual. He loved it. No doubt he believed our ideas were his because he had convinced us to join his ranks.

That afternoon, Alex looked strained. I took pity on them. "Want to walk with me into town for an ice cream cone?"

I could smell their relief and excitement. "Yes!"

Sierra, Oscar's wife, asked if she could join us. "I know you two want to get away, but I'd like to check out the police station, see if they have any openings."

I looked at Alex, but they shrugged and seemed to be okay with the idea. "Sure. But you should know there's a wolf at the local station. Carlos. You can ask for him. It may be a way to get faster answers. He's on the fence about joining the Pack. I don't know where lone wolves get such weird information about Pack life."

The three of us hit the road. The walk to town took about twenty minutes. Alex and I pointed out some of the landmarks along the way, helping Sierra learn about her new territory. Once we hit downtown, we pointed Sierra in the direction to the precinct. She said she'd meet us back at

Were House. We then made our way to the ice cream shop.

We found Milli working, but today she had help. Donna and Ruby were back there with her. She looked up when we walked in, and yelled over a gaggle of kids roped together with their adults, "Your usual?"

Alex and I nodded and found a seat. A minute later, Milli plopped down, handing me a sugar cone with chocolate marshmallow and malt amore. Alex was handed a cone with peanut butter cup and cookie dough. Milli smiled as she sat. "It's crazy in here today. I bet you two want to skedaddle, but before you do, the painting for the wedding is done. You can pick it up Wednesday from my studio."

She pulled out her phone to show us the images. She'd painted a surreal image in blues, grays, and greens. There was a landscape and wolves, but you had to know to look for the wolves to see them. It was beautiful. She'd put in each of my requests spectacularly. It was breathtaking.

A shake of my shoulder pulled me out of my trance. Alex laughed. "We have to let her get back to work, and your ice cream is melting. Let's go."

We said our goodbyes and headed to campus to walk around. It was empty, yet familiar, and let us decompress from all the people at Were House and the ice cream shop.

Alex sighed and their shoulders dropped. Their expression softened as they finally started to relax. I slipped my arm around their waist. "You doing okay with all the new Pack members?"

They wrapped their arm around me. "It's good. I'm just more used to being ignored and a loner. This being asked questions—like I know what's what—like I'm in the 'in crowd' is…a lot."

I gave them a squeeze. "Popularity for our young Alex. What's a person to do?"

"I know, right? Even Brooke is somewhat nice to me."

I choked on my ice cream. "Say it isn't so."

They laughed.

"Are you still doing your meetings at the Youth Outreach Center? Did they find someone new for you?"

Alex nodded. "Yeah, they're good. I think it's important to continue. Learning how to be Pack has been important but learning to be me…I can't explain it."

Their scent changed to the sweet scent of snickerdoodles—wonder.

"I'm really glad. I wish I'd pushed you to go sooner."

"I don't. I wouldn't have become a wolf. I probably would have ended up back home and who knows what would have become of me. I think I'm glad about the way everything turned out."

"You know your positivity makes my teeth hurt, right?"

They laughed. "That and the ice cream?"

"Yeah, of course. When's your next meeting?"

"I go in every Tuesday and Thursday morning. I set it up after finals, but you've been at SSLD when I go, so you probably didn't notice."

"Sorry." I smiled at them and scrunched up my nose. "I didn't mean to be so absent."

"No worries! We just need to talk more. Get ice cream more. Leave the den and relax."

"Is the den too much?"

Alex sighed. "No, I adjusted to the dorms and that was more people and less privacy. I just need a bit of time to adjust again. This is nice."

I gave them a squeeze. "I agree."

The wind shifted and I thought I could smell a familiar scent...*is that Greta?* But the campus was empty and there weren't any people around. I was starting to imagine her everywhere I went. I shook my head and focused on our walk.

Unable to get the scent from my mind, when we stopped in front of a fountain to finish our cones, I had to ask, "Did you smell...anyone?"

"No. Why, did you?"

"I just thought...never mind. My mind is playing tricks on me. It must be because we're on campus."

Off in the distance, I saw someone walking towards the parking lot. It looked a lot like Greta, but again, I figured my mind was just playing tricks on me. She was home in San Mateo. Why would she be on campus?

Once our cones were done, we headed back home. As we walked, I asked them, "Feeling better? Less over-saturated?"

"Yeah. I think I'm ready to face the wolves."

"You did *not* just go there."

"Oh, but I did."

I couldn't help myself, I doubled over laughing.

The next morning, as Bevin and I were getting ready to leave for work, Alex and Sierra headed to town together. Alex had a session with one of the counselors at the Youth Outreach Center and Sierra already had an interview at the police station. I guess they had a few openings they needed filled right away, after all.

After Second Breakfast—pancakes with bacon—we went into the library for our hour-long talk with Sammy.

Continuing to learn about the ways Sammy had problem-solved her first few days as a swan was fascinating. I mentally took notes to compare to my one flight. The merging of the human thought process and, as Owen would say, the bird brain filled pages of my notebook. She continued to regale us with anecdotes that had both Bevin and I chuckling.

We were about an hour in when my phone rang. Pebble. Gulping, I bit my lower lip and gazed at the display. I stopped the recording and apologized. "I really need to take this; my sister doesn't usually call me."

Bevin's hand landed on my shoulder with a squeeze, felt his concern.

's cool. I need to use the restroom, too much

coffee. Be back in a few." Sammy ran out.

Answering the phone, I was a bit nervous. My sister had been bitten by a werewolf far too young. My parents believed this caused her to receive premonitions. She knew I was working; normally she wouldn't call when she knew I was busy. I tried for a nonchalant tone. "Heya, sis, what's up?"

Her voice sounded airy and distant. "The jealousy you thought was, wasn't…your friend is in danger…help!"

A cold chill ran down my spine. "Pebble?"

There was a crashing sound and a thump as if Pebble and her phone both hit the ground. Then Dad's voice. "Jade, pumpkin, is that you?"

"Is Pebble okay? She called with a premonition."

"She'll be fine. Did it make sense?"

My breath hitched. "I don't know, but I'm scared. I'll call you back once I've figured anything out."

"We'll let you know if we figure anything out on our end. Good luck, pumpkin."

Bevin and I gathered our stuff and headed for the door. Before we reached it, Sammy burst in. "Are we continuing?" She saw that we'd packed up and her brow furrowed. Her scent shifted to confusion. "Everything alright?"

I shook my head, my heartbeat so fast in my chest I was surprised she couldn't hear it.

Her eyes narrowed and she gently sniffed the air. "You're freaking out." She sniffed again. "And your heart rate is elevated." She continued to sniff. I wasn't sure why the sniffing helped with her analysis. "You're both scared. It smells…almost like decay?"

It intrigued me that fear smelled like decay to a prey animal, something to avoid, whereas it smelled like something sweet and attractive to predators. I shook my head, I didn't have time to think about that now, I had to go.

Proud and frustrated, I sighed. "Nice work. We *really* need to go. It's a family emergency. Can you let the director know?"

"Yeah. Phone call. Emergency. Got it. Go, go, go." She waved us off.

We told Anastasia on our way out for good measure. The traffic was light, and we made it home in record time. Sarah and Owen met us by the door. They were holding the green go-bag, a bag filled with food I may need if I were to use my abilities on the run. And their faces said business.

My face contorted. "What's up with you two?"

Sarah's brow rose. "We're connected, love. You've been on high alert. You tell us."

Drooping, I shook my head. "I don't know. Cryptic message from Pebble. I was hoping we could work it out."

Sarah and Owen each approached, their scents spiking with the lemon-drop scent of anticipation. Owen reached me first, grabbed my shoulders, and rubbed, as if he needed the contact. His voice was low and full of concern. "What did she say?"

"When I got back from Iowa, I smelled jealousy." I shot a glance over my shoulder to Bevin, needing his support.

"I was sure it was Quinn seeing me and Alex walk in arm in arm. Pebble said the jealousy I sensed was 'not.' I can't think of any other jealousy. Then she said, 'Your friend is in danger, help.'" Shivering at the memory, I shrugged and shook my head as I rubbed my chest. "I don't know who I need to save, but my animals are pacing, and it hurts."

Bevin snarled low in his throat. "Has she told you Greta's been texting her all summer?"

Before either could answer, Quinn drove in, pulling up to the garage. What was he doing here? And where was Greta? She would have come with him.

Quinn cleared his throat. "It's Alex. Alex and Greta. Boden called me after his meeting with Jerry. Greta picked Alex up this morning. I don't know what Greta plans, but we need to save Alex. I think Greta has lost it. She took Alex to Jerry, and, from what Boden told me, it didn't end well for either of them. Jade, I need you to come and help me. I can't do this alone. She's my twin. I know I sound weak…I…I just can't alone. She's been talking about how to win you back. Have you been texting with her? I think if she sees you, she'll calm down." Tears ran down his face as he finished speaking.

"It's fine—no it's not fine, it's the opposite of fine, but I get it. And no, she's been texting me, but I haven't responded." I headed for his car.

Bevin growled. He was all alpha. A wave—so strong that Owen had dropped to his hands and knees—blanketed

193

the area. "I'm coming."

Sarah turned to him. "No."

"Yes." This time, even I almost fell. I'd never felt his power so strong.

Owen whimpered as his two alphas faced off.

"You are the alpha here. If you go, it's war, full-on war, Bevin. If you go and get hurt, what will José do? You are *not* going. I, too, am an alpha. Owen and I will go as back-up. Let me do this."

Bevin roared, his fists at his side shaking.

Sarah pulled him into a hug, kissing his cheek. She whispered, "I'll protect them."

Owen slowly got up and grabbed the green bag. He made it into the back seat of the car, panting. I got into the front seat, waiting for Sarah to make things right with Bevin.

Finally, Sarah slid in next to Owen and Quinn got into the driver's seat. Bevin's eyes glowed. As Quinn peeled out of the driveway, tires screeching, Bevin knocked on my mental door.

Yes?

"I don't like this. If you get hurt, if you don't come back…"

I know.

"Come back to us…to me…we need you as our third. And start eating from the go-bag now."

Love you, too.

As we sped away, I watched him recede into the distance through the rear window. I could feel his alpha power blanket the land farther than I thought possible.

CHAPTER 20

Quinn explained everything as we drove from Were House to San Mateo, where all of the Dynasty wolves lived. They had taken over a solid block of homes backed onto a grassy knoll that led to a lake. Part of the grassy area was the backyards of the homes, but the rest was an underground bunker—a sanctuary—for the Dynasty headquarters.

He stopped us before we got to their property. "This is the old meeting spot for the wolves, the old headquarters. There's a new one downtown, but from what Boden told me, this is where they brought Greta and Alex."

I whirled to him. "Both of them were taken here?"

Quinn slumped. "From what Boden told me, yeah. My uncle is less than impressed with Greta. He wanted you, not Alex. This is his way of punishing her."

"Is the layout here similar to the place you held me in Santa Cruz?"

Jaw tightening, Quinn shook his head. "No, this is different."

We sat for a few minutes and Quinn gave us a basic layout. The bunker held an office, a gym, a school to teach new wolves what the leader thought they knew about werewolves, rooms for the wolves to sleep or play in, a medical suite, and a dungeon. There weren't sleeping quarters, per say. This location was in a neighborhood, and all the wolves owned homes. But they could keep prisoners there for as long as they wanted. It also included a torture chamber, though Quinn didn't know much about that room; it was locked and their leader, Jerry, always kept the only key on him.

Quinn stared at me. "They still use this location for some things. The new official cooperation has too many non-werewolves. This is used for the—*unsavory*—side of their business. Though everyone is in the downtown location, we need to get in and out as quickly as possible. We're in the Dynasty's backyard and someone could come home."

Quinn parked a couple of blocks from our target. The underground sanctuary had a single locked door. All the Dynasty wolves had copies of the key. Quinn snuck in the back door of Jerry's house—which was usually unlocked because no one came to this area but 'family members'—and grabbed it. I was a bit dubious on how easy this part was, but also relieved.

We then moved as stealthily as we could towards the hidden door. The door opened silently to a long set of stairs that ended at an even longer hallway.

I started to head down the long hallway when Quinn reached for my hand. "They won't be on this level. This is just the gyms, office, and member rooms." He pointed across the hallway where there was another set of stairs going down. "We need to go down one more level, to the dungeons."

A shiver of foreboding traveled down my spine as I eyed him. "The Dynasty really has dungeons?"

Quinn continued down the stairs. "They butt up against the lake. It leaks a bit, but the original leader didn't care if the prisoners were left in a moist dank cell."

Despite being able to smell we were alone, we all walked quietly, whispering. The air wasn't stale, letting us know that indeed, this place was still in regular use. The lighting on the main floor of the compound was bright. Once we got to the bottom of the second set of stairs, the dungeon level, the cells were damp, dark, and smelled of mildew and rot. A shiver of dread crawled down my back.

Sarah's hand landed on my shoulder, steading me.

"We're here with you, sis. You're not alone." Owen's voice was like a cool breeze, relaxing me before the tension took over.

Greta's voice floated to us from the far end of the long

line of cells to the left. "You're my little pet. Tell me your secrets, and the suffering will end."

Heart in my throat, I took off at a run, I could hear the others close behind me. As I neared, the smell of the two of them finally broke through the stench of the mildew. There were dozens of cells. When I got to the last cell, dark with no lights of its own, I found Alex curled up in the corner. Greta was in the cell with them, cavorting around like a crazed street performer.

Jerry had locked the two up together in one tiny cell. It was easy to determine his end goal. Two in, and only one would exit—if that.

Greta's hair was up in a ponytail, but the band was slipping out. Her light blue shirt and jeans were ripped and dirty. A bruise was forming on her cheek, and dried blood stained her face and neck from a cut. Alex wore the same jeans and dark green button-down they'd left in that morning. Their clothes were dirty, but beyond the sweet scent of fear, they appeared unharmed.

I focused on the dancing girl. "Greta, what are you doing in there with Alex?"

Greta's face lit up with an airy smile as her voice floated my way. "Oh! I knew you would come to free your girlfriend!"

Recoiling as if slapped, I asked, "My what?"

Next to me Quinn moaned and I heard Owen whisper something to him. Sarah stood behind me, her heat warming me.

Greta's features sharpened. "I saw you two after you returned from Iowa. You were inseparable. I smelled how much you love her."

"I care for them, but Alex and I are not a couple." My mind whirled with the accusation.

Her eyes narrowed and she stopped dancing. Hands on hips, she said, "I *saw* you. When you came back from Iowa. When you got ice cream together. You can't lie to me. You are *replacing me! Replacing me with her!*" She ended in a scream then began pacing in the tiny cell.

As I watched the scene play out, the others crowded in close behind me. Quinn grasped the bars next to me and whispered. "Oh, gods, Alex." I shot him a quick glance. His face was pale, and it didn't look like he was breathing.

On his other side, Owen looked from Quinn to Alex, as if trying to figure out how to solve the puzzle.

"Let me in, Greta. We can talk." I had to do something to distract her from my friend.

"You don't want to talk. You don't care about me, you made that *very* clear. You want to come in here to save *her!*" She jabbed a finger at Alex and scowled.

Lowering my voice, I spoke with my eyes on her. "Just let me in."

"I can't. I'm locked in with her. I came back with a gift for Jerry, and he locked us in here together, after slapping me around a bit." She lowered her voice to mimic Jerry,

"'*No girl is going to have a place in* my *Dynasty.*' Me and my gift, together, together." She started singing and spinning around the cell again.

Sarah gasped behind me. "Oh, gods, she's crazy."

My breathing grew ragged as I tried to figure out what to do. I grasped the bars, watching as Alex lay curled in a ball and Greta danced around. I could hear Alex's heartbeat, but I wasn't sure if they were conscious. Was the fear I smelled recent?

Sarah put her hand on my shoulder, and I relaxed. "Stay here and try to talk her down. Try to get through to Alex. The three of us will find the key." Her words had me tensing again…left alone to save Alex?

Quinn's fingers whitened as he held on tighter. "I can't leave them."

I didn't think he was talking about his sister.

Sarah leaned in closer to his ear. "We can't get Alex out without you. We need a key to open this door."

Quinn audibly gulped. "Right. Jade, please, save them, and if you can…don't kill Greta."

I nodded as they ran off. *Kill Greta? I don't want to kill anyone.* I gulped.

After a moment, I heard the door at the top of the stairs bang shut.

Greta stopped dancing. "Good, now we're alone. I'm going to kill her, you know. Then you won't have anyone to love but me. She'll be my gift for you; she's not worthy of you."

200

"They are worth more than you, Greta. They are smart and fierce and they are good. What are you?" Grasping the bars, I wanted to scream, but I'd already said too much. I knew I shouldn't let my emotions out, but I was scared and angry.

Greta grabbed Alex and pulled them up. Alex whimpered but made no other sound. "This? This is better than me?" She threw Alex to the floor. There was a meaty sound as their head hit stone. Greta stomped her foot and shrieked, "Why won't she shift?"

I kept my attention on her, though my heart skipped a beat. Alex still had a slow heartbeat. A trickle of blood spread from where Alex's head had hit the ground. I growled through my clenched jaw. "Do you want to die, Greta?"

Greta laughed. "I'm not going to die. Alex will." She moved to the back of the cell and grabbed a knife hidden in the filth. It looked like a hunting knife. It wasn't huge, but it appeared dangerous. When she faced me again, her eyes burned with madness. "I knew you were going to come for your girlfriend. I asked Jerry to leave this as a gift from the Dynasty to you. He agreed. I just had to wait for you. I'm going to push this into her heart, and then all you'll have is me."

Her voice pulsed with sincerity. She meant what she said. Hot tears traced their way down my cheeks. "Greta, listen to me. Don't do this. Alex doesn't want me; they've never wanted me. They don't like girls. Even if you kill them…I won't want you back."

Greta slowly sashayed to me. When she reached the bars,

she looked down into my tear-stained face. "Of course she doesn't love you. She isn't smart enough to see what's right in front of her. Don't waste tears on that. She isn't worth it, my love. She isn't worth it. Soon it will be just the two of us."

I felt lost, her emotions reminding me of another time I faced someone broken in a cage so many years ago. My heart tore as Greta and Cody, two people lost to their own madness, collided in my mind. My voice came out low. "Greta. What happened? Why are you doing this?"

She leaned down low, tracing a finger up my chin and then across my lips. "It will be over soon, my love, and then we can be together." The back of her finger rubbed my cheek. Her soft motions made me shiver in fear and in disgust.

This close, I could smell her excitement. She exuded the chocolate of lust, vanilla interest, all mixed together with an overall excited citrusy scent of lemon. Her emotions were all over the place. It made me want to sneeze. Her joy overwhelmed the dank depression of the dungeons.

She truly meant to kill Alex. There was nothing I could do to dissuade her.

A shiver of fear raced through me. "No…"

She leaned down as if to kiss me, then whirled and moved to Alex. Kneeling next to them, she caressed Alex's still form.

My eyes stung with unshed tears. "Please, don't do this."

Greta's lips spread in a beatific smile. "It's done."

I tried to release my calming to deescalate her, maybe get Greta back into her right mind, but nothing happened. *Right, you have to have calm to give calm.* The staccato of my heart beat faster. *Why can't I find my calm? I need to save my friend.*

I wanted to reach out and warn Alex, but they were unconscious, and what could I do if they weren't awake to hear me? Hope lost, I fell to my knees, tears freely flowing. I couldn't get in the cell, and I couldn't stop her. The only thing I could do was watch.

Greta leaned low and placed a gentle kiss on Alex's lips. "You are so lovely, but you tried to take what is mine." Greta stroked their cheek as her gaze traveled down at their body. Slowly, she placed her hand over Alex's heart. "Pretty soon, this will stop and so will all your pain. You'll no longer have to feel the rejection of your family or your Pack."

Is she talking about her family or Alex's? She doesn't know anything about Alex. Stop Jade, focus . . . you need to keep Alex alive.

Greta moved to straddle Alex, almost like a lover. Her feet were close enough for me to touch. An image of Matthias in a cage, and what I'd done, flashed through my mind. On impulse, I reached in and grabbed one heel. Here was my chance. Panther pounced. I collapsed on the floor, too focused on Greta to hold on to myself as well.

Panther and I raced inside Greta. We had mere seconds to stop her—to save Alex. We got to Greta's heart and defied our alpha's orders. We stopped her heart. We stopped the heart of a woman we'd loved, a woman we still, in some part of our soul, had feelings for. We waited to make sure the heart wasn't going to start back up, then we rushed out so as not to get caught in the death wave.

Quicksand clutched at my paws. We fought our way back through Greta's dying body. Like last time, I wasn't sure we'd make it. We were weakened and moving too slow. It was so far. Too far. Greta was pulling us back. Her soul called out its siren song.

Jade! What have you done to me? Stay, we can live out our final moments together. All your pain will be gone if you stay with me!

I paused. Everything felt so heavy. What she promised was so enticing—no pain, no worries—everything just stilled. And then Panther pulled. I warred with myself. Panther pulled again. Defeated, I followed her.

A part of me wondered if I had been too late. Had Greta's words slowed me down for too long? Would her death wave swallow me whole? Had she pushed the knife into Alex before I stopped her heart? Had she done it as soon as she felt me killing her—one, final blow to teach me a lesson?

My mind felt like mush. Was I dying? I felt my alpha calling me, demanding I answer. I groaned as my vision darkened. I couldn't breathe. My motions grew sluggish. So much quicksand; it engulfed me. I reached for the salvation of my body. I had to get out.

Could I survive? I had to survive. My Pack needed me.

CHAPTER 21

"Jade, you have to let go of Greta."

My face was pressed against cold bars, and my left arm cramped in an odd position over my head. I grasped a cold rock. My right arm was bent, and when I lightly yanked, it too was caught in the bars.

Panic flooded through me; they'd captured me again.

I whimpered, but stayed calm as I'd been trained. My head pounded in a slow rhythm, matching that of my heart. My breath dragged in and out raggedly. My stomach cramped. I tried to tuck my body into a ball, but my muscles wouldn't follow simple commands.

A hand began to rub my right shoulder. Another one gripped my left arm. Panther sniffed and invited them in.

I sat cross-legged in my mental landscape outside of the small log cabin. Panther and Wolf paced near me. Shifting slightly, I hugged my knees to my chest and rocked in place, my head tucked down. The world reeled around me, out of control.

A warm presence sat beside me. "Sis, you have to let go of Greta. We need to leave. You're blocking the door and we aren't sure if Alex will make it. Please." Owen wrapped an arm around my shoulders.

Whimpering, my mind was in shambles. "I killed her."

"But you saved Alex."

As I swayed in my mental landscape, my hand released its hold on the cold rock. Owen slowly vanished and without him there to hold me up, I collapsed onto my side. Panther and Wolf curled in around me. And then I felt the tickling feathers of Swan as she too settled in close.

Someone lifted my body and a loud clicking sound reverberated around me, but my animals continued to protect me.

Owen's voice rumbled. "Sarah, if you can carry Alex, I have Jade."

Quinn's sad voice almost broke me away from my animals. "What about Greta?"

Sarah, as alpha, took charge. "We leave her. The Dynasty can clean up their own mess. Are you coming with us or staying with her?"

"She was all I had here. With her dead…I have nothing."

Sarah's voice softened. "You have Alex, and you have us."

And then things grew hazy as unconsciousness embraced me.

I ate. I drank. People spoke around me. The words flowed in and out of my ears, but I couldn't focus on them. I looked down at my plate. It was still full of food. I lowered my head and slowly drew a slice of Swiss cheese to my mouth.

The voices were like flies. They kept buzzing, buzzing, buzzing. I shut my eyes, but they wouldn't stop. I rubbed my forehead and grabbed a cashew. If I continued to eat, I was pretty sure no one would bother me. I washed the nut down with a sip of soda.

The buzzing stopped. It was quiet. I stared at my hands, waiting for the noise to start up again, but the hum that came with deepest silences took over. Finally, I raised my head. Violet sat across the table from me. Like me, she was focused on her plate of food, on her hands, on anything but the people around her. I let my gaze wander to my left. Bevin and José were watching me. My heart began to race and my hands trembled. My eyes snapped to my right where Sarah and Owen also sat staring at me. Next to Violet, Fred had his eyes on me as well. Everyone, except for Violet, was looking at me.

They were caging me in.

Why did I kill again? Did I leave part of myself behind? Did I take part of her crazy back? Am I broken?

My mouth went dry. I tried to swallow but couldn't. I grabbed for my soda and would've knocked it over if Sarah hadn't beaten me to it, handing me the glass. I took a sip. "Why is everyone staring at me?" My voice was rough.

José placed a hand on my leg, and I almost jumped out of my seat. Only the pressure from his hand held me in place. "Fred asked how you were. When you didn't respond, both Sarah and I tried to reach you. Then Bev. We're all worried. That's all."

It was too much; I closed my eyes before their burning created a trail of tears. "I need to go lie down. I just…I need a few minutes alone. I…I know you all are trying to help, I just…" I leapt up and ran to my room.

Bevin said he wanted to follow but others raised their voices in debate. I ignored it, slipping into my room and onto my bed. I didn't bother getting under the covers. The tears already flowed. It was just too much. It hurt too much. Greta's specter floated behind my eyelids, hurt and accusing.

I know I wasn't in love with her. I know she wasn't the one. But the betrayal of someone who I had cared for, someone who had cared for me…I couldn't breathe. A weight compressed my chest. I gasped from the pain.

My door opened and I buried my head in my pillow.

I wanted to scream in agony. The door shut quietly. "Jade, I'm here to help."

My body convulsed. My mind nearly exploded. Brooke, of all people? "What are you doing here?" I croaked out. "Are you here to gloat about how you knew she was bad news the whole time?"

She sighed, the floorboards creaking as she made her way across the room. Then the bed gave under her as she sat. "Jade, you know what I am, right?"

So many answers came to mind, none of them appropriate. I almost laughed. Why couldn't she leave me in peace and solitude? I continued to hide under the pillows with my back to her. My body shook in pain. I couldn't subdue.

She lightly placed a hand on my shoulder. "I'm the submissive of this Pack. Everyone seems to forget what that means. I feel…gods, Jade…I feel *everything*. I know about the emotions all around me. I even took some classes to become a therapist last year to help me figure all this out. I know it isn't enough, but it's a start."

"I don't know what you want me to say, Brooke. Good for you? Despite that, you're always nasty to me. So, what?" I wanted my words to cut so she would hurt like I did. But no one could hurt like I did. My soul was breaking…dying, like Greta had died.

She started to rub my arm, and despite it all, it felt good. My body finally stopped trembling, and the bits inside me that felt off and out of place began to settle. It was like when José and Bevin became my pillars of strength, but so much more. The tears ran hotter and harder, though I tried not to make a sound. I wouldn't give her the satisfaction.

"That was Brooke the person, not Brooke the submissive werewolf. You know that I, as a wolf, honor and respect you. I'm…I don't know. It's hard to have your worldview shift under you without any warning. I'm trying to change, but being reminded on a regular basis that you're a jerk makes change hard."

While she spoke, I heard shuffling sounds. Then I felt the bed shift. I realized she was lying down behind me. As her body spooned mine, I relaxed more. My mind didn't want to accept this, but my body, my animals, my soul knew better. A sound of acceptance escaped me, against my better judgment.

"I'm learning how to do my job for the Pack. It's hard to be the heart when everyone treats you like a villain." Her arm slipped under mine and around my waist. "But with the wolf…came an instinct. I know what is needed. I know—I understand—what everyone's feeling. Strong emotions have become the backdrop of my day-to-day life. Everything in me wants to be there for the other Pack members…even when all of you seem to want to push me away." Her other arm slipped under the pillow my head was resting on. "I don't think I'm explaining this well. It's just that…I have a need to help, and I'm tired of fighting it…fighting all of you."

With a sigh, I melted into her. I finally could breathe evenly. A small whimper left me as my tears soaked my pillow.

"This time, when the Pack tried to keep me from you, I had to lay down the law. I know what my place is around here. I'm not just a pretty face. I am the submissive werewolf, the heart of the Pack, and I have my role. No one else can do for you what I can do. And this time…this time, there is too much need to let others try to do my job."

I rolled over, tucked my head into her chest, and sobbed. She wrapped her arms around me as all my pent-up emotions poured out.

The next morning, I woke up curled up in the protection of Brooke's arms. I froze for a second, and then it all returned to me. I relaxed. I ran a mental inventory and realized I was feeling better. I let my forehead drop against her for another few minutes, taking in a few more moments of healing. But I had to get up and face the day.

Groaning, I rolled away from Brooke and instantly a cold emptiness crept in. I plodded into the bathroom and cleaned myself up. Heading back into the bedroom, I found Brooke sitting on the bed.

"You okay?"

I nodded. "I think so. Thanks."

She smirked. "Did that hurt?"

My face fell and I walked into my closet to find clothes. "Can we please call a truce? I came into my room last night not knowing if—when—I'd be able to focus on life. Now I think I can function." I grabbed jeans and a t-shirt that said, *I don't like morning people, or mornings, or people.*

I cast a glance at Brooke as I returned to the bathroom. "I know that the Pack hasn't been fair to you, but you haven't been working with us. Can we start over? Here and now?" My reflection made me grimace. My eyes were a bit puffy, and my black curls sprang out everywhere. I wet my hands and tried to tame my hair a bit. It was mostly a failure, but I got the locks going somewhat downward. I washed my face with cold water and called it good enough.

As I exited the bathroom, Brooke watched me closely. One of her eyebrows rose. "Fine. We can call a truce. I'll stop fighting with my wolf and start going with my instinct."

I stopped mid-step. "You've been going *against* your instinct?"

She sighed, slumping against the headboard. "Yeah. I knew everyone expected me to be the mean girl. I knew you were the only one who could handle it. Even when I was nice, people still judged me negatively. So, I played it up." She stared at her hands. "I *feel* everyone's emotions." Her voice grew small. "It would be easier if everyone treated me like I belonged."

Guilt slammed into me. I knew this was partially my

fault. From the beginning, I should have worked harder to make sure she had been accepted, had been given a chance to be part of the Pack. Biting my lower lip, I nodded. "I'll fix this, Brooke. I promise."

She shook her head. "No, Jade. It isn't your job to fix everything, but we can start by being decent to each other." She got up and moved to the door. I followed; I needed food. It had been too long since those nuts and cheese.

She left and headed to her room. I turned towards the kitchen. In the hall, I ran into Bevin. His shock at seeing the two of us walk out of the same room in the morning was hilarious.

He grabbed my upper arm. "What…um…did she…?"

I pulled away. "Breakfast. I don't really know when I last ate."

"But, Jade, what did I just see?"

I gave him a half-smile and a wink before walking away. Yes, I was definitely feeling better.

CHAPTER 22

Somewhere along the way I'd lost a day. It was Friday morning and I called in sick. Well, another day of family emergency. According to Bevin, that had been happening ever since Pebble's phone call telling me about the emergency surrounding Alex.

After breakfast, I asked to be briefed on what happened while I had been with Greta. Bevin and José took one loveseat, Sarah and Owen settled on a couch, Quinn sat in a recliner, and Alex and I flopped on the second couch.

It was a beautiful day and staying indoors seemed a shame. Most of the rest of the Pack was out exploring the area or swimming in the pool. We could hear the squeals and shrieks from the kids as they splashed and leapt in the water.

José faced me. "I know you want to get caught up, but I'd like you to start."

"Don't you know the full story by now?"

"I do, but I'd like to hear it from beginning to end."

Slumping into the couch, I sighed but did as he asked. I gave my side from Pebble's call until I reached into the cell to stop Greta's heart. Most of the time I stared down at my hands, but at that point in the story I paused and looked up. I shifted my gaze between the sad blue eyes of one alpha to the concerned brown of the other. "I know I went against a rule the two of you set for me after Matthias. I'm…I apologize. You didn't say it was an alpha law, though it did sorta feel that way. I just…I didn't know what else to do. I had to stop her."

My gaze returned to my hands which were tightly holding onto each other. A tear burned its way down my cheek. Gods, I had to get control of myself.

José's soft voice flowed over me. "We didn't set that rule for us, chica, we set it for you. Each time you do that, stop a heart, we fear you lose a piece of your soul, or that you may not make it out. It hurts us to see you come back so broken. In *most* cases it won't be worth it. But, Jade, we understand why you did it. I can't say that any one of us in the same position wouldn't have done the same thing."

I hadn't heard him move, but suddenly my hands were

in his. His eyes caught mine and he gave me a small smile. "Please don't agonize over this decision. You saved Alex, and that's a miracle." He leaned in and gave me a hug. I melted into it, needing the comfort more than I realized.

After returning to his seat, he asked Sarah to share her part.

"I'll start in the dungeon. We headed out knowing we needed to get a key. Quinn took us to the new San Mateo Dynasty center, hoping Boden could help us find the key. A way to get Alex out. We knew Greta was crazy, but she hid the severity."

I shook my head. "Boden? Really?"

Quinn sighed. "I know he isn't your favorite person, but he's been roped into the Dynasty now that they've lost so many wolves. He hates it. He's still my friend and I knew he'd help." He shook his head. "I know you don't understand him working for my uncle, but he's tried to have my back my whole life."

Sarah continued. "So, we went in. No one knows me or Owen, so we could play off being friends of Quinn's without being a part of this Pack. We found Boden and he came up with a key." She gave a wry smile. "Well, he *had* a key. Apparently, it comes with werewolf membership."

Sarah sneered and took a sip of her soda. The thought of giving all wolves access to cells to lock anyone away seemed creepy to me, too. "Getting in and out wasn't a problem. Everyone we ran into, save Boden, were norms. They seem to be trying to run a legitimate security business. When we got to the car, we realized we were being followed, so there must have been some sort of surveillance, because I can't see Boden telling Quinn about Alex, giving us a key, and then ratting us out...unless he were trying to get in good with this Jerry guy."

Quinn jerked in his seat. "No, he wouldn't do that."

Owen huffed. "We know, it doesn't seem his style. From what we've heard, he's much more direct. Not devious."

Sarah turned to Owen, and they smiled as she continued the recitation of their adventure. "There were two men, both in corporate Dynasty attire, forest green slacks, and an off-white button-down shirt. On the pocket was embroidered Dynasty International. One was a wolf, the other a norm."

Quinn turned to me then José. "I didn't recognize the wolf. He wasn't part of the family, which is weird. Jerry must be getting desperate. So, the wolf was probably newly-turned, as well."

Sarah nodded. "They approached with their hands on their guns. They asked Quinn who we were and if we'd head back to the compound to answer some questions. When we refused, they pulled out their guns."

At that, I raised an eyebrow. "That's weird. Quinn, did you know them or recognize them? Did they call you by name? Oh, and where are the bodies?"

Quinn shook his head. "I didn't know them, but they did

know my name. I wouldn't put it past Jerry to pass around our pictures so all the new 'employees' know who we are."

Owen snorted. "They were idiots. Sorry, Quinn, you kinda were, too. Sarah and I each disarmed one with a quick arm-swipe-kick combo. The norm I expected, but the werewolf? He should've been faster. Then we slipped into the alleyway next to us and they followed. I tell you, idiots. Quinn backed the car into the alley, and we put the bodies into the trunk."

Once Owen was done, Sarah turned back to me. "Anyway, when we got back to the old compound, all three of you looked dead. It was only your heartbeats that let us know you and Alex weren't, thank the gods for that. Jade, you have *got* to stop doing this to us. You are shortening all our lives, I tell ya."

Owen mumbled, "Tell me about it."

Bevin snorted, and José nodded.

I snarled, "Can we just finish the story, please?"

"Right, so, you let Owen into your head space. He got you to drop Greta's foot, and here you are."

"Oh, no, what about all the blood? How did Alex survive all of that?"

Alex took my hand in their cold one and smiled at me. "After Greta took me, I was scared, but I tried not to antagonize her. When she threw me on the floor, I did pass out for most of it, but I regained consciousness before the end. I was there for the kiss, unfortunately. She was crazy."

They faced Quinn. "Sorry." Rotating back to me they finished. "My situation looked a lot worse than it really was."

I shook my head. "Wait, I have anoth—"

There was a knock at the door. As one, we all swiveled to face the noise.

Oscar's voice came from the kitchen, low and soothing. "Sorry. There was a buzz from the gate and since you all disconnected for your meeting, I took it upon myself to deem the person worthy." He headed for the door to let the guest in.

Unfolding myself from the couch, I followed. When it opened, a huge man—he must have been close to seven feet tall—stood there, with violet eyes, and a wide smile. "My loves, the party has come to you! Raquel has arrived!"

Slightly behind Raquel stood a shorter man, probably under six feet tall, with mousy brown hair, brown eyes, and a charming smile. Before I could say anything, Raquel entered the house.

"We're from Florida, and I am tired of sitting in that car." He bent dramatically at the waist. "Oh, honey, is that a pool I see out back? Child, we may get along yet."

"Do you two want a single room or a suite upstairs?" I bit my cheek to try to keep my smile in check.

"Raquel needs space, honey child. We'll take a suite."

José came up behind me. "Welcome Raquel. I'm José and this is Bevin. We're the alphas. I can show you to a suite of rooms and afterwards we can show you around the grounds."

"Well, aren't you the cutest couple with the mostest. I had heard the alphas were a sweet gay couple, I just couldn't believe it until I saw it with my own eyes. Ben, come and check this out." He turned to the rest of us. "I was out of town doing a show when your lovely alphas were visiting my Pack."

The other man wasn't a wolf, but the rings on their fingers told me they were definitely a couple.

Ben held out his hand. "Hi, I'm Ben. I'm glad to finally be here. That was one heck of a drive."

José and Bevin led our newest wolf upstairs and I headed to the kitchen. Before I could enter, Oscar blocked my way. "No, ma'am. You are not permitted into *my* domain. I'll bring a plate to the dining room for you."

"I am *not* that much of a disaster in the kitchen! You let the others in."

"I do. And you can just sit and be served."

Pretty soon, I was joined by the others. We enjoyed grilled cheese sandwiches and tomato soup.

Owen sat across from me. "Did I hear you were banned from the kitchen?"

"Hush, I don't want to hear about it."

"You know, *I'm* not banned."

Growling at him, I dug into my food. Owen had *always* been the scourge of the kitchen, and *I* was banned?

José turned to Quinn. "Do you feel safe getting your stuff and moving it here, or do you think you need people to help you? Maybe Boden could help?"

Quinn's eyes widened. "My stuff?"

Bevin smiled. "We don't think it's safe for you to go back to San Mateo. Welcome to the Pack, Quinn. Welcome home."

CHAPTER 23

Saturday morning, I woke up early to get my Owen torture set done and over with. Outside my door, a paper tacked to my pegboard informed me my training would be out by the structure. Groaning, I grabbed a muffin from the counter and headed out.

Owen was waiting for me. I eyed him suspiciously. "It's a quarter to six. What are you doing up?"

The left side of his mouth quirked up. "I'm applying for a job with you and Bevin at the SSLD. Bevin's been asking around and they don't have a good trainer for the werewolves. The director has been doing his best, but he doesn't really know what he's doing."

"Did Bevin ask while I was out? Huh? And I thought you were looking for a job at a school."

"I was, but the job market's tight."

"Isn't a third member of the Pack at this government facility a risk?"

"It is, but Bevin and José weighed the risks, and they decided it was worth it."

"Okay, but that doesn't explain why we're both out here at the crack of dawn."

His smile widened. "I've been studying the tapes of Sammy's interviews. We're going to spend the next hour or so teaching you how to bank. I want to be a trainer of wolves and swans, but I need to get a bit of practice first."

I groaned. "Really? Now?"

"Suit up...or down. And then connect to me. I need to be in constant communication, recruit."

I mumbled, "I'm not a recruit..." But I did what he asked.

"Okay, go up to the ten-foot platform, and this time, don't aim for the trees. I want you to land in the field if you can't bank. The first jump, I just want you to glide down. If you don't mind, I'll lift you up to the five-foot platform and have you climb from there to save time."

As he filled me in on his plans, I stripped and shifted. It was nice how quickly I figured out the swan, versus the months it took to figure out the wolf. Between a new shifting paradigm and utilizing the tricks I used to differentiate

Wolf and Panther, this third animal was *almost* a breeze.

My first glide was smooth and the landing more pleasant than hitting a tree. It wasn't the most graceful transition from air to ground, but at least I didn't use a tree, and I ended up on my feet.

"Next jump, I want you to focus on the air currents. Feel them. Shift your wings just a bit and feel how their movements affect your glide."

The next hour continued with Owen slowly adjusting my movements, changing each glide minutely. After an hour, I could change course, but my wing muscles ached. I waddled over to my clothes, found my humanity, and dressed. I lounged on the ground, unsure if I could get up.

"You okay, sis?"

"My arms hurt. So does my head."

"What have you eaten?"

"A muffin."

"No coffee?"

I collapsed onto my side with a grunt. Owen grabbed my hands and pulled me up. "Come on, ya idiot, let's get you fed. I have just a bit of time before my job interview."

We made our way back to the house and flopped into dining room chairs. I turned to the kitchen where I could smell coffee brewing. "Oscar, would you allow me in to get my own coffee and breakfast?"

"Nope. You stay right where you are, child. This is my territory and I like it how it is."

"What have you heard? I have never harmed a kitchen!"

"Mm-hm."

"It was Owen who did all the damage. I'm good in the kitchen…well, as a helper."

"I'm sure."

Snarling, but not with enough gusto to actually get up, I waited. A few minutes later Oscar appeared with a mug of coffee and a plate with eggs, bacon, and a sliced-up apple. My snarl morphed into a moan, and I dug in.

I was halfway through my plate of food, when the front door opened and my parents walked in, followed by Tanner and his family. I ran to give them all hugs.

Mom dropped her bags and returned my hug, taking in the place. "I can't believe how wonderful your den is."

Dad came up beside her. "This is spectacular. I know you all described it to us, but it's perfect."

Stepping back to let them in, a whirlwind of energy threw herself into my arms, and I hugged my sister. She dropped to the ground. "I know this place is huge, but can I stay with you in your room?"

Smiling down at her, a bubble of happiness erupting in my chest, I said, "Of course." I pointed to my door. "That one. I even have a private bathroom. There's plenty of room, as long as you've learned to not kick at night, scamp!"

I hugged Tanner, his kids, then his wife last. Before they all scattered to rooms, I asked, "Do you want food or a tour first?"

As one, they agreed. "Food!"

Everyone settled around the table, and Oscar came out with a couple of platters of toast, bacon, and scrambled eggs. He placed the food down, but before he could head back into the kitchen, Tanner grabbed his hand. "Sit, join us. It's been too long, brother."

We spent a few minutes catching up. The question arose of the wedding plans.

Everyone looked at me. "I don't know why you think I know anything. Sarah is the wedding planner. I only know that I have to wear the same dress as her, and that's not fair."

Mom smiled as Owen snorted.

Tanner stared at me, then shifted to Oscar. "Do you know who's catering the soiree?"

Owen had stood to clear his plate but paused. "Sarah has been looking for a caterer who would provide the food, but not need to stay the night. It's a tricky set of requirements. I don't think she's found anyone yet. Since the wedding is in two weeks, she's a bit freaked out. I think that's the one piece she's been struggling with."

Oscar and Tanner just faced each other. Their blank expressions hid their thoughts, but their eyes held a conversation only they heard. The rest of us watched, shifting, and shrugging at each other, not sure what was going on between them.

Finally, they just nodded, and Tanner huffed. Oscar smirked and returned to the kitchen.

My hands flew out to the side. "What? What just happened?"

Tanner slumped a little. "We will cater the event. Oscar and I."

I stopped breathing. "Really?" A smile broke out across my face. "Will this be a friendly family competition? Like, who can produce the most popular selections?" I waggled my brows at him.

"I did *not* miss having you around."

I blew him a kiss. "I bet you did!"

Owen plopped back down next to me. "We have to set up separate tables for them so we can keep track of whose food people like better."

"Oh, and we can't let people know. This should just be between us. If they know, it could become biased."

Owen nodded. "Yeah. Just the appetizers, or the whole meal?"

I thought about that. "Probably just the appetizers, the meal will be integrated."

"Fact. Okay, how abou—"

"Kids, to your rooms!" Mom shouted.

Owen laughed as he cleared his plate and headed off to dress for his job interview. I just leaned back in my chair as I enjoyed seeing my parents and catching up with them after so long.

A few minutes later, José and Bevin joined the party. Bevin's plan was to accompany Owen for his interview, so he grabbed a quick bite. However, it didn't take more than a few seconds to realize living with four strong alphas under one roof was going to be an issue.

An electric tension built in the air. My skin began to prickle, and I saw Tanner's hand begin to tremble. As dominant as he was, that was a huge tell.

Nothing like this happened when we traveled to Wisconsin, probably because José and Bevin felt that they were part of my parents' Pack when they were there. But here in California, we were on our territory. The problem was, many of the wolves presently were—or had been— part of my parents' Pack.

José gave Bevin a kiss and a shove when it looked like he wanted to stay to help figure out the problem. "We'll deal with this. You go. The two of you have an appointment. We're all adults. Well," he shot me a snarky look, "we usually are. I have an idea, so you go."

Bevin gave José a pained look, holding his hand for a few extra seconds before bending down for one extra kiss. "Okay, fine. But call if you need me."

"Go. This is a good opportunity for Owen. And it gives him someone else to focus his torture routines on."

Dad laughed.

Once Owen and Bevin were out the door, José joined the rest of us at the table.

Mom cocked her head. "So, what's your great plan? I'd love to say having the four of us under one roof will work great, but there's too much family and historical bond overlap between our Packs."

José leaned back and took a lazy sip of his coffee. I could feel the strain coming off him, even though he tried to play it off. Before he could answer, Brooke came out of her room, sauntered over, and sat down next to José. She nonchalantly placed a hand on his knee as Oscar came out with a clean plate for her. Immediately, the tension drained from José, and he took a deep breath.

Nodding at her, José slid a bit closer but faced my parents. "We have another property—Pack House. It isn't as nice, but it should suffice. It's about a five-minute walk from here and has two rooms."

My mom nodded. "If we stay there with Jackson and Allison, I think things shouldn't come to a head during your wedding." She nodded at Brooke. "I see you've already learned some of the advantages of having submissive wolves around. Jade is great for calming a Pack, but for managing your temper while not feeling drugged, you need your submissive wolves."

Raquel, wearing pink biker shorts and a green halter top with a duck on it, came bounding around the corner with Ben in tow. "Oh, thank goodness someone dealt with that blast of tension. I know we have some of the most fabulous submissive wolves in this new Pack," he winked at Brooke, "but I was getting my beauty on when that wave of za-za-zoom hit." He looked around at everyone. "Well, aren't you all a sight for sore eyes; it has been too long. I'll be performing tonight in town at Boylesque at The Queen's Bee. You *all* must come to watch."

I gaped at him. "You just arrived yesterday. How could you possibly already be performing?"

"Honey child, I *am* Raquel!" He whipped around on his heel and left the room.

Dad's jaw dropped a bit, and Mom was holding back laughter. Ben didn't follow Raquel out. "Hi, Hazel, River. Long time no see."

Mom lifted her hand, and her laughter became more audible. "Raquel has certainly amped up the…" She waved her hands, seemingly at a loss.

Ben came to the table and sat. "Yeah. Ever since the alter-ego took over, it's been Raquel all the time. It's been a hoot."

Dad looked up as if he could see Raquel through the ceiling. "Does he—she?—ever go by anything but Raquel?"

Ben leaned back as Oscar brought him a clean plate. "He, and no. He likes the name and the persona of Raquel too much. Raquel has brought out his extroverted nature, and he enjoys it."

Dad's head tilted. "What about when he's in drag? Is he still 'he'? I just don't want to offend him."

Ben nodded in understanding. "No, I get it. It can get complicated. When in drag, go with 'she.'" Ben started eating and the conversation came to an end.

I got up. "Can I show you to your private cabin?"

José looked at Tanner, Monica, and their son Easton. "I

can show you to a two-bedroom suit, or two single rooms."

My parents followed me out the door. We each grabbed some bags.

Mom breathed in the clean air. "What you all are doing here is amazing. Do you realize all the firsts you're doing? A new Pack, run by two men, west of the Rockies, an epsilon to help them out. And this wedding…all the alphas in one spot. We talk over the computer…but together? That hasn't happened, Jade. You three did this."

I didn't know what to say. I was proud of our Pack, the land we'd found, and the den we'd built. The pride from my parents, my old alphas, overwhelmed me.

Dad asked, "When can we see your new animal?"

Grumbling, I rubbed my arms. "Owen has set up a new training schedule and he has me flying in the morning. My arms are really tired. I can't actually do much with the flying. If all you want to see is the swan, I can show you after we drop off the bags. If you want to see me fly, and not hit a tree, that will take a bit longer."

Dad stared at me. "I flew in this morning, and boy are my arms tired."

I groaned and Mom punched his arm. "No!" we both said together.

When we got to the cabin, I showed them around. By the time we finished the tour, Mom and Dad decided they wanted to rest. My swan could wait until later.

When I got back to Were House, Alex was up, and

they smelled nervous. I dragged them out by the pool.

"What's up?"

"Quinn is heading back to San Mateo later today to get his stuff."

"Is he taking anyone with him?"

"We haven't discussed it."

I smiled and Alex backed up a step. "What is it, Jade? You have a mean look about you."

"I just had a most excellent idea."

"Why do I have a feeling I won't like this idea?"

My grin softened as I looked past them, through the glass doors, to Tanner who was collecting his bags. "Don't worry, this is an idea you'll love."

"May I present: Raquel." Ben bowed, leaving an arm out in presentation form. He wore a white tuxedo for Raquel's first night on stage. We all stood outside, ready to leave for downtown. Raquel was about to present herself from the double front doors of Were House.

Everyone attending tonight's event had dressed up for Raquel's California debut performance. The men all wore slacks and nice button downs, even Dad. José had a sapphire blue shirt that matched Bevin's eyes, and Bevin wore a brown button down that matched José's. She and Brooke had both gone all-out with skirts and tops, makeup, and accessories. They looked ready for a photo shoot. Even Alex had dressed up. Sarah had wrestled me into a lavender wrap dress, but I refused the makeup. I was starting to reconsider my choices.

I thought I was prepared for Raquel in all her splendor. I wasn't.

Raquel came out wearing a dark blue tank dress that ended just above her knees. She wore silver fishnet stockings and matching blue, five-inch stiletto heels. On her head was a blood-red wig in slight waves that dipped down past her ample décolletage. She wore a large tiara and huge white wings flowed from her back. She strode out of the house like she owned the place, stopped at the top of the stairs, hands on hips, and took us all in as if we were her entourage. "Tonight, you may see things new to you, but know, you will grow and return here better people. To the coaches!"

At the venue, Bevin, José, and I took one of the small tables. Sarah, Owen, and Violet took a second table. Alex, Quinn, and Brooke took a third, and Ben and my parents took a fourth. I wasn't sure if anyone else from the Pack would show up for Raquel's debut extravaganza. We sat through the first two numbers, enjoying the first round of the two-drink minimum. I ordered a frozen grasshopper. By the end of the second round, when the waitress arrived, José ordered a pitcher of margaritas for the table.

Raquel was the third act. When she came out, she had

accessorized her outfit. Blue gloves, trimmed in white fur that matched her dress, covered her arms. She dripped with silver jewelry: earrings, necklace, bracelets, rings. She had completed her makeup with over-the-top eyes in shades of blue and purple, a red lipstick the color of blood, and crystals decorating her cheek in an upside-down wave under her eyes, almost touching her mouth. The total image shimmered under the lights.

The music started as she sauntered out, lip-syncing to Natural Woman, and I swear I was falling in love.

CHAPTER 24

I couldn't believe it was happening again. A person I loved was going to die. The only way I could save them would destroy a piece of my soul. José had said it was up to my discretion, and as much as I knew it could break me, losing a Pack member wasn't an option.

Panther and I ran in and found the beating heart. I paused. I knew that time was an issue, but it hurt. Both times I'd done this had hurt so much. *I have to save them! Stop wasting precious seconds, Jade. Do it fast, in and out.*

Taking a fortifying breath, we stopped the heart, but I couldn't wait this time, not again, I had to get out. We ran. The quicksand grabbed at me and pulled. I was going under. I couldn't move fast enough. Trembling, I crawled, but the pull was too strong, the person's will so much stronger this time. It dragged me down with them. I wasn't going to make it.

Panther pulled. I crawled. I felt Wolf pulling, too. Death held on to my feet and dragged me back. I was stretched in two directions. My body was being pulled apart. Pain ripped through my gut. My face wet with tears, I screamed. I couldn't see my goal. I had to make it.

I dug my fingers into the sliding sand and crawled, tears mixing with the grit. My nails broke as I strained to make it out. I had to survive. My failure would break my alphas…but could I do it this time? Was I strong enough? I didn't know if I could fight the yanking of my body as it was torn.

My eyes cracked open to see if the fight was over. The hand in mine was limp. Something was wrong. Blinking to clear my vision, I focused on the arm I grasped. I recognized the plaid shirt—Bevin!—and my heart stopped. *No!*

How could this happen? How could I be holding the wrong hand? This was wrong. I had stopped the wrong heart.

Frantically, I connected to José and screamed out, *Help me! He's dead, I killed him!*

"Jade, it's the middle of the night. What's wrong?"

He's dead, he's dead, I killed him, oh, my gods, I killed him!

Suddenly, I couldn't breathe, hyperventilating with the

realization of what I'd done. Tears pooled where my head lay. *I killed him. I'm so sorry. I killed the wrong person. What have I done?!*

A door slammed and there were hands on me. Someone shook me. They must be furious with me. I screamed.

"Jade! Wake up!"

The voice, the shaking. I shot awake. Pebble was curled in a chair on the other side of the room. José, Brooke, and Bevin—oh, my gods, Bevin!—stood around my bed. I just stared at Bevin. He wasn't dead?

I started shaking. "But I ki-ki—" I couldn't complete that statement. Bringing my knees up to my chest, I curled into a ball and cried harder.

Bevin crawled in next to me and pulled me into a hug. Brooke sat down on the other side, taking my hand.

Brooke rubbed my hand. "What happened?" Her voice was low, soothing.

"His heart." Wild eyed, I gazed at Bevin, then started to tremble.

José watched over us. "I don't care what's happening. No more stopping hearts."

I groaned, curling closer to Bevin, trying to get my head to believe he was really sitting next to me. Hoping this was reality and not the dream.

The next morning, Owen had a new challenge for me.

He wanted to continue flight school Monday afternoon. He suggested moving my torture routines to the SSLD compound, but Bevin and I vetoed that for a myriad of reasons. The biggest was keeping most of my abilities a secret from the agency.

We headed out to the middle of the field earlier than I thought my brother ever woke up. Poles were set up down the field at ten-yard intervals. There were four images on each sheet, a gray flower, a red flower, a purple flower, and a yellow flower. I could see the images on the first pole and almost make out the second, but after that the images were blurry.

Owen came up next to me. "Okay, I want you to focus on Wolf. Bring her forward, have her enhance your vision."

Wolf came forward, but nothing changed. I shrugged.

Owen nodded. "That's what I thought. You see four flowers and the gray one is with the wolf ink. Did you know that Sarah can't read that ink?"

Wolf ink was an ink calibrated for werewolves. I'd always thought it was something all wereanimals could see. After I'd been changed from a norm to a wereanimal, I could see this ink on the pictures I'd drawn for my dad in his office. I always thought the panther bite had been enough, but I'd been attacked by Candice, a member of my parent's Pack, shortly after my return to Wisconsin. It never occurred to me it wasn't the 'were' that saw the ink, but the were*wolf*.

That shook me and I stared at him as my brows came together. "Really? I thought she could."

"Nope. Panther next."

I shook my head. This was something new. I'd never really thought about which animal I had riding my senses. If anyone asked, I would have predicted Panther, but I guessed Wolf made sense, since Panther was always available to travel to other people.

I closed my eyes and focused. I asked Panther to take over, and when I swayed, Owen wrapped an arm around me to keep me steady.

When I opened my eyes, the world had changed. "The gray flowers are gone, but I can see three sets of flowers. The world smells different, too. Good gods, Owen, I had no idea." I started to get dizzy.

My eyesight had improved, but my sense of smell had worsened. There were still a lot of scent markers coming in, but what my mind focused on were different: birds, trees, rodents. Some of the same things as the wolf, but I could sense more of the airways and what was in the trees. Things Panther cared about but Wolf didn't.

"Hang on. I know this is trippy. I tried it myself last night."

"Have you ever done it before last night?"

"Nope. It wasn't until Sarah looked at a sheet of paper written in the wolf ink that it clicked for me. It took a few tries; I'm not as close to the animals as you. But the shift tripped me out. Can you stand on your own?"

"Yeah, I think so. This is just…whoa." I started to move around, and everything was off. I tried to leap, and I soared, but landed on my face. Rolling onto my back, I laughed. "I think I'll need to practice. This was what it was like before I got my wolf, but it's completely new again."

"Come on, panther-girl, I'm not done with you. Back to the start. I'll set up a weekly rotation on Sundays where you figure out how to move around under each of your animals so that you can switch to the form that gives you your best advantage. But, for now, stay focused. I still have a second day of interviews."

"Wow, brother mine. I didn't even have one interview, and they offered me a job."

"Ha, ha. Now, let's see if you can bring up that swan of yours to the forefront."

I complained under my breath, not looking forward to the headache when I was done. I closed my eyes and focused. It took longer because the swan was new, and not a wereanimal. When I opened my eyes, I felt drunk and would have tipped over if Owen wasn't actively holding me up.

"The world is bluer and sharper, and I may be sick. When I'm in bird form this different view seems natural, but gods above, there is so much extra visual information. But the scents are almost muted. I have almost nothing."

"Jade, stop moving."

I hadn't even realized I shifted in his arms. I focused on my feet and keeping them still. Then I straighten up, holding my wings—no, my hands—out to the side. Owen had his arms around me, keeping me from hitting the ground. I was panting. Slowly, ever so slowly, I took deep breaths, calming my heart from a racing staccato to a reasonable rhythm.

Owen smelled scary. He was a predator and I had to escape him. Oh, gods. My nose worked so much better in human form than swan form…though not as good as my other forms. Using the swan's senses, I could get all the nuances of his scent. How did Sammy filter all of this?

Owen sniffed, then squeezed me tightly to him. "Jade, you have to calm down. You smell sweet, and it's hard for me to control myself."

"You aren't helping. You smell like a predator, and my instinct is to flee. I don't know why this doesn't happen when I have feathers, except I can't really smell then. Just drop me and back up."

His hold tightened. "I don't think I can." His mouth lowered to behind my ear and his breathing became rough. "Jade." He was struggling.

I tried to tamp down my growing panic. "Owen. You need to move away from me."

A soft growl reverberated through his gut, sending shivers up my spine. He took a slow, appreciative sniff and groaned, squeezing me tighter. "Your scent. I haven't smelled anything so compelling. You are prey…and too addictive. It's worse than hunting as a wolf. Gods above, Jade. I physically can't. I am fighting everything in myself…help me."

I shivered at his words. They were light, almost a caress. I swallowed hard and his hold began to cut off my breath. Digging deep, I tried to slow my breathing, my heart, my… everything. I shut my eyes, pulled deeply on whatever calm I had and released it.

His arms loosened and I landed on my hands and knees. I rolled far away from him. After a few minutes I looked up at the images. "I…I can't see the gray, but I can see four sets of flowers. There is much more blue…and I'm going to be sick." I threw up. Afterwards, I rolled farther away and called up Wolf. I lay whimpering, shaking, with my head pounding.

Owen came over and knelt next to me. "Are you okay?"

Recoiling, I gave a single shake of my head. He picked me up and I groaned. "No. I can make it back myself."

"I know. Just let me get you to your feet, sis."

I shook but curled my head into his shoulder, shivering. I knew he didn't believe me, but the world still spun. Despite being human and channeling Wolf, I was afraid of being left alone in the field for predators to find. I felt exposed and weak. He placed me on one of the pool chairs and disappeared, reappearing a few minutes later with a mug of coffee and a chocolate shake.

"I wasn't sure which you'd prefer so I asked Oscar for both."

Taking both, I switched back and forth until my head

decided it was safe to use again. "Go, you have your interview."

"I don't want to leave you alone."

"I'm fine."

"You're lying to me."

"Fact. But you need to leave. I *will be* fine. Go, then we can get sick of each other while working together."

His brow rose. "Huh, I hadn't considered that angle… maybe being late isn't a bad idea."

I threw a pillow at him. "Go!"

He left. I sat with my pounding head, wondering if I'd ever feel able to function again. Between the nightmare and the morning training, I didn't want to think or move ever again.

Before long, Alex and Quinn came outside. They took my empty cups and a few minutes later returned with them topped off. "You don't have to serve me. I was just about to fill them myself."

Quinn sat on a chair next to mine. "You do know you look like death, right? Not even death warmed over, just plain death. I don't know what you did this morning with your brother, but if I were to make a suggestion, don't do it again. You're pale as a ghost and look like if you tried to stand, you'd collapse."

I shivered. Between the nightmare and my morning with Owen, I was sure I did. No one knew about the nightmare, and I didn't want anyone knowing about what happened with my brother. I needed to change the subject.

"How was moving out?"

His old smile came back, and a twinkle sparkled in his hazel eyes. "It was almost fun. Thank you for asking Tanner to join. He's just so…impressive. At my house, my dad was about to say something when Tanner came up behind me. My parents just slowly backed up into the kitchen."

Quinn grabbed Alex's hand and pulled them down to sit next to him. He gave them a gentle smile. "I ran to my room and Tanner just stood outside the door, like a sentinel. I packed all the important things in three suitcases. I was about to grab them all when he took the two big ones. There were four wolves by the car, but I only recognized two. Tanner threw the bags in the trunk and just stared them down. Like, he didn't even have to fight them. They all crashed to the ground onto their knees. No words, no fighting, just a look."

Shifting to a sitting position, I finished my coffee. Then I started on the shake. It tasted different. It took me a few sips, then I shot a glance to see it was Tanner in the kitchen, not Oscar. He gave me a smirk before returning to his play.

I swung back to Quinn. "I'm glad he went with you. He's good backup."

Quinn continued to gush. "I'll say! It was magnificent."

Alex giggled. "Have you seen José or Bevin when they let out their alpha-ness?"

"Alpha mantle."

"What?" Alex turned to me with their brow furrowed.

"Nothing."

Quinn paused. "Well, no. Maybe. Was that what happened that day my dad asked us to bring him here?"

Giving a small smile, I nodded.

He sat and thought. "I guess I did then, though I didn't really understand it."

Alex blushed. "You'll see it again, and when you do…" Their eyes glazed over for a second. "It's fantastic."

I finally got myself into a fully upright position. "Okay, fan club. Your wolf club spirit is getting all over me. Enough is enough. Anything else you want to talk about?"

Alex paused and their face grew serious. "I have a silly question."

"Ask away, oh, silly one."

"I know that José and Bevin are a couple, and so are Sarah and Owen, but, well, is it okay if Quinn and I date? I mean, I just…well…" They ducked their head, blushing.

This day was already too long, and it was still morning. I fell back down in my chair. "Alex, we are a pack, not a business or in any other way in control of you or who you date."

Quinn grabbed Alex's hand. "I told you, hon, we're fine."

Alex dropped their head but scooted closer to Quinn.

I closed my eyes to enjoy the sun's warmth. Suddenly, I heard the door slide open and closed, a few squeals, and loud splashes. Cracking an eye open, I saw Pebble, Easton, Ginger, Seth, and even Maddy all running and jumping into the pool to play. Monica and Sierra grabbed the pool toys and threw them in before climbing into the hot tub. I wonder how long it had been since Tanner's and Oscar's wives had sat down and talked without their husbands present.

About an hour later, Pebble landed on me, wet and giggling. I yelped. "Goodness, child, you're wet and cold! What do you want?"

"I want to meet your newest animal. I want to see you fly! Please, Jade, can I?"

The thought of moving hurt my head. But how could I say no to her? "Let's have lunch first."

"Yippy!" she squealed. Leaping up, she grabbed my hands and pulled me up to follow.

"Oof, girl. When did you become so strong?"

Giggling, Pebble dragged me into the house. She led me into the kitchen. I got one foot onto the gleaming tile floor when a deep baritone filled the house. "Tanner, if you let your girl into my kitchen, you will be banned as well."

Tanner spun from the stove and pointed towards the dining room. Grumbling, I stomped out. I turned towards the living room and shouted, "What did I ever do?"

"Just stay out of that room and we'll get along fine, child. Remember the chocolate shakes."

Confusion, anger, and desire for more shakes warred in me as I dropped into a seat. A few minutes later, Pebble bounced out of the kitchen with two plates of spaghetti and meatballs. She set the plates down and ran back for garlic bread. Oscar moseyed into the dining room, calling for his kids. Soon, the table filled with Pack members. The eating and talking got louder and louder as everyone dug in. After two plates, and several slices of garlic bread, my stomach called for a cease and desist.

Owen and Bevin had returned during the meal. Seeing everyone was done, I asked my parents and Pebble to join me out in the training area. Owen, Bevin, and José came as well. As we walked out, Owen pulled me aside. "Bevin told me about the nightmare. I know you didn't want anyone to know, but he thought you might need another person to talk to."

"Not really, and not now. I'm fine."

"You keep saying that. I don't think you know what that word means."

"Fly now. Avoid nightmares later."

At the structure, Owen knelt next to me. "Okay, flying. I want you to go up to the fifteen-foot platform for the first leap. I want you to catch the air current and try to flap up to a higher altitude. Then bank. First left, then right. From there I want you to back-flap to slow and land. You do have an interested audience, so be brilliant."

I stopped moving and gaped at him. "I was with you until the end."

"Can you connect with me and see if I can give the explanation better that way?"

Narrowing my eyes, I grumbled, "I think I got it. Most of it we did yesterday. The slowing to a halt is new, but I've seen Sammy do it." I touched his hand to make the connection easier.

I stripped down and shifted. I heard a gasp from the Wisconsin contingent as the swan cloud enveloped me. Then I stood, feathers ruffling in the wind. I waddled up to the structure. Before I got there, Pebble ran up and scooped me up into a hug. I laughed, though it sounded more like a singing honk, and wrapped my neck around hers in a swan hug.

"That was the coolest sound!" my sister squealed.

She was about to put me down when Owen patted the five-foot-high platform. From there I made my way up two more landings. I jumped and flapped my wings. Owen's voice in my head guided me through the steps he wanted me to take. It was comforting and helped me to stay focused.

As I first gained altitude then banked and finally landed, I heard Pebble cheering me on. At one point I peeked down at her and saw her jumping with her cheers, but, like a new driver, the distraction made me wobble.

Owen's rich voice filled my mind. *"Eyes on the road, young padawan, eyes on the road."*

Snorting, I replied. *Where I'm going, I don't need roads.*

"Dude! You're mixing up your movie references. I may have to take away your sister card."

Mine was totally better. Now, am I ready to land?

That night, Brooke slept in my room to keep the nightmares away. I hadn't been sleeping well, and she wanted to ensure I had a good night's sleep. That, or she figured it was less far to travel when I eventually had a nightmare. Pebble slept in her room.

For the first time since Greta's death, I slept soundly through the night. She agreed that whenever I needed it, she'd help me with my sleep.

The next day, Bevin, Owen, and I drove into work together. I wasn't surprised that Owen was as excited as I was for Second Breakfast. While Bevin and I interviewed Sammy, Owen went off to start his job training the troops.

"Sammy, I want to start our interview talking about senses you have in your human form."

"Okay, yeah, sure. What do you want to discuss?"

"Well, first of all, let's talk about sight. Have you noticed any differences?"

Sammy's eyes started taking in the room, as if the plain, seafoam-green walls and ceiling held any answers. "Sometimes, I guess."

Leaning back, I focused on her. Her scent turned minty, she was frustrated or confused. Then, it shifted to something garlicy, as if she were trying to hide something. "What are you hiding? Why are you hiding?"

She hunched in on herself. "I...I don't really know. The werewolves all talk about all these sense changes, but except when you got that call and you were really emoting a lot, I just feel like me. Nothing different."

Owen and I hadn't shared my training with anyone in

the Pack. It wasn't that we were embarrassed or keeping secrets or anything, it was just that there was a lot going on, and there hadn't been time. I connected to Bevin but kept my eyes on Sammy.

On your drive in here yesterday, did Owen tell you about our training?

"*No. He said that something happened, but he wasn't sure exactly what. He wanted you to tell me and José. I also wanted to discuss your dream. Sorry if I overshared.*"

Slumping a bit, I wanted to scream in frustration while being thrilled I had some secrets of my own. Finally straightening, I reached over and grabbed Bevin's hand to strengthen the connection and make it easier. I had the energy, but I needed the connection for this. In my peripheral vision, I saw confusion flash across his face momentarily before he put his blank mask back in place.

Owen had me call each animal to my forefront to control my senses. Apparently, I normally have Wolf in front. Panther hit hard, but I'll train her. Swan? I didn't handle it well. My vision overwhelmed me. I threw up. I…I couldn't handle it. The scents were all wrong. Swans don't normally smell much. I just…I couldn't.

I didn't realize my hand was trembling until Bevin squeezed it to remind me I wasn't alone. I took a deep breath and realized Sammy was watching us closely. "You two smell weird. Like, Bevin, you smell like Jade's trees and river smell. Why is that? What are you two doing right now?"

Trying to hide my exasperation, I huffed and smiled. "Swans don't have a strong sense of smell, but they do have good vision. You may be able to train to pull the swan's senses up to yours so that you can see better, but it may be too much for you, I don't know. Werewolves can pull up their wolf senses. It helps them to see and smell more keenly. That said, you may feel like prey surrounded by predators. If that happens here, the wolves may sense that feeling and treat you like prey. It may be dangerous."

Bevin's head snapped to mine, and he squeezed my hand again. His mental voice snapped in my head, *Jade, what happened to you?"*

This time, I kept my poker face in place, waiting for Sammy to work through her thoughts to decide what she wanted.

Nothing. Owen moved away from me before anything happened. I smelled like prey, he smelled like danger. It was hard for both of us. When I pulled the swan up, I couldn't stand, so he had been holding me up. It was...awkward.

"*Good gods! I don't know if anyone else could have controlled themselves. Jade, I don't know if I could.*"

I know.

"*Don't do that again. Please, promise me. Don't let her guide your senses again.*"

I won't.

"*Are we really going to encourage and help Sammy to do this?*"

What if she stumbles upon this without us? What if it happens when she's surrounded by a pack of wolves?

CHAPTER 25

Bevin and I left after lunch. Owen stayed. Sarah would pick him up later.

When we got home, Maddy and her parents sat in the living room with José, waiting for us.

José smiled. "Jade, Bevin; would you two mind joining us?"

Halting in my path, I eyed José. "Aren't you supposed to be at work?"

He smiled. "Working from home today. So, late lunch. Join us so I can get back and not upset my fiancé by working all night."

I snorted, then, sharing a look with Bevin, shrugged,

and flopped down on one of the couches.

José leaned back, watching us. "Holly and Nick have a request for the three of us. I know what it is so I'm going to stay neutral while they plead their case to you. Jade, this becomes especially important for you to consider."

I kept a neutral face. I was pretty sure I knew what this was about, but wanting to be fair to them, I sat cross-legged on the couch and waited. Then, smelling Maddy's fear, I gave her a gentle smile before shifting my attention to Holly and Nick.

Holly took a calming breath before starting. "I'm sure you can guess what this is about. From what Bevin's told me, Maddy isn't going to become a werewolf naturally. We'd like to…she'd like to become a werewolf. And Jade, she'd like your help with her wolf—for the miracle you can provide."

My first reaction to her request was a bit of annoyance. I hadn't done anything; it was all the wolf's doing. But saying that wouldn't help, so I bit back my immediate response. I knew our answer—and I knew this was something Maddy wanted—but I wanted, needed, to hear her ask for herself. Thinking back, I wasn't even sure I'd heard her talk before. Had she said anything at the airport when Alex and I met her? I couldn't remember.

I got up, knelt in front of her, and took her hands. Panther confirmed she was human with no werewolf seed. "Hi, Maddy. This is a huge life-changing request. Both of them, really. Although I'm sure you're the one making the requests, I really need to hear all this from you."

She smelled nervous, a nutty carnival smell, but she maintained eye contact with me. Her hands shook as she nodded her understanding. "I, um…" Her voice dropped for a second and she cringed. "I would like to join your Pack. I've always hoped to become a wolf one day and learning from Bevin I didn't have the potential…well, it sucked. Being a wolf in this pack seems like a dream come true. I never thought there'd be a pack like yours."

She pulled her hands from mine and rubbed them on her pants. Then she rubbed her face. Shaking out her fingers, she looked at her parents then stared at Bevin, a deep sense of yearning in her eyes. "If you could do for me what you did for Bevin…I can't imagine."

During Bevin's senior year in high school, his wolf came out to play. With his transformation from teen to werewolf, his wolf saw his binder as a bandage, and tried to heal him, giving him half the body he'd always wanted as a trans kid. Together with Owen, we taught his wolf how to complete the 'healing.' We'd needed Owen, because I just didn't have the parts to show his wolf the fixes.

"It wasn't me, it was his wolf. I just know how to talk to them. But yeah. I'm in. I know the boys are, too, even if they haven't said so."

"Jade!" they both snapped, but I heard the laughter in their voices.

I shot them a quick glance over my shoulder. "What?

You're not going to keep her waiting a minute longer, are you?" Then I gazed directly into her green-blue eyes. "You can see the hurt and need as much as I can."

José sighed. "She's right. We'll have to do some planning, but we'll get it figured out, then either Bevin or I will discuss the specifics with you."

Maddy's body began to tremble as she stuttered out, "Oh, my gods, thank you. Thank you so much…I just…really?"

Her mom's mouth opened and closed, but nothing came out as Nick wrapped his arms around her. "I…we… we can't thank you enough. I know this won't happen right away, but…thank you."

Tears, happy tears for once, falling from all their eyes, Holly and Nick collected Maddy, and the three of them headed to their apartment to whisper about celebratory ice cream. *Now that is my kind of celebration.*

I turned to the boys. "None of it can happen the day of your wedding, which will be a crazy day. She can get bitten earlier, though, and then the morning of your wedding we can see what we can accomplish. It will be a full moon. Man, that will be a crazy busy day."

Bevin snorted. "You are a wicked woman, Jade. Are you also going to decide who bites her?"

"Honestly, it should be you or José. The strongest wolf is best." I finally broke my gaze away from the direction Maddy had gone. We'd connected, and I felt she understood a bit more about me. "I can't do it. I'll never be able to do it. Her parents are strong, just not as strong as you two." I stood and spun and was face to chest with Bevin. I hadn't realized he'd come so close to me. I grabbed his arms to steady myself. Looking up, I smiled. "You handle blood better." Reaching up to tap his nose I said, "So, you."

He stepped back a half-step to give me maneuvering space, then he faced José. "Told you so."

"Why ask me, if you'd already decided?"

"You grew up with alphas. It's nice to double check our reasoning."

I banged my head against Bevin's chest a couple of times. "So, when are you doing this, and do you need any other pointers?"

"Probably Friday, after your Aunt Allison gets into town. Having another healer seems the best plan. And sure, what help can you give?"

"Well, my parents are a five-minute walk away. That's the best advice I can give."

He pushed me and I fell. My heart almost stopped as I thought I was going to land on the floor, but, instead I landed on the couch, laughing hard enough I couldn't stop.

That evening over dinner, we discussed the ins and outs of biting a norm. Sarah had bitten Owen, but that was to give a werewolf a second animal, which required a near-fatal attack. To infect a norm took more than piercing skin, but nothing as severe as what Owen or I had survived.

As Bevin and Mom made a plan, Quinn pulled José aside. I followed them and wasn't shooed away.

"I was wondering if there was any way I could be bitten, too." Quinn threw his hands up in a double stop towards José's chest. "I totally get it if you're still hesitant because of my family and background. If you want to wait before making this decision, I can be patient."

José placed a hand on his shoulder. "Quinn, breathe. Let me speak with Bevin and Hazel. We need to work through some logistics. I'm not opposed to you becoming one of our wolves."

Quinn's eyes widened as José left to join Bevin and my mom. He faced me, eyes alight. "Did you hear that? He didn't say no. It's actually a possibility." Spinning on his heel, he bounded off.

Chuckling, I rejoined the others to listen in about Friday.

Mom was speaking. "As long as we have both Jade and Allison here, I don't see why you couldn't do two. It's tricky, but having an extra healer is key. Using your healer as the biter is ironic, but I understand why you're doing it this way. The power level between you two is pretty even."

José's brow furrowed. "Do you think I should do the biting so that we have three healers available?"

Bevin started to protest, but Mom spoke first. "I doubt you'll need any healers, but since you hold the majority of the Pack, I'd assumed you would do the biting. That said, I know you like to avoid the more violent nature of the beast, so I don't see that it matters. Choose, bite, move on. It's your Pack." She placed her hands on both cheeks of first Bevin, and then José, pulling them each in to kiss on their forehead. "I am so proud of you boys and everything you've accomplished here."

José stood a bit taller. "Our Pack has three leaders." He glanced at me with a small smile.

My mom smiled gently. "It's felt by anyone walking through the doors. Your Pack is different, but so strong. You're all doing something amazing here."

Bevin shot me a look over his shoulder. "That is, if your daughter doesn't do something to drive us all mad."

Before I could respond, Owen popped in from outside where he'd been swimming. "Bevin, José, next Saturday we're having a bachelor party." I perked up. Owen rolled his eyes. "Sorry, sis, guys only. I know, sexist, but them's the rules."

"*Your* rules. They're stupid rules. You're taking out both the grooms," I waved my hands. "Sarah and I should be able to go."

Owen smirked. "Where we're going, Sarah would have more fun than I will...or you, for that matter. If you really want to go..."

Narrowing my eyes, I made my prediction. "A male strip club?"

My mom snorted. "I think my part in all this is done. I'll

see you all in the morning." She headed out the front door.

Laughing, Owen wrapped a cold, damp arm around me. "So, what do you say, sis? Want to come and see naked men dancing?"

Imagining the night, I shivered. "Do you?"

"That isn't the point, now, is it? I'm catering to my man here." He slapped José on the chest. "We're heading out to Vegas, and we're having a night of it."

Scrunching up my face, I narrowed my eyes. "Why not just go to the Queen's Bee and have a night in town? That was fun, and I bet if you call and tell them about these two, it would be way better."

Owen's eyes widened. "I'm gonna find Raquel," he yelled as he ran off.

CHAPTER 26

Thursday morning was the last day of our interviews with Sammy. She informed us that she didn't want to try to pull the swan up.

"Every once in a while, I feel a bit of her senses…and…" She searched the room to make sure no one but Bevin and me could overhear her. "I freak out. One day, it got so bad I ended up huddled in my room, terrified. The director found me and said a couple of the wolves said the hallway smelled like a candy shop. They didn't know why it was so overwhelming. They were clustered near my door, like they couldn't control themselves. To me…I felt surrounded and thought I was going to be attacked, eaten, killed. If I bring her out fully, I think it would just be worse."

Her heart was beating fast, her pupils dilated. I grabbed her hand, but she was beginning to lose it. After a few seconds, the sweetness of her scent started to overpower the room, and I saw Bevin grasp the table. His lip started to separate from his teeth, and a low growl came from his belly.

Closing my eyes, I ignored my growing need to attack the prey—a need stronger than any I'd felt in the wild—and sought my calm. Taking a few breaths, I released it. I tried to blanket as far as I could, having heard some shuffling in the hallway. It was a larger release than I'd ever done before. Once the calm was rolling throughout the compound, I slumped, slipping to the ground, my head pounding.

Sammy collapsed, passed out. Bevin dropped to his knees next to me. "I'm so sorry, Jade. I couldn't control my wolf." He rubbed my arms and bent down to touch his forehead to mine. "Please tell me you're okay."

"My head hurts. I…gods, Bevin, I know, I felt it, too. I need…gods…so much. Can you help me up? Slowly?"

He did. The room spun, but he got me to my feet. With Bevin half-carrying me, we got the door open. We left Sammy. She'd be safe enough.

As we made our way to the mess hall, people were looking confused and dazed. A few, like Sammy, were passed out.

Owen came running up to us. "What happened? You two okay?"

Bevin nodded but handed me to him, his arms trembling. He'd gotten hit with a massive blast of the epsilon calm; only his alpha willpower kept him upright. "Food."

After they got me settled, Owen and Bevin went to grab food. As we ate, Bevin filled Owen in on the basics of what had happened. Owen figured out the rest.

"Well, hell, that sounds oddly familiar."

Bevin nodded. "That's what I was afraid of."

The director dropped down in a seat at our table. "What sounds oddly familiar, son?"

Dizzy, I groaned and looked down at my empty tray. Using the table for stability, I started to stand when Bevin reached out and stopped me. "Owen?"

Owen leapt up. "On it, boss." He headed off to get me more food.

Once Owen returned and I started to feel a pinch less dead, Bevin explained what we'd learned.

"Having a prey animal live amongst the wolves may not be the wisest move. She's managing, but as her defenses slip, this will happen more."

The director's face went blank, and he smelled dubious. "Do you mean the drugged-out response of half the compound?"

Bevin rubbed his forehead. "No, that was Jade. As the swan begins to present more when Sammy's in human form, you and she will have problems. The swan's prey nature is somehow amplified when she's human. I could barely contain myself, and I tend to have good control."

"Is this why my wolves were acting strangely the other day? They said the corridor smelled sugary."

Bevin nodded. "Yeah. Sammy told us about that. Her fear smells sweet, but it's more than that, it's compelling, addictive. It's like there's an uncontrollable urge."

"But not when she's in bird form?"

"Not at all. For some reason, in her natural form, she doesn't call to the wolf at all, at least not when I'm in human form."

"So, we need a place outside the compound where she can get away and relax."

"That would be my suggestion."

The director nodded. "Noted." He then gazed into the distance for a minute, eyes narrowed, before he turned to Owen. "That latest obstacle course, my men say it isn't possible."

Owen turned to me with a twinkle in his eye. "Heya, sis, wanna prove some overconfident men wrong?"

Groaning, I dropped my head onto Bevin's shoulder.

I pulled myself up a rope with knots for hand- and foot-holds. At the top hung a rope suspension bridge, which I ran across to reach eight-foot high poles spaced three feet apart. I called on Panther's balance to navigate that precarious path. A peg-maze attached to the far wall with a couple of metal hoops to hang from that had my legs dangling over a ten-foot drop. The pegs were barely over an inch long. Once through that obstacle, the only path was a wall with a series of two-inch finger-holds.

Right then and there, I vowed to take my brother's TV away from him.

With a soft groan, I made my way across, pushing myself for speed before my arms gave out. I dropped onto a cushioned landing pad with my arms held high above my head in a V formation, and smirked down at the observing crowd. Then I fell onto my back and tried to slow my racing heart.

"Two minutes, twenty-two seconds."

Using my ab muscles, I sat up and glared at Owen. "Really? You timed me?" I stood and marched over to him. "Why don't you go up there and do better?"

Before Owen could respond, Bevin's hands landed on my shoulders and rubbed. "I'll give it a go."

Owen's eyes gleamed.

Bevin and I didn't look athletic when we showed up at work. I usually wore jeans and a snarky t-shirt; Bevin wore jeans and long sleeve button-down shirts. We'd even gotten him some dorky themed ties. We came in our nerd personas. That said, we had been training for years. These people didn't know that.

Bevin, in all his lanky wonder, moseyed over to the start of the obstacle course. Owen and I couldn't keep our smiles from our faces. The other wolves would have been able to smell our anticipation and excitement if it weren't for the bear soap we both used before we came to work.

Bevin began. Watching him, I realized why the SSLD wolves were so frustrated by what my brother had put together. Running the course had been hard but fun. Watching Bevin, it looked more dangerous. Once he landed, Owen announced, "Two minutes thirty-seven seconds."

Laughing, Bevin returned. "Slow poke!" I teased.

He nudged my shoulder with a laugh.

Agent Vern gaped at me. "Will one of you please tell us what she is? Both their runs were incredible but *come on!*"

Surveying his victims…er, the trainees, I poked Owen in the chest. "Shouldn't you be able to beat me by now?"

Owen's eyes danced. "You think I can?" He handed me his clipboard and timer and trotted over to the starting line. "Tell me when you start the timer."

"Go!"

He went. I watched my brother in awe. He'd been an athlete his whole life and, like me, had two wereanimals. *Though I guess I now have three, huh? I wonder if she helps or hinders in these situations.* He flowed over the course like a dream. Once he landed, I stopped the stopwatch and snorted. "One minute, fifty-eight seconds. You're slowing down, slacker."

The trainees' jaws gaped in shock. The citrusy scent of excitement filled the room.

Owen jogged back to where we stood and collected his

gear. "That was fun. It makes me wonder…" He stared at me then darted a quick look at Bevin before staring at me again. "We should have a foot race."

I narrowed my eyes at him. *He may be more athletic, but I'm pretty sure I can take him in a race.*

CHAPTER 27

I had another nightmare on Friday morning. Somehow, Brooke entered the dream before it fully developed, and when I woke up at five-thirty, I couldn't remember what most of the nightmare had been about.

After lunch, Bevin and I brought Maddy and Quinn out behind Were House. Others came with us to help.

On one side of Were House was the garage, the other the gym. Between the gym and the house was a small patch of grass and a path leading to a door that accessed a hallway which led to the meeting room and a medical suite with four beds.

I stood by Quinn, and Aunt Allison near Maddy. Maddy's parents as well as my own were available to help as well. Bevin planned to bite Maddy first, then Quinn. He would bite down on the hip hard enough to cause bleeding and to mix his saliva in the wound, but nothing life threatening. Before we pulled each bitten member inside, I'd check for the potential wolf. Any streamlining of this process was a boon.

José crouched beside Bevin's black wolf, hugging and petting him, whispering what I assumed were words of love. Bevin's eyes were closed, and his muzzle rested on José's shoulder.

A combination of sadness and excitement wafted from Bevin.

Both Maddy and Quinn lay on stretchers. Maddy's heart was beating fast, but her joy was infectious. Her mom rubbed her shoulder, whispered words of encouragement to her as they waited.

The looks of delighted terror that Maddy and Quinn kept sharing, their squeaks and smiles, spread to the rest of us in the backyard. They'd both been waiting for this their whole lives.

Based on my watch, Bevin and José had spent almost ten minutes mentally preparing. "Okay, boys, it's time."

Holly gave Maddy's shoulder one more pat before walking back. "I'm so proud of you, dear."

José nodded and stood. He stepped back. He had a

hard time with the violence that came with the wolf side of our nature, but he would support both his mate and his new Pack members. He would be the rock we all needed.

Bevin moved forward and, faster than expected, shot towards us and clamped down on Maddy's hip. Maddy let out a small shriek, froze, and watched with wide eyes. Snarling, Bevin dug in for a few seconds, ensuring his saliva had time to mix with her blood. Then he licked her wound clean and stepped back.

Once Bevin was clear, I took her hand. After a moment, Panther confirmed Maddy now had the potential. "One week, werewolf."

Her wide eyes rotated to me. "Oh, my gods." She lay back and let her parents lift her and move her to the medical suite. Aunt Allison followed them.

Quinn gulped audibly and reached out a hand to me. Just before I grasped it, Bevin was on him. I held his hand throughout the process and felt the moment the potential dream became a reality. Smiling warmly down at him, I said, "One week, werewolf."

José and my mom carried Quinn's stretcher. In the medical suite, I rinsed out the wound, but did little more. It was already healing.

Alex came crashing in. "Did it work?"

Bevin followed, wearing only a pair of jeans. If those SSLD guys saw him like this, they'd never assume he was only a nerd—his body was solid muscle. He tucked Alex under his arm, kissing the top of their head. "Yes, hon, it worked."

They squealed.

We all winced but smiled at their excitement.

Saturday morning, both patients were up and eating breakfast with us. Oscar and Tanner presented a brunch of bacon, eggs, waffles, sausage, oatmeal, and a fruit plate. Platters were set up along a buffet at the back of the room and we all sat and enjoyed our meal.

Quinn, shifting a bit off his sore hip, leaned back. "Okay, Owen, I've arranged tonight. A place in the Castro."

Owen started filling his plate again. "Perfect. I don't know why I was thinking Vegas when we're so close to San Fran."

Bevin and José both shook their heads as I filled up my coffee cup. "Who all's going?"

Quinn darted me a look. "I was told the boys. Owen, Luke, and me, along with Bevin and José. I don't know who else wants to go, but it isn't like I made reservations."

Brooke leaned back. "Let the boys have their night. They'll have more fun without us there. We'll go out and watch Raquel again."

Sarah whooped and I agreed.

Brooke's eyes narrowed. "But, Jade, if we're having a girls' night at a drag show, Sarah and I are dressing you up. No jeans and t-shirt for you." She waved her hand at me, disapproval oozing from her. "This…whatever you call it… it won't do."

Suddenly, my night didn't seem nearly as exciting.

Over the next week, beginning on Tuesday, the alphas from the other four U.S. North American Packs, and José's family members from Mexico, descended on our territory. Like my parents, they showed up with their more dominant wolves and families. Unlike my parents, since they didn't have any real connection with the leadership of our Pack, staying in Were House wasn't an issue.

Most of the Wisconsin Pack came. Their reaction to what we'd built was heartwarming. Pebble became the tour guide, assigning rooms and showing people around the property. She somehow acquired a notebook—probably from Sarah—and kept track of everyone. As always, the book had a banana split across the cover. She had organized kid-free areas for adults and adult-free areas for the kids, and a space for food and entertainment to always be available, courtesy of Tanner and Oscar. She even scheduled tours into town. I was dumbfounded.

The only Pack member not staying at Were House was Piper. How she obtained permission to invite Julez, her human girlfriend who didn't know about werewolves, was beyond me. There was no way she could stay at the house.

They got a room at the local hotel.

The wedding was on Saturday, July 21st. The full moon. It would be a typical wedding, starting in the late morning with the attendees sitting in a beautifully set area and the couple walking up the aisle.

The morning of the wedding, we set up gray chairs decorated with purple flowers in the field behind the house. There was a gray and purple runner between the seats that looked like water flowing down a sea of flowers. At the front of the seating area stood a metal arbor large enough for the couple to stand under with the officiant. The design on the sides of the arbor were wolves howling at a moon in the woods, reminiscent of the gate to the Mondaris Estates, made in the same dark wrought iron.

During the ceremony, a submissive wolf, a bearer of the hearts of the Pack, would lead the group in a prayer to Sonnara, the sun god, protecting our humanity and blessing the union. Bevin and José had asked Aunt Allison to officiate.

After the prayer, the couple each stated their vows in front of family, friends, and Pack. The formal ceremony would be followed by food, dancing, and mingling. Then there was the prayer to Mondara, the moon god. That was done by running under the full moon in our animal form.

We planned to have over fifty wolves running on our property. It was going to be insane. The food offered beforehand had to be ample enough that the run didn't need to include a hunt. A hunt beginning with seven sets of alphas would not end with seven sets of alphas. I hoped a huntless run would be safe.

Saturday morning, I woke up early. It only took a few minutes for José, Bevin, Maddy, and Quinn to join me for coffee. It was the boy's wedding day and there was a long list of things to do, so we all needed to complete this one thing before the horde of guests awoke.

We headed to the small grassy area outside the medical suite. First, José collected Maddy and Quinn into the Pack. Closing my eyes, I visualized their connections. Then Bevin knelt by Maddy, and José squatted by Quinn, and the alphas each called out a wolf.

I stood back and watched their slow transformations. Quinn completed his first. Snarling, he leapt at José, who grabbed Quinn's muzzle and rolled with him on the ground. Once the snarling subsided and his tail was tucked, José chuffed him on the nose. "You did good, Quinn. That was the right reaction."

Quinn's wolf was dark gray with an almost black muzzle and black paws. Once he was over his shock at attacking José, he yipped and ran in circles. His excitement at turning furry made me giggle.

Maddy took a few more seconds, and before she

finished, her parents came out wearing robes and holding steaming mugs of coffee. They both looked tired as they stood and watched, big smiles on their faces.

When Maddy's wolf emerged, like Bevin, her wolf knew the soul of her human. The female wolf snarled at Bevin but tucked her tail, shaking. She snapped her teeth twice before shaking her head as if to clear cobwebs, and then she whimpered, slinking to Bevin as if to apologize.

Bevin dropped and Maddy all but crawled into his lap. "Maddy, it's fine. You should know that a new wolf's instinct is to attack. It's *not* the attack we worry about, hon." He kept petting her and speaking calmly until she relaxed.

Her wolf was red with a black diamond on her forehead. She had some gray streaks down her sides, and a black-tipped tail.

Half asleep, Alex stumbled out the door. "Did I miss it?" They took in the two new wolves and did a happy dance. "Okay, okay, okay...I'm on new wolf duty. I'll shift and take them for a run. I'll bring them back for breakfast so that we can all attend the ceremony. You three go; you have too much else to do."

They pushed us through the door before they began to strip down.

José grumbled. "We're going to be managed all day, aren't we?"

Grabbing his arm, I kissed his cheek. "Yep. Welcome to my world. And what did you expect for today? For it to be a day to do your own thing? You have every alpha imaginable here. You will do as you are told, soldier, and like it."

He glowered at me. "You know, you aren't in a much better position."

I shrugged. "I rarely get to manage my own things anymore. You all think I'll get into too much trouble. I'm used to it by now. I swear I used to be better at managing my own life."

They both snorted.

We took the final turn into the living room. Sitting on the love seat was Piper and Julez. They'd obviously been waiting for us for a while, though it was only seven in the morning. They were kissing, and, like the last time I'd seen them, the love emanating off them was palatable, almost as intense as that from José and Bevin.

Something in my head snapped.

CHAPTER 28

Before anyone could stop me, I slipped around the furniture in the living room and out the front door. In the back of my head, I was aware of people calling my name, but I had to get out of there. My heart was...I hurt. My head pounded and before I knew it, my feet were hitting the ground to the same beat...I was running. I didn't know where I was going, but I ran.

When I got to Pack House, I knew I was close, but this place wasn't quite right. The thought of being around people made me recoil. Heal...I needed to heal my broken parts. Gods, I had three animals in me; certainly I could heal these wounds.

Searching, shaking, panting, I moved to the tree that I'd collapsed behind when I shifted to Panther all those weeks before, when Mathias invaded our property. With a jerk, I dropped down, landing on my butt. I leaned my back against the tree, facing out into the woods, hidden from anyone who may have been looking for me. I had done enough sweeps through this area that my scent shouldn't be out of the ordinary.

I pulled my knees up, tucked my head in, and took calming breaths. First, I had to slow down my heart. Closing my eyes, I headed into my mental mindscape and found my animals. Swan normally stayed in the lake behind the small structure, but right now, all three stood with me.

As a group, we gazed at the spot where the cone of silence once stood, but was gone, shattered, obliterated. We gaped at the ghost-Piper, where she had broken free from her jail, and stood taking over my mind. *If she gets big enough, will she start to feel me, too?*

She became my…everything. Taking over my senses. My entire body trembled. I could feel what she felt, smell what she smelled, I could practically see and hear through her eyes and ears. If I merged into her ghost, could I become her? Would she take me over? I didn't want to find out.

I backed away from the ghost. The more I focused on it, the bigger it became. There was a tingle and I realized that I was feeling Julez's hand on my arm. Then I heard her speaking in my ear. "I wanted to ask before, but there were too many people in the room…What do you think that was all about?"

My fear spiked, and I shivered. This had to stop. If I didn't control my emotions, the others would find me by scent. Overwhelmed, I knew I couldn't do this alone. But I couldn't call José; it was his wedding day, that wasn't fair. He didn't deserve my problems. He needed to worry about being with Bevin and nothing more. Sarah would help, but she was running the wedding; she too had too much to do today.

I had to figure this out on my own. Everyone else had too much on their plates.

Even my image of myself in my mental landscape was shaking, trembling as it sat, hugging its knees. In my mind, I lay down and tried to think my way out of this.

I tried to rebuild the prison, but because I hadn't eaten anything yet today, I didn't have the energy. I felt myself—my physical self—start to waver, as I used up whatever strength I had fighting with this connection. Finally, I just lay down and let it wash over me.

There were sounds around me. A click as I heard a door open and close. Talking.

The voices got quieter. I wanted to yell out for help, but I no longer had the energy to move. My escape plan had worked. I had removed myself from the wedding so I wouldn't be a burden, and it worked.

More talking…a fight?

"No, I will help her."

"I've been helping her her whole life."

"But I've been helping her for the last few months. I know the issue. Let me do my job."

"If you were doing your job, she wouldn't be out here."

There was a huff of annoyance. I envisioned toe-tapping. The thought made my breath escape in a laugh. "She freaked out. She's been having nightmares. This was a kind of nightmare come to life. We can talk about all of this later. Let me help her now. I know what I'm doing."

"Do you two even get along? She's been coming to me for help and advice, again, her whole life."

"Allison, please. You are amazing. Honestly, I'd love to sit and talk to you; I'm ready. But for now, let me pass."

I was starting to figure out voices. My mom finally cut in. "Allison, let Brooke work. If they aren't back at the house in an hour, you can go help. She's right. Jade isn't in our Pack any longer. She isn't ours. She's theirs."

Aunt Allison let out a strangled cry and I heard her storm off.

"Brooke, I'm trusting you with my daughter. I don't know what has happened, but I can smell that she's broken. Fix her." It was an order. An alpha order. Mom's power blanketed the area and I whimpered.

"Hazel. I appreciate your love for your daughter, but you're hurting her. Please stop that."

The energy push stopped, and I sighed. A moment later,

I was being lifted until I leaned on Brooke. "Good gods. I leave you for five minutes.... What did you do to yourself?"

I moaned. I was still mostly in my mental landscape and before I knew what was happening, Panther invited Brooke in.

"You're curled up here, too. This place is...trippy. I've heard others talk about it, but...why do you have a fake fire?"

I rolled my head to stare at her.

She smirked back. "Right, campground. You have a building you can't get into. A fake fire. And way off in the distance, a pond for the bird. And a huge freaky ghost wolf. Swell. Now, the ghost is getting bigger. Can we work on containing it?"

My attempt must have looked pitiful, or desperate. Feebly, I shook my head. Brooke sat down next to me, hauling me up so I was practically sitting in her lap. "You're miserable. Pull some of my energy and lock her up until the alphas can do more."

After doing as she asked, I could finally sit on my own. Then I commanded the ghost back into prison, and she disappeared. I let out a groan at the cessation of extra stimulation. "Thank you," I choked out.

With a small push, we were both out of my head space. I found we were in pretty much the same position in the real world. "We should get back."

"No. We should talk."

"About?"

"Really? You see Piper and Julez, freak out, and you don't know what you need to talk about?"

"I'm fine."

"Bevin's right, you really don't know what that word means. You had to stop Greta's heart—you still aren't over that—and then you see your first love in bliss with somebody else. You had a panic attack. You aren't fine. You're grieving, but you won't let yourself feel emotions or let any of your Pack or friends help. You keep trying to push it off and be strong. You're trying to be a role model, but Jade, you need to let go. Let your heart heal."

Slowly, I just looked up at her. "It hurts when I think about it. Any of it."

"I know."

"I don't want anyone else to feel my pain."

"I know."

"If I grieve, everyone will feel it. They'll know that I'm hurting."

"That's what *Pack* is for. It's one of the lessons you taught me. Right at the beginning. You're never going to be alone. It will suck, it will be hard, but it will be good, because when you're hurting, the Pack will always be there to help you."

My eyes widened. "That is almost word for word what I said to you…years ago."

"I know. They were the most terrifying things anyone ever said. I sat and contemplated them for hours. I couldn't believe anyone would be there for me. Maybe Owen… but a whole Pack? Then, I started watching and learning. Ironically, the only person who doesn't actively take advantage of the Pack bonds is you."

I dropped my head onto her shoulder. "I feel like that's all I do."

She turned my face so that we looked at each other. "No, it isn't. We force you to utilize us, but you don't lean on us as much as you should. Maybe José and Bevin, but you should be leaning on me and the other submissives, like Raquel, maybe Owen as well. You have people, use them."

She leaned down and kissed me on the lips in the same way Bevin or José would. Then she pulled me up. "Come on, let's get food into you before your Aunt Allison comes and kicks my ass for doing this all wrong."

I snorted. "The women in my family can be fierce. I would say you could learn a lot from her, but I'm not sure I want you to be any meaner." When Were House came into view, I stopped. "Brooke. I don't know if I can handle seeing them together."

"Stick with me or Raquel, or any of the other submissive wolves here. After breakfast, you need to get Sarah and José to reset your ghost wards."

I blinked at her. "Are you asking to be my date for the wedding?"

She rolled her eyes. "Oh, gods, you're awful."

We reached the doors and made our way to the table.

I could almost hear it groan, it was so overfilled with food. People were all over the house, at the dining room table, in the living room, at the kitchen stools, and even outside. There really wasn't anywhere to sit.

Oscar's voice flowed out from the kitchen. "Child, I saved you and Brooke seats at the counter. Come in here and sit."

I narrowed my eyes. "I thought I wasn't allowed in the kitchen."

"You have three seconds to get your butts in here."

We ran.

CHAPTER 29

After brunch, José, Bevin, and Sarah followed me into my room. They demanded to know what had happened when I'd run out of the house.

I didn't tell them everything, but then Brooke strode in and gave a quick rundown of her take on the situation.

After everyone was up to speed and in agreement, I sat in the middle of my bed with all three of my alphas around me. Sarah and José each took one of my hands. Bevin put his hands on my shoulders, so his fingers touched the skin of my neck. I'd never done this before, but I shut my eyes and slowly invited each of them into my mental landscape.

I got a bit dizzy with so much action in my head, but once there, they helped hold me up.

"A party in my head. I mean, I've heard of hearing voices, but inviting them in is something new."

Bevin came up from behind and wrapped his arms around me. "Relax."

My hands shook. "I don't think I can. This is a lot."

He rubbed my shoulders. "Okay, let's get this done then. I've never done a capture. Should we try to expel the ghost?"

José circled the jail, inhaling deeply. "She's too integrated. I don't know if that's an option. Okay, Sarah, you first."

Sarah closed her eyes. A pulse of power flowed through my body and her jail for Piper appeared. I whimpered and would have fallen if Bevin hadn't held me up.

Watching me, Sarah said, "I'm out; this is too much for her." She slowly faded. It felt like I could breathe a bit easier.

José closed his eyes and a second wave of power rocketed through my body. I turned and curled into Bevin. He held me. I heard José walk up though the grassy terrain I'd created in my landscape, then felt him touch my head. "It should be better." Then he faded from my senses.

I relaxed. One person in my mental landscape was fine. I pushed away from Bevin. "I'm okay now." Spinning from him, I eyed the cone of silence.

He placed his hands on my shoulders again. "I hate that she's in your head. I'm sorry that you had to experience that today. It hurts me that you had to face Greta alone.

We're Pack, and as a pack we'll figure this one out. You aren't facing this ghost alone." His hands slipped around my shoulders into a tight hug. "I want to take the pain away from you, and I know that I can't. But maybe I can help with this." There was a beat and then his power pulsed within me. My mom was wrong; it was so much more than the others. He must hide his power from everyone. It almost floored me. I couldn't breathe for a few seconds.

When I could see, there was a dome over the jail, shimmering. "Wh-what did you do?"

He chuckled. "It's made from the same metal as Thor's hammer."

I huffed. "How long have you known how strong you are? And does José know?"

"I've always known. And yes, he does. I just asked him not to let others know. I can usually tamp it down. I just want this shield to last."

"Will everyone know now? Gods above, Bevin."

"Sarah might, but most people won't. I kept that blast contained to this room—I hope."

"Thank you."

Then Brooke and Sarah kicked the boys out and did their best to prepare the three of us for the wedding. Pebble came in to dress with us and was just as critical of my lack of style as the other two.

After a quick shower, Brooke braided my hair; creating loops and adding flowers. Once she'd designed something that was stunning and baffling, she began on my makeup. Eventually, she was done torturing me, and I slipped into the dress.

By then, Sarah had completed her own primping. She wore her makeup subtle and her hair in braids similar to mine. We complimented each other nicely. When I saw our reflections together, I was less worried about standing beside her for the next few hours in a matching outfit.

Brooke dropped a couple bags on my bed. "Okay, here are the accouterments. I'm heading to get myself ready. You both look great." Spinning on her heel, she exited my room.

As I gazed at myself in the mirror, Pebble started pulling out accessories. We each had a tiara, a silver headband with small wolves racing across the band. From a distance, you wouldn't be able to see the wolves, but from a foot or so away, the image became clear. There were matching necklaces and earrings with teardrop diamonds set in white gold.

Once done, Pebble stepped up beside us in her pale gray, A-line dress. Sarah looked down at her. "Can you go check out the other bag, by the pillow?"

Pebble ran off and came back with a third tiara. "You got one for me?"

Sarah smiled at her. "Of course, we did, sweetheart. You're

not standing up with us, but you're absolutely one of us!"

The three of us headed out together to make sure everyone knew where to go. We found Aunt Allison and sent her to the arbor with Owen and Luke. We asked Owen to cue the music.

Before we could start walking down the aisle, Bevin grabbed my arm and turned me around. "You two look amazing. I still can't believe you kept your dresses a secret!"

José's smile was just as big. "I love it!" He carefully pulled us each in for a hug.

I pushed on his chest. "The music has started. You know that's our cue."

He snorted. "It isn't like they'll start without us."

"Fine." I held my finger up and twisted it in the air, signaling him to turn so I could check out his outfit. The boys each wore a gray suit, tailored to show off how buff they'd gotten over the years. No hiding today. Their shirts were the same deep purple as our dresses. Their ties were gray with a purple shadow of a howling wolf. "You two look sexy. Who knew you cleaned up this well?"

José's eyebrow shot up. "Look who's talking, missy."

I smiled. "Does Pebble have the rings?"

Sarah sighed. "Really? Now? When the music starts to play, you actually pay attention to something?"

I winked at her, then grabbed my bouquet of flowers and headed for the door. "See you two at the head of the party."

A few wolves with musical talent played stringed

instruments. Sarah and I marched our way towards Aunt Allison and the groomsmen. The seats were full of friends, family, and allies. There was no groom A and groom B side, everyone got to decide where they wanted to sit. Fred was sitting up front with Bevin's sisters, Heather and Hanna, and had an open seat next to him for his wife. On the other side, Alejandro, José's dad, sat with Estrella and an open seat as well. Behind Fred were my parents and others from the Wisconsin Pack. Behind Alejandro were people from the Mexico Pack. After that, everything was random.

Gazing over the seats, everyone's lovely outfits looked like a jewelry case of stunning pieces. My focus was on marching to the music and enjoying the day. A rock—missed by whoever had put out the runner—caught my toe, and I would have gone down if a hand hadn't grabbed my arm.

A gravelly voice whispered in my ear, "Ms. Stone, you're better than this."

I bit my cheek and moved on from Mr. Nelson, my old gym teacher. Who had invited the bears?

Arriving at the front of the aisle, we took our places to the left of Aunt Allison. Across from us stood Owen and Luke, looking handsome in their suits, similar to the grooms.

Then everyone turned to watch the real show. José with his mom, Clare, and Bevin with his mom, Janet, both walked down the aisle. Clare and Janet had chosen matching dresses in complementary colors. Clare's was burnt orange and Janet's was sapphire. Once they reached us, the moms gave a tearful hug and kiss to both grooms before finding their seats.

José and Bevin grasped hands and approached Aunt Allison. Her face softened as she gazed at them. Her eyes glowed an ethereal gold, and her voice took on a resonance a bit deeper than normal. I wasn't sure if people who didn't really know her would notice. "It has always been the way of Sonnara to shine down on us, guiding our way through the maze of challenges life throws at us."

Both boys smiled a bit at those words. We'd already had challenges; hopefully we were close to the end of them.

Allison continued. "At times, we are lucky enough to find someone who will be our partner to face those challenges. And, seldom, Sonnara touches down upon the hearts of two souls and deems them more than just partners, but mates."

At Aunt Allison's words, there was a collective gasp from the audience. The Packs coming to celebrate with us knew they were welcoming a new Pack and new alphas, but apparently, they didn't know that these leaders were a mated pair.

Aunt Allison smiled at the crowd, and then shifted her gaze back to the boys. "When this special bond is applied to leaders, it is more powerful than at any other time. It is a sign of things to come. Sonnara has doubly blessed your partnership and your Pack. There will be trials that Sonnara herself will present in one form or another, but nothing that you and yours cannot face together."

She lowered her head and when she looked up again her eyes had changed back to their usual shade. "On a personal note, I am so proud of you two for everything you have accomplished. May Sonnara bless you—as all of us do—on this day of your joining."

She faced Bevin. "Bevin, your words to José?"

Bevin dropped his chin for a minute before looking up. Without breaking eye contact with José, he gently swung out an arm, and Pebble ran up to place a ring in his hand. He slipped it on José's finger, then grasped both his hands. "You know that I have loved you for as long as I can remember. You were my fantasy when I was young, my best friend when I was older, and now my partner, my lover, and my mate."

His voice wavered and he licked his lips. Pulling out one of his hands, José rubbed his fingers down Bevin's cheeks, then down his arm, and back to their clasped hands. All the while, he smiled up, nodding encouragement.

Taking a bracing breath, Bevin licked his lips again. "I'm not sure how I became so blessed by Sonnara and Mondara to have won you as a life partner, but in you that is what I have. Someone who will help me to grow to be a better person. Listen when I have worries and let me help when there are burdens to share. A partner in all things." He leaned down and gently kissed José.

The crowd tittered and Aunt Allison cleared her throat.

"Well, it *is* their ceremony. I'm here to help guide, not to judge. José, your words to Bevin."

José repeated Bevin's gesture, swinging out his arm, and again Pebble ran up with a ring. After placing the ring on Bevin's finger, a flash of power emanated throughout the field. A joining that I didn't think anyone expected. A stillness permeated the on-lookers for a moment as the potency of the joining settled over them.

José leaned in close. "My journey wasn't as clear as yours, though I think part of my heart has always belonged to you. You have always been the most amazing person I've known. The fact that you've chosen me to share your life with makes my breath catch every time I think about it."

Bevin trembled, his love and wonder pooling out of him. José rubbed up and down his arms to squeeze his wrists, love coming from him as well. "*You* are the person I want to share my joys and pains with. *You* are the person I want to lead with. Without you, none of this would make sense to me. You are the partner I love and desire. Together, we will create a Pack, a home, and a territory that will make Sonnara and Mondara proud." Then he, too, leaned in for a quick kiss.

Aunt Allison smiled this time. "I present to you all José and Bevin Cortez-Green. Now," she chuckled, "you may kiss the groom."

A cheer went up from everyone assembled as the two stepped together for a third kiss.

CHAPTER 30

Everyone wanted to congratulate the new couple. I knew I had time later, so I made my way to one of the two tables laden with food. I grabbed two plates and assembled a selection of treats. Plates full, I found an empty table in the field on the edge and watched the interplay of people mingling. It was like a living painting with all the beautifully attired people and the comings and goings.

Food melted in my mouth as I ate delectable after delectable bite.

The chairs from the ceremony were being swept away so that people who wanted to dance could. We didn't have a long break—maybe two or three hours of dancing and eating—and then we'd all change for the run. My heart raced just imagining all these wolves prowling the woods together.

Halfway through my first plate, Piper and Julez joined me. I watched them set their plates on my table. Doing a quick check-in on my head space…nothing. Tension inside me released as I told myself I could do this. "Hey." I gave them a slight smile.

Piper met my eyes. "Mind if we join you?"

Considering them, I shrugged. "Not at all."

Julez was taking everything in. "That ceremony was…well, I don't know. It was similar to, but different from any wedding I've ever seen. And I didn't know your aunt was ordained."

Nodding, I made a noncommittal sound. "I'm a bit surprised you made it, honestly."

Julez's eyes shone. "I know, right? Originally, I didn't think I could make it either, my grandma's birthday and all. But she lives in San Jose, which is so close. It's funny, when I heard about the wedding, I just assumed that the celebrations would be all night, but Piper explained it would be earlier and that I could come to see this part and slip away. Who knew two such young, hip guys, would have a wedding so early in the day?"

Trying to keep a neutral face, I said, "Yeah, how much *has* Piper told you about all of this?" Piper's anxiety dripped from her as her eyes widened. *She must be trying to contain her stress.*

Julez shrugged. "Not much. She explained it would be

big. There *are* a lot of people here. So many from Wisconsin. Almost feels like you should have come back home instead of forcing everyone to fly out here." Julez sounded almost angry.

Piper placed her hand on Julez's arm. "We talked about this. They wanted everyone to see where they lived."

"So, they rented a resort?" Julez snapped out. It sounded like an argument they'd been having.

Covering my mouth, I coughed and then took a sip of juice.

Julez continued. "I mean, it isn't like we've even seen where they live, Piper. I was hoping to visit, see their home, check out their new digs. Instead, we come to this posh resort, Mondaris Estates. Or is it apartments? I wasn't quite clear. Where do they live? And what's more, Jade's dad told me I couldn't return after my grandma's party. I really don't get that either. Like, the ceremony's done, can't I come back for the after-party? What's happening that I can't drop back in for?"

Searching the clouds for answers, I finally dropped my chin and faced the hurt and confusion in Julez's eyes. "The ceremony was early, because in a few hours we'll head out into the woods. The ceremony is not just this." I waved at the place people were now dancing. "As the sun sets, we'll all get on our game faces and head to the woods for a night hike and camping. We'll probably end up sleeping out there. We'll return in the morning. We have a day celebration and a night celebration. We celebrate the marriage under the sun *and* the moon."

Julez's ire shifted to contemplation. "I hear all of your family say gods instead of god. And Allison talked about them in the ceremony. Two gods then, sun and moon. You're looking for both to bless this union?"

Impressed, I was a bit nervous at the intelligence of Piper's chosen love. My parents were going to have to decide about her, and soon. Julez, like Piper's mom, was going to figure things out on her own.

"Something like that. Now," after staring pointedly down at my empty plates, I gazed back up at the pair, "I need to check out the second table's selections." There was a cooking competition after all.

Julez looked scandalized. "You had over a plate of food left. When? How? I didn't even see you eating." She faced Piper. "How was that even possible?" Then she stared at me. "And how can you still be hungry?"

Piper lifted up on her tiptoes and kissed Julez's cheek. Thankfully, I felt nothing. "You get used to it."

Blushing a perfect shade, Julez quickly backtracked, "Oh, I'm sorry. I didn't mean to sound rude. I just—"

I shook my head. "No worries, I'm used to it." Not wanting to experience more, I slipped away to fill two new plates with the second table's offerings. Before I got there, I ran into Pebble. "That was so amazing, Jade! Can you believe it? They did it!" I gave her a squeeze and pushed her towards the dance floor.

Looking around, I saw Quinn dragging Alex toward the dance floor as well. There seemed to be an impromptu meeting of all the alphas in the far back area of the field.

Seven sets of alphas. I contemplated what the topic of discussion could be and was glad I didn't have to join. I sent a pulse of support to my new alphas and a pinch of amusement, then moved to grab a couple of clean plates.

Deciding Oscar had done well with his selections, and happy to have Tanner's, I found a new table on the other side of the gathering. The dance floor was filled with kids from all the different Packs showing off new and wild dance moves. Owen was out there with Sarah, just as free and crazy as any of the kids. Alex was a bit more reserved with Quinn, but Piper had made it out there and she danced with as much abandon as she always did.

Maddy and her parents joined me this time. She looked heartsick.

I placed my hand on hers. "What's wrong?"

"I...Bevin...my..." A tear traced down her cheek.

"You're worried because your body didn't change after your first time becoming a wolf?"

She nodded, taking back her hand to wipe her tears.

We really didn't explain this enough to poor Maddy and her parents. She's so quiet, I'm glad she didn't hold this in, agonizing for days before approaching me.

Sighing, I surveyed the strained and worried faces of her parents. "It wasn't instant for Bevin either. We had to show the wolf what needed to be done. It was..." I shrugged, not knowing exactly how to explain what I did. "A process."

Maddy's green-blue eyes were more green when she

cried. "Help me, Jade, please."

Stroking her arm, I smiled. "Of course, I will, hon. We promised you this."

She took a shaky breath then grasped my hand. "Now?"

Scrunching up my face, I gauged my two plates of savory delights. There was plenty of food to be had, so that was a good start. I'd chosen a table with backed stools, but I was still wary of my overall success of staying in the stool. "Nick, can you come support me? Holly, support your daughter. After this is done, we'll both need more food."

Holly eyed my plate. "I know you're a teen, and have a few animals, but you just downed two full plates of food."

"And I'll probably need more. So will Maddy. She's going to be shaking. Don't worry, she won't get hurt, just a bit freaked out. If you want, we can wait and have Bevin or José here to help."

Maddy's scent spiked, almond, citrus, and a bit sweet. Tense, excited, and a bit scared. "No, now. I don't want to ruin their wedding with this. Please, Mom, just do as she asks."

Holly smelled frustrated but stepped up behind Maddy, placing her hands around Maddy's waist. Nick did the same for me.

I took Maddy's hand and Panther ran forward. *No. Wolf.* We entered Maddy and found her red wolf cowering.

What is wrong, friend? Why do you fear us? You shrank from Bevin yesterday as well.

"I am unworthy. For a week I have prowled my person's

body trying to find the wound and have found none to fix. She hurts, she is injured, but I find nothing."

Why do you think she is injured?

"All week she has asked me to fix her, to heal her, to make her better. I do not understand what she means."

Sitting down, I coaxed the red beauty to me, earning her trust. My black shadow of a wolf lay next to her, creating a bond of friendship, making her feel loved, needed, welcome—and worthy.

I will help you to understand, though it will be strange to you. Bevin's wolf did not understand fixing a wound that wasn't a wound. But he'd fixed a hurt that was.

First, I took her wolf throughout Maddy's body, showing her and instructing her on anatomy. Teaching a wolf who could heal anatomy was bizarrely fun. I felt Maddy tense and whimper as we moved through her body. She started to shake as the lessons continued. Some areas that were private seemed painful.

Next, I took her wolf to my body and showed her how my body was different.

This is what typical female anatomy looks like.

"This is not what my Maddy has."

No.

"This is why she is heartbroken?"

Yes.

Maddy's wolf disappeared, and I felt her slump.

I opened my eyes, and my stomach grumbled loudly.

CHAPTER 31

The run was chaos.

Alphas led their wolves, for the most part, but there were some issues when alphas clashed. Too much power flowed through the woods. Ours was the first new Pack in generations, and the first time all the Packs had come together in written history. At one point, the Massachusetts alphas and the Tennessee alphas came head-to-head in a snarling confrontation. Bevin released his mantle, proving he was the biggest, baddest wolf in the forest, before running off to rejoice in Mondara.

Near morning, there was a disruption with about

twenty wolves. They were tired and snapping. The night was waning, and I knew José and Bevin had slipped off to return to their rooms. Blood would be shed. The last thing I wanted was another kerfuffle.

My parents trotted up to me, flanking me.

I quickly connected to mom. *Thoughts?*

"*Can you knock them out?*"

Too tired.

"*Take from me and Dad, we can sleep out here as well as in our room. Stop this before something happens that no one wants in the Packs history books.*"

I pulled power from them as I blasted the forest with a wave of calm. Many of the wolves fell where they stood, collapsing in a pile of sleeping beasts. Others began a wobbling trot back to Were House. I made it back to my room with Pebble and we collapsed on the floor next to my bed. Brooke, Owen, Alex, and Quinn joined us in a big puppy pile.

The first to wake in the morning, I threw robes over all the bodies asleep on my floor. I tiptoed to the bathroom to wash up and slip into clean clothes. Today's shirt reflected my mood. It read: *Sometimes I pretend to be normal, but it gets boring. So, I go back to being me.*

There were too many people around to bother with training. I had also decided the wedding was reason enough to take the weekend off. I was about to sneak into the kitchen when Oscar's voice stopped me. "And what makes you think your restriction from the kitchen is lifted, child?"

Freezing, my foot inches from touching the kitchen tiles, I slowly backed up. My stomach grumbled in protest. "I just need food, Oscar. And coffee. Can't I come and sit at the counter like I did yesterday? I don't get this ban you have on me occupying the kitchen."

He came out and bodily turned me, guiding me into a chair. "Ever consider it has less to do with your destructive nature and more to do with someone wanting to take care of you, child? Now sit." He placed a mug down in front of me and an assortment of leftovers from the day before.

"But I can do things in the kitchen."

"I'm sure you can. But I enjoy being in the kitchen, so you will allow me my peculiarities."

Holding my mug for a minute to enjoy the heat, I finally sipped my coffee, and then dug into my food. When either got low, Oscar refilled them. Slowly, I began to feel human again.

Finishing off my second cup, I pulled Oscar down to join me at the table. "Do you ever sleep? You seem to always be in there." I tilted my chin towards the kitchen.

"Oh, I sleep, but I get up early. It's always been that way. As long as I'm up, I may as well be useful. Especially once I figured out I'm not the only early riser. That whammy you laid on the Packs last night was impressive. Is that why you're so hungry?"

I nodded. "I should've eaten last night, but I just wanted to curl up and sleep."

José and Bevin were the next to join us. I eyed them. "Why are you two up so early?"

José snorted. "I know. I love to sleep in, but we have guests. Most of them are leaving today. We've taken the week off and can sleep in then. I plan on not leaving the room…"

Plugging my ears and shutting my eyes, I ignored him. When I finally opened up, he was laughing at me.

"Do you know what that wave of power was during the ceremony?"

Bevin took the plate of food Oscar offered him. "I've been thinking about it. It happened at the end. I mean, Allison had a few more words, but it was after our vows but before the final kiss. I think it was the mating bond coming into full force. Neither of us did it."

I rubbed my chest. "Good gods. If you two can work together to join your power, you can knock down buildings."

José snorted. "Or possibly keep you in line?"

Turning to face him, I rolled my eyes.

Bevin grabbed my hand. "Did I see you with Piper and Julez?"

Sneering, I nodded. "Whatever you did worked." Shaking my head, I felt both relieved and sad. "I didn't feel a thing…even when they kissed."

He squeezed my hand, looking relieved.

Maddy plodded into the dining room. She looked different. She smelled different. She had a shy smile as she sat across from me and blushed. "Jade...can you...um..." She looked over at Bevin and José, her color deepening.

Bevin bit his lips, then smiled. "You know, I wolfed out over spring break. The next thing I knew, I was like a toddler all over again. Owen was the one who ended up teaching me how to use my new body."

A wave of gratitude came from Maddy as she kept sending me hopeful glances. Smiling at the change of subject, and for a task I could do, I said, "Of course. Let's spend the day together. I have work tomorrow morning, but any time I'm not at work, we can hang out. I'm sure Sarah will help, too, especially if you want help with shopping or makeup. I'm really not good at those things."

Maddy nodded along as I delineated options.

That afternoon, Owen challenged me—and anyone else who wanted to participate—to a foot race. There was a ten-mile path near the school that I used for track. People utilized it a lot during the school year, but it tended to be free during the summer.

About half the guests were leaving, but the rest lined the running path, curious to see what this race was all about. Sarah and Brooke decided to take the run with us. Neither of them believed they'd beat us, but claimed the idea of stretching their legs sounded great. They'd both been part of track in high school and college.

As the four of us lined up, Maddy came over and tapped me on the shoulder. "Would it be okay if I ran with you all? I'm not the fastest, but I like to run."

Owen's eyes started to glow as a smile took over his face. He wrapped an arm around her. "Maddy, all are welcome. I want you to run and turn once we've all passed you coming back. That way, your time will be close to ours. Use your watch so I know your distance."

She smiled shyly up at him.

We all lined up. Bevin took out the official timer. "Go!"

I took off. Sarah was in the lead at the start with a mind boggling sprint. Owen was right behind her. A minute later, Owen and I passed her. I stretched my legs and let my speed out. It had been a few weeks and running gave me the same thrill these days as flying. Owen stayed close, but I knew I had more speed as the faces of the spectators blurred.

It took surprisingly few minutes to get to the turnaround point. Looking at his watch, Owen huffed. "You're not breathing hard enough, so smoke it back!"

We were flying over the pavement, but I realized he was right. The run felt good, but it was more of a workout, not a strain.

"Jade, run!"

I shot him a grin, dug deep, and ran!

I wasn't sure what happened between the grin and the finish line, but the next thing I knew, I was grabbing my knees, panting. There was a stitch in my side and my vision ebbed and flowed. José handed me a bottle of water. I splashed it over my head.

"Chica, that was for drinking." He handed me another one. That one, I drank.

A few minutes later, Owen came up behind me. "Good gods, sis, you blurred."

I shook my head. "I don't know what happened. I was with you, then I was here, and my body feels abused."

Owen patted my soaking body. "This, sister mine, will be a fun challenge to train."

Muscles sore, I looked up at his smiling face and groaned. What had I gotten myself into now?

Over the next few days, we got our house back in order. Once all the guests were gone, the Pack presented Bevin and José with tickets to Hawaii for the following weekend. It was only for Friday through Monday, but it was a getaway and they needed it. By Wednesday, everything was cleaned up and back to normal.

Thursday morning, Owen and I were headed out to

work. I was leaving as he cleared the dishes. I skipped out the door, and there, in the center of the driveway, ten feet from the front door, was a dead body.

I froze.

Sniffing the air, I knew there weren't any other people around. "Owen…there's a body…a, um, dead body."

"Don't approach it."

"It's dead and there aren't any other people or wolves around."

"Jade! Don't approach it."

A growl bubbled up from my gut, but I stayed put.

From behind me, I heard him knocking on José's and Bevin's door and speaking softly. A few minutes later, Bevin stood next to me. His quiet voice flowed over me. "Thank you for listening and asking for help." He grabbed my hand. "Thank you. Let's do this together."

We moved towards the body. I felt Owen behind us. Once we got close enough, I swore. "It's Boden."

Bevin froze for a second before continuing. "Are you sure?"

The body lay on its back, facing the street, but I recognized the profile. I'd had much more contact with him over the last few months at school than the others. He wore jeans and a green Dynasty United polo, both ripped and bloody. Pinned to his shirt was a note with my name on it.

Grabbing it, I opened it up and read.

Jade Stone,

You soiled our land with your presence and killed one of our daughters. We aren't sure how, but we know it was you. You left your scent behind. You took one of our sons from us and turned him against us. You turned another one traitor, and he lies here before you.

In the past months, your people have taken from mine. Now it will be our turn to take from yours. This is your only warning.

This is war.

Jerry Verater – Leader, Dynasty W.

Please review to help other readers to choose Jade Stone Chronicles!

Continue Jade's adventure:
Book 6: Battlefield: mybook.to/battlefield

Find back stories and updates on my website: https://huckleberryauthor.wordpress.com

Find me on:
Facebook: https://www.facebook.com/Huckleberry-Rahr-Author-129482262301549
TikTok: https://www.tiktok.com/@huckleberryrahr
Instagram: https://www.instagram.com/huckleberryrahr/
Twitter: https://twitter.com/huckleberryrahr

If you missed the first four books, find them here!
Book 1: Wolf Healer: mybook.to/WolfHealer
Book 2: Epsilon: mybook.to/Epsilon
Book 3: Alphas: mybook.to/Alphas
Book 4: Traitor: mybook.to/jade_traitor

ACKNOWLEDGEMENTS

The list of people I want to thank is ever increasing. As always, the top of my list includes my family, especially my son Gavin Rahr. He saw something in my writing when I'm not sure there was anything to see. Then came along Angela Grimes, who took my slapped-together words and found beauty, or at least something that could be cleaned up to form something fun to read. You add a bit of Wes Imrisek, and then my writing comes to life. The Jade Stone Chronicles takes a village. To this book I add the YA readers group, Monica Boothe and Sarah Welch, who added their thoughts and comments to the story, and finally Corona Rivera, who's taken on a bigger and bigger role as family supporter, reading the stories and giving her support before the book is finished. the book is finished.

ABOUT THE AUTHOR

Huckleberry Rahr is a mathematics instructor at the University of Wisconsin-Whitewater. She spent many years teaching math around the Midwest and in Papua New Guinea with the Peace Corps. Her parents instilled a love of reading from a young age.

She grew up with lesbian moms who had a huge collection of women authors with heroines as the protagonist. Her favorite genre was fantasy and science fiction, that is, until she discovered urban fantasy. What her mom's library lacked were books with characters that looked like her family: diversity in background, gender identity, and sexuality. She decided if she couldn't find that series, then she would write it.

Printed in the USA
CPSIA information can be obtained
at www.ICGtesting.com
LVHW042031110124
768771LV00039B/555